"Albert," Horatio said reasonably. "Let me get this straight. You're telling me that Mulrooney was executed—"

"Not executed. Struck down," Humboldt said. His voice was as exact and prim as the rest of him; he reminded Horatio of a white rat that spent too much time grooming itself.

"Struck down, then. By—"

"God."

"You heard a thunderclap."

"Oh, yes. I'd been hearing thunder all day, but this was loud enough to rattle the windows. And it was a sort of double explosion, almost like an echo."

"Did you note the time?"

"Yes. It was two forty-five. I had just finished my break."

"You're sure?"

"I'm sure."

Horatio leaned forward. "And you were the one that discovered the body. The other employees had varying theories on why Mulrooney was the victim of divine retribution . . . care to share yours?"

"He no longer believed in the rightness of Doctor Sinhurma's teachings," Humboldt said. "He'd lost his faith."

"And then his life," Horatio said. "Seems like an awfully big price to pay."

CSI: MIAMI™

CULT FOLLOWING
a novel

Donn Cortez

CSI: MIAMI produced by CBS Productions, a business unit of CBS Broadcasting Inc.
and Alliance Atlantis Productions Inc.
Executive Producers: Jerry Bruckheimer, Ann Donahue, Carol Mendelsohn, Anthony E. Zuiker, Jonathan Littman
Series created by Anthony E. Zuiker, Ann Donahue, and Carol Mendelsohn

POCKET STAR BOOKS
New York   London   Toronto   Sydney

An *Original* Publication of POCKET BOOKS

A Pocket Star Book published by
POCKET BOOKS, a division of Simon & Schuster, Inc.
1230 Avenue of the Americas, New York, NY 10020

This book is a work of fiction. Names, characters, places and incidents are products of the author's imagination or are used fictitiously. Any resemblance to actual events or locales or persons, living or dead, is entirely coincidental.

ISBN-13: 978-0-7434-8057-4
ISBN-10:   0-7434-8057-0

This Pocket Star Books paperback edition January 2006

10 9 8 7 6 5 4 3 2 1

POCKET STAR BOOKS and colophon are registered trademarks of Simon & Schuster, Inc.

Cover design by Patrick Kang and cover photograph by Angelo Cavalli/Getty Images

Manufactured in the United States of America

For information regarding special discounts for bulk purchases, please contact Simon & Schuster Special Sales at 1-800-456-6798 or business@simonandschuster.com

This book is dedicated to my Kate—an investigative sort.
I love you.

1

LIGHTNING FLASHED IN THE SKY like paparazzi chasing angels; the detonation that followed an instant later sounded more like dynamite going off than thunder. A September storm in Miami, Horatio Caine thought as he pulled his Hummer over to the curb and parked, was more like an aerial assault than a natural phenomenon. It could explode overhead with a *boom* so intense it sometimes jolted tourists into an involuntary shriek in response.

Horatio's only reaction to the explosion was a slight narrowing of his eyes. Years of living here had acclimatized him . . . but he still preferred the quiet of the Miami-Dade crime lab. His time on the bomb squad had given him a somewhat negative perspective on sudden, loud noises.

He gloved up, translucent white of the latex incongruous against the sleeves of his Hugo Boss suit jacket; in Miami, a sense of style was almost as important as a grasp of the subtle and ever-shifting politics that went with being head of the CSI unit. Horatio usually wore a good suit—no vest, no tie, shirt open at the collar— that was stylish but informal; it helped him blend into the background of casual chic that had evolved in South Florida, where even a T-shirt could be considered high fashion if it had the right label. Appearance was a useful tool, and Horatio was willing to use whatever tools were available to get the job done.

He grabbed his CSI kit and got out, the afternoon air like the moist breath of a large animal after the AC of the Hummer. Coral Gables, once a suburb of Miami and now a city proper, was an affluent and distinctive place, home to over twenty consulates as well as a thriving theater and shopping district. West of Little Havana, the Gables was a designed city, planned in the twenties by an eccentric citrus millionaire named Merrick. Wide avenues, towering banyan trees and more Spanish architecture than a bullfighters hometown gave it a memorable look: red-tiled roofs, marble fountains and terra-cotta arches in every shade of pastel available.

A few warm, fat drops of rain spattered on the sidewalk as he walked toward a Mediterranean-style storefront cordoned off with yellow tape, an art gallery on one side and a women's boutique on the other. The neon above the door read, THE EARTHLY GARDEN, with a smaller sign beneath it proclaiming *Vegetarian Cuisine*. The uniformed officer stationed at the door recognized him and nodded as Horatio ducked under the tape and went inside.

Horatio stopped and looked around, taking in everything. The restaurant wasn't large, seating no more than fifty; decor was simple, consisting of a few watercolor paintings on whitewashed walls. Oval-shaped tables of blond wood that sat four, with a cut-glass light fixture suspended over each. Only one of the tables was occupied, and from their clothes Horatio guessed all four were employees. A tall, olive-skinned woman with curly black hair spilling down the back of her tailored gray suit stood next to them, but broke off her conversation when Horatio walked up. Detective Yelina Salas motioned Horatio toward the door to the kitchen with a nod and fell in step beside him.

"What have we got?" Horatio said.

"Vic's name is Phillip Mulrooney," Salas said. "He's a waiter here—or was. Body's in the staff bathroom, back here."

She led him through a swinging door and past the stainless steel glint of the cooking area. The ghosts of garlic, ginger and curry hung in the air, cut with something sharper. Burnt plastic, and a touch of ozone.

The door to the bathroom was open. It was a small room, with barely enough space for a sink and a toilet. The victim was on his knees, slumped across the toilet bowl. His shirt, pants and socks were in tatters, one shoe in the far corner, the other in the sink. Horatio could smell burnt flesh now as well. Little bits of plastic and metal were scattered across the floor.

Eric Delko picked that moment to arrive, CSI kit in one gloved hand, camera around his neck. He was dressed in shorts, sneakers and a Miami Heat T-shirt. *Probably out running when he got the call,* Horatio thought.

"What's up, H?" he said.

"Just got here myself," Horatio said. He reached

over carefully and picked up a mangled piece of plastic from the floor. "Looks like our vic had a cell phone in his hand. Not much left of it now."

"Think that's what killed him?" Delko asked. "Cell phone batteries sometimes overheat and explode."

"Especially third-world knockoffs sold at a fraction of the price. Like playing Russian roulette every time you make a call . . . but I don't think that's the COD. It wouldn't shred his clothes like this."

Delko picked the shoe out of the sink, studied it. "Laces are still tied."

"And the floor is wet." Horatio pointed out a trail of moisture that wound from the bathroom to a metal drain set in the kitchen floor a few feet away. "If he had a seven-iron in his hand this would be easy."

"Sure—lightning strike," Delko agreed. "Voltage vaporizes the moisture between the skin and fabric, winds up blowing people right out of their clothing."

Horatio squatted down, took a closer look at the commode. "Stainless steel toilet."

"Industrial grade," Delko said. "See those more in high-traffic public restrooms—airports or malls."

"Maybe the contractor got a deal," Horatio said. "Looks to me like the rest of the plumbing is polyvinyl chloride—cheaper to install, and since it's in a staff-only area the owner doesn't have to worry about appearance. But not all the pipes are visible, are they?"

"So the bolt came through the plumbing, passed through the vic and the water on the floor and grounded out in the drain?"

"And caused his cell phone to explode on the way," Horatio said. "But the position of the body is unusual . . . let's take a look at the roof. We know where the lightning went—let's see if we can pinpoint where it entered."

"I'm going to finish talking to the staff," Salas said.

The access hatch to the roof was at the back, at the top of a white-painted steel ladder bolted to the wall. Horatio studied the rungs. "Looks awfully clean, don't you think?" he asked. "No smudges, no dust, no grease."

"The rest of the kitchen's pretty clean. Maybe they wipe it down every day," Delko said.

Horatio pulled a nearby chair over and climbed up on it. He peered at the uppermost rungs. "All the way to the ceiling? That's above and beyond, even for a restaurant. . . ." He grabbed a rung and climbed up the last few feet. The trapdoor had a simple latch and no lock; he opened it and stuck his head outside.

The roof was a flat, tar-and-gravel deck, with an air-conditioning stack on the north end. A short pipe stuck up a few yards away, approximately over where the bathroom was—probably for venting built-up gas in the sewer lines.

Horatio examined the area around the trapdoor carefully, hoping the intermittent rain wouldn't turn into a sudden downpour, before climbing out on the roof. He made his way slowly toward the venting pipe, checking the surface of the rooftop as he went.

"Anything interesting?" Delko asked, peering out of the hatch.

"Several things," Horatio said. "First off, the most obvious electrical path would be down that venting pipe—but like the rest of the plumbing, it's made of PVC."

"Maybe it hit the air-conditioning unit? Jumped from a vent to a pipe somewhere in the wall?"

"Possibly—but listen." Horatio paused.

Delko cocked his head, then nodded. "Still running. No way the AC would be working if it had channeled a lightning strike."

"Right. Which means it entered through some other means. Either a means we haven't found . . . or a means which has since been removed."

"Lightning sometimes enters through a window or an electrical appliance," Delko pointed out.

"True, but it always follows the easiest route to ground . . . and I'm having a hard time imagining a route involving plumbing that seems to be mainly plastic." Horatio walked over to the air-conditioning stack and looked it over. "No obvious strike marks . . . hold on. Eric, get up here and take a look at this."

Delko clambered up through the hatch and joined him. Horatio hunkered down and touched a gloved finger to the blackened pattern on the gravel beside the AC unit. "Looks like a burn mark," he mused. "But a very oddly shaped one." The pattern was a jagged mass of angled lines, radiating from a central point.

Delko frowned. "Why would the lightning hit there? It doesn't make any sense."

"No, it doesn't. . . ." Horatio reached down and picked up a small, triangular shard of material. He held it up and examined it; it was white on two sides, charred black on another. "Looks ceramic," Horatio noted. "The pattern suggests something circular that fractured—maybe a plate?" Delko handed him an evidence envelope and he slipped it inside.

"Take a picture of this, will you?" Horatio scraped a small amount of material from the burn into another envelope. He held the envelope up to his nose and sniffed, then passed it to Delko. "Smell that?"

"Yeah. Definitely an accelerant, but there's something else there, too. Almost like cotton candy."

Horatio nodded. He could see from the thoughtful look on Delko's face that both of them also smelled something else.

Murder.

"All right, let's process the kitchen," Horatio said. "Eric, you take the storage space, I'll start in the food prep areas."

They worked slowly and methodically. While Delko searched drawers, cupboards and shelves, Horatio sifted through bags of flour and cornmeal and lentils. They checked beneath and behind anything that could be moved, and inside anything that couldn't.

Nothing.

"Maybe we're looking too hard," Horatio murmured. "Maybe what we're after is in plain sight. . . ."

He moved around the room, trying to get a feel for what was out of place. Pots, pans, cooking utensils. Plastic buckets, buspans. A sandwich bar with a cutting board and a row of plastic condiment containers. Each of the containers had its own wooden-handled knife sticking out of it, presumably so the mustard wouldn't contaminate the margarine and vice versa.

Except for one of them.

The container was full of a thick, dark liquid. He

leaned over and sniffed: sweet and almost smoky. *Black molasses. Now why would the rest have their own knives and not this one?*

There was a buspan full of dirty dishes next to the dishwasher. Horatio had already gone through it, but now his memory tugged at him and he went back. In among the other dirty cutlery were two wooden-handled butter knives with blades coated in a thick, black goo.

Delko came over and joined him. "What do you have, H?"

"I'm not sure," Horatio answered. He carefully wiped a tiny amount off the tip of one blade. The metal underneath was scorched black. The other matched it.

"Possible conductor?" Delko asked.

"Maybe," Horatio said. "But why two of them? Eric, I want you to keep looking. Pay extra attention to the electrical outlets and appliances. I'm going to have a chat with the staff. . . ."

Horatio Caine had a secret.

It wasn't of the deep, dark kind—those that knew him well would claim it wasn't a secret at all. But many of the people he encountered in his job either wouldn't appreciate it or would find it inappropriate, so Horatio had learned to keep it concealed most of the time.

What Horatio had was a sense of humor.

It tended toward the dry and ironic (at least the parts of it he said out loud) but—as all CSIs eventually found out—it was impossible to do the work without one. Not that he found suffering funny, or even that he didn't empathize with those experiencing it—some days, Horatio felt their pain so strongly it was all he could do to keep going—but one of the most basic coping mechanisms humans had was turning pain into laughter, and you couldn't work around death as much as Horatio did without developing a sense of the absurd.

He kept it pretty much to himself, though, partly to set an example for his CSIs but mainly as a matter of respect. He dealt with people in pain every day, and whether they were victims or suspects, they all needed to take him seriously. So he allowed himself the occasional wry smile or comment, and left the jokes to the other members of his team. They needed the release more than he did.

That's what he told himself. Most days, he believed it.

Horatio glanced down at the notes Salas had made and back up again. He and Salas sat side by side at the employees' table, talking to them one by one while the others waited outside. The man sitting across from them was small and neat, wavy white hair combed back along a narrow skull. His hands were clasped in front of him, his fingernails trimmed. His apron was white and stain-free over a blue chambray shirt with the sleeves precisely rolled to just above the elbow. Albert Humboldt looked more like a waiter than a dishwasher.

Maybe he has aspirations, Horatio thought, though he doubted coveting the lofty position of waiter at a vegetarian restaurant was motive for murder. In any case, Humboldt had just told Horatio more or less the same thing the two waiters had, and he was getting tired of hearing it.

"Albert," Horatio said reasonably. "Let me get this straight. You're telling me that Mulrooney was executed—"

"Not executed. Struck down," Humboldt said. His voice was as exact and prim as the rest of him; he reminded Horatio of a white rat that spent too much time grooming itself.

"Struck down, then. By—"

"God."

He glanced over at Salas. Her eyebrows had been arched for so long he wondered if she was getting a cramp.

"All right. Leaving theological matters aside for a moment, let's go through the sequence of events again. You say you saw Mister Mulrooney go into the bathroom?"

Humboldt nodded. "Yes."

"Was he talking on his cell phone at the time?"

Humboldt hesitated. "Not that I noticed."

"Did you hear a cell phone ring or hear Mister Mulrooney talking to anyone while he was in the bathroom?"

"No. But the dishwasher makes enough noise that I might not have heard anything anyway."

"But you heard the thunderclap."

"Oh, yes. I'd been hearing thunder all day, but this was loud enough to rattle the windows. And it was a sort of double explosion, almost like an echo."

"Did you note the time?"

"Yes. It was two forty-five. I had just finished my own break."

"You're sure?"

"I'm sure."

Horatio leaned forward. "And you were the one that discovered the body."

Humboldt met his eyes and licked his lips nervously. "Yes. I knocked on the door when I noticed the smell—I'm very sensitive to . . ." He swallowed. "I'm a vegan."

"Doesn't eat meat or consume animal products like eggs or milk," Salas said.

"And Mulrooney?" Horatio asked.

"He was vegan too," Humboldt said. "All of us are. It's part of the Vitality Method."

"New fitness craze," Salas said. "Giving the South Beach Diet some serious competition. Uses vitamins to replace what you lose when you stop being a carnivore."

"It's more than that," Humboldt said. "It's a whole philosophy—it changed my life."

"It change Phil Mulrooney's life?" Horatio asked.

"The Vitality Method changes *everybody's* life. Doctor Sinhurma believes that inner beauty is brought out by nurturing our physical *and* spiritual selves."

"That's very commendable," Horatio said. "The other employees had varying theories on why Mulrooney was the victim of divine retribution . . . care to share yours?"

"He no longer believed in the rightness of Doctor Sinhurma's teachings," Humboldt said. "He'd lost his faith."

"And then his life," Horatio said. "Seems like an awfully big price to pay for breaking a diet."

Humboldt turned his hands palms up in a what-are-you-gonna-do gesture. "I don't claim to know the mind of God. What I do know is that Doctor Sinhurma is a very wise, insightful man, and when Phillip turned away from that wisdom he was killed by a bolt from the heavens."

"In a toilet," Salas said. "If God threw that thunderbolt, he has a nasty sense of humor."

"Or maybe," Horatio said, gazing at Humboldt mildly, "someone else has."

The last interviewee was Darcy Cheveau, the cook. He was well-built and swarthy, with dark curly hair cut short and a five-o'clock shadow that looked closer to midnight. He had a small, crescent-shaped scar just above his lip. He was the kind of person that exuded menace like an expensive cologne; you couldn't quite recognize what it was, but it got your attention.

"Mister Cheveau," Horatio said. "Where were you when the incident occurred?"

"You mean when Phil was fried?" Darcy said, flashing a grin. "Same place I was all day—in the kitchen, crankin' out grub."

"You don't seem terribly upset by it," Salas said.

"Me and Phil weren't that close. It's like the Doc says—everybody's karma gets 'em sooner or later."

"By 'the Doc' you mean Doctor Sinhurma?" Salas asked.

"Yeah. You on the Method, too?"

"Hardly," Salas said.

"So you think Mulrooney deserved what happened to him?" Horatio asked.

"Hey, *I* don't know—that's between him and the universe, right? But getting zapped like that—*somebody* up there didn't like him much."

"I'm more interested in the people down here who didn't like him," Horatio said. "Did you and Mister Mulrooney have any friction between you?"

"Nah, we just weren't buds," Cheveau said, shrugging. "Didn't know him that well, honestly. And it looks like that ain't gonna change anytime soon. . . ."

Calleigh Duquesne, dressed in dark slacks and a white blouse, blond hair in a ponytail, arrived while Horatio was still interviewing the staff; she had a wide smile on her face and a Makita power saw in her hand. "All right, who ordered the blue plate special?"

Delko grinned and held up a gloved finger. "That would be me. Medium rare, please."

Calleigh sniffed the air delicately. "I would think 'well-done' would be more appropriate, don't you?"

"It was worse before they took the DB away," Delko said. "Lightning doesn't turn people into sooty silhouettes like in the cartoons, but the internal temperature of a bolt can be four times hotter than the surface of the sun; that's definitely enough to barbecue flesh."

"Where can I plug this in?"

"Anywhere but here," Delko said, brushing fingerprint powder onto an outlet over a counter. "I've checked the breakers, and this is the only outlet that the lightning affected."

"Was there anything plugged into it?" Calleigh asked. She crouched down, set the bright orange tool case on the floor and snapped open the latches.

"Nope. No prints, either—but look at this." Delko pointed to a spot near the top of the outlet. "Looks like a pattern melted into the plastic."

She came over and studied it, holding the saw. "Hmm. Doesn't look like the outline of a plug. Maybe something resting against the outlet?"

Delko put down his dusting brush and picked up his camera. "Yeah, and I think I know what." He told her about the knives Horatio found. "I'm betting one of them was jammed between the wall and the plug," he said, snapping a picture of the pattern.

Horatio walked into the kitchen. "Calleigh, glad you're here. I need you to look behind the wall in the bathroom, see if you can trace the path the lightning took. Eric, you find anything else in the kitchen?"

Delko showed him the outlet. "Interesting," Horatio murmured. "You test all the appliances?"

"Every one. They're all working."

Horatio looked around the room, hands on hips. "Okay, this is a vegetarian restaurant in Miami. I would imagine that fresh fruit and vegetable juices feature prominently in their menu . . . so what am I not seeing?"

Delko glanced around. "No blender."

"Right. Check the Dumpster, see if we get lucky."

"I'm on it."

Calleigh slipped on a pair of safety goggles. "Okay if I start, H?"

"Go ahead. I'm going to make a call."

Horatio stepped back out into the main area of the restaurant; the employees had been told they could go home. He pulled out his cell phone and hit the first number on the speed dial: the Miami-Dade crime lab.

"Mister Wolfe? Horatio." He had to speak up over the ratcheting clatter of the saw. "I need you to find out everything you can about a Doctor Sinhurma and any possible connection to a restaurant called The Earthly Garden. That's right, the diet doctor . . . also, I need the cell phone records for a Phillip Mulrooney for the last twenty-four hours. Okay, thanks."

He snapped his phone shut and slipped it into his pocket. The sound of Calleigh's saw biting into plaster sounded like an angry animal; outside, the rain began pelting down in earnest.

Horatio Caine knew Miami. He knew her the way a sailor knows the sea, the way a man knows a temperamental lover; he couldn't tell you what she was going to do, but he could tell you what she was capable of. She was a city of extremes—on the surface all neon dazzle, golden-brown skin against white sand, parrot-bright *fashionistas* slamming back *Mohitos*, hot bodies in hot clubs on hot tropical nights. The cutting edge of the East Coast, sharp as a Versace suit, quick as a supermodel on Rollerblades.

But underneath the glitter, darkness.

Horatio knew how short a trip it was from the warm glow of nightclub neon to the hard, fluorescent glare over the autopsy table. He knew that despite all the money flowing through, Miami-Dade remained one of the poorest counties in the country. He knew that hot weather led to hot blood, and a certain segment of the population thought "tourist season" referred to carjacking.

Horatio thought of Miami as a borderland, a place between. Some people found it hard to see, that line between the dark places and the light, but it was where Horatio lived. Not in some nebulous gray area, either; he had a foot planted firmly in both realms, and to him the demarcation was as clear as the difference between life and death. It was a line that ran through everything, and it was always there. Where other people saw sunlight, Horatio saw shadows.

His job was to take care of those who crossed that line. *And they always cross it going the wrong way,* Horatio thought as he entered the observation gallery. *Too many of them end up down there.*

He looked down at Doctor Alexx Woods and keyed open the mike. The Miami-Dade coroner's facility was also a teaching lab, with a number of high-resolution screens in the glassed-in area overlooking the autopsy room itself. Horatio sometimes monitored autopsies from there, not because of any sense of squeamishness but because the cameras in the room below could magnify any detail he wanted a better look at.

"Well, Alexx?" Horatio said. "What can you tell me about our vic?"

Alexx smiled up at Horatio, then down at the body on the table before her. "Poor boy suffered facial trauma and burns from the exploding cell phone, but that wasn't what killed him. COD was cardiopulmonary arrest, probably caused by lightning."

Horatio frowned. "Probably, Alexx?"

"Well, there's some contradictory indications. A lightning strike can be anywhere up to two billion volts, but since skin has a relatively high resistance the charge usually travels along the surface."

"Flashover," Horatio said.

"Yes. It's the reason why most people survive lightning strikes—the bolt travels over the body instead of through it. Along the way it vaporizes any moisture present, causing distinctive linear or punctuate burns. You can see them here, under the arms, more down the inside of the thighs, on his feet and his forehead."

"Which is what shredded his clothes and blew off his shoes."

"There's also this." Alexx pointed to a feathery pattern on his chest. "It's called a Lichtenberg figure, sometimes shows up in lightning strike victims. Extravasated blood in the subcutaneous fat causes fern-shaped lesions on the skin. Nobody understands the exact pathogenesis, but it disappears from the body within twenty-four hours."

"So what doesn't add up, Alexx?"

"Patichiae in the eyelids and the visceral pleura." She pointed out the telltale red dots of tiny burst blood vessels in the whites of the body's eyes.

"Asphyxia? That *is* unusual."

"You see it sometimes in cases of low-voltage electrocution. If the current is above what's called the 'let-go' level—about sixteen milliamps—the victim's flexor and extensor muscles in his forearm contract. If the flexor is the stronger of the two, the hand spasms closed, sometimes preventing the victim from breaking the circuit. The current induces tetanic paralysis of the respiratory muscles, so he can't breathe—if it goes on long enough, the victim suffocates."

Horatio leaned forward and studied the image on the monitor. "Sixteen milliamps. You can get that with house current . . . so if his heart hadn't stopped he would have died of respiratory failure?"

"Not from lightning. A thunderbolt's an extremely short event—the whole thing's over in two hundred milliseconds or less, and peak current duration is maybe point one percent of that. In most cases of tetanic paralysis the lungs start functioning again as soon as the current's interrupted; it would have taken two or three minutes of continuous contact for him to asphyxiate. These hemorrhages aren't pronounced enough for that—I'd say he was without oxygen for a minute, maybe less. I also found these." Alexx pointed out a series of small red dots on the upper thigh. "Needle marks."

"Odd place for tracks. Junkies usually go for an easily accessible vein."

"Well, these are intramuscular and at least a week old—looks like whatever he was taking, he stopped taking it. If so, the tox screen probably won't tell us what he was on."

"No," Horatio said, "but it will tell us what he wasn't on . . . and that might be just as useful. How about stomach contents?"

"Results just came back. Partially digested chili, looks like."

"Vegetarian?"

"No—definitely animal protein."

"So our boy was backsliding," Horatio mused. "Giving in to the temptations of the flesh . . . thanks, Alexx."

Alexx looked down at the body with the same tenderness she always showed to those under her care. "We all give in to weakness now and then," she said softly. "Nobody stays strong forever."

2

"How's THE RENO GOING?" Horatio asked. Calleigh had cut away a large part of the wall behind the toilet, extending all the way up to the ceiling. The exposed pipe was copper from the bowl up to head height, where it joined to a piece made of PVC.

Calleigh grinned and pushed her safety goggles up on her forehead. Bits of drywall dust speckled her face and arms. "Well, I may not be ready to host my own TV show, but I think I found what we were looking for." She pointed to a spot just below the join, on the copper pipe.

Horatio stepped up and took a closer look. "Burn pattern—and something else."

"Tool marks," Calleigh said. "I think something was attached at that point—probably some sort of clamp. And I can tell you how they got access, too."

She motioned for Horatio to follow her and stepped around the corner into the kitchen. She walked to the opposite side of the wall, where a first-aid kit hung. She took it down, revealing a small square of plywood attached by screws. "This was probably put in by a plumber after he cut through the wall to get access to the pipe. The copper looks pretty new—I'm guessing that section of the plumbing was replaced after a leak."

"Or maybe it was put there for a more specific reason," Horatio said. "See if you can find out when it was installed—and I want the panel, the first-aid kit and that section of pipe in the lab. The question now is—how did the lightning get from the roof to here?"

Calleigh pointed at a small window set high in the wall, propped open a few inches with a broken-handled coffee mug. "No screen—I'm thinking some sort of wire was fed through it. I've already checked it for trace, but didn't find anything."

"Okay—good work."

"Carpentry *and* plumbing," Calleigh said cheerfully. "I guess this is power-tool day. Things keep going like this, I'll be working a jackhammer by the end of my shift."

"If I need any concrete broken up," Horatio said with a smile, "you're first on my list."

The rain had come down in a torrent, but it was over now; orange-red light gleamed through the breaking clouds over the freshly washed streets, the kind of presunset glow that could make even the industrial backside of an alley look pretty. Horatio walked up to a Dumpster that sounded like a bear was thrashing around inside and rapped on the metal. "Is that my CSI or am I addressing Oscar the Grouch?"

Eric Delko's head popped up over the lip. "Hey, H— think I found something." He reached down and pulled up an industrial-grade blender. "Burn marks on the plug end."

"Well done." Horatio took a closer look at the plug. "Anything else?"

"Yeah. An empty package of ground round."

"And Alexx found meat in the vic's stomach. . . ."

"Anyway, I bagged it and sent it to the lab for processing. Maybe we can get a print off the plastic."

"Good job. I'll have the restaurant staff come in for prints and DNA, see if we can find a match."

"Y'know, I hate to say it, H, but . . ."

"Yes?" Horatio gave him an inquiring look.

"I'm getting kinda hungry."

Horatio chuckled. "Okay. Run that blender over to the lab and then grab some dinner."

"Yeah? How about you?"

"I'm going to go talk to someone about a diet. . . ."

Ryan Wolfe sat at one of the lab's computers, intent on the screen, and didn't look up when Horatio walked in. Horatio knew Wolfe wasn't being rude or unperceptive—it was just that the young CSI tended to totally focus on what he was doing to the exclusion of all else. Wolfe had a mild case of obsessive-compulsive disorder, which to Horatio's way of thinking made him a perfect fit for his job.

"Mister Wolfe," Horatio said. "What have you got for me?"

"Quite a bit," Wolfe said. "Do you want to hear about the doctor or his diet first?"

"Let's start with the man," Horatio said.

"Doctor Kirpal Sinhurma. Originally from Calcutta, came to the States on a scholarship and graduated from Johns Hopkins with a psychiatric degree in 1975. Settled down into private practice in New York State, wrote a few self-help books that made a lot of money, went back to school in the early nineties and got a degree in nutrition. Relocated here five years ago."

"Uh-huh. What's he been doing since he got to Miami?" Horatio leaned against the edge of the desk and crossed his arms.

"Founding his own movement, apparently. His web site reads more like New Age manifesto than nutritionist." Wolfe tapped a few keys. "See for yourself."

Horatio leaned over and scanned the screen. "Hmm. Quite a few celebrity endorsements listed."

"Yeah—models and actors, mainly. He seems very popular with the young, rich and pretty crowd. His philosophy leans heavily toward appearance reflecting spiritual enlightenment."

"What can you tell me about the diet itself?"

Wolfe frowned and tapped a key. "Not a lot of hard data. I've read several articles and interviews, and it seems to be a regimen that varies from person to person. The only universal is the elimination of all animal products from your diet and periods of fasting and meditation."

"Okay, what about vitamin supplements?"

"That's where it gets interesting. The 'Vitality Method' is a two-step process; anyone can buy the book and follow the diet, but that's just preparation. When you feel you're ready—and have the cash— you sign up for one-on-one time with Doctor Sinhurma at his clinic. You spend two weeks there, during which time they supply their secret blend of 'vitamins, exercise and counseling' that will presumably keep you young and healthy far longer than you have any right to."

"Any connection to The Earthly Garden?"

"Yeah. He owns it. He's got another in Queens and one scheduled to open in L.A. next month."

"So our Doctor Sinhurma is building himself an empire," Horatio said. "One where presumably the unattractive and carnivorous are not welcome. . . ."

"That's not all. There was too much on the site to read through everything, but I did a representative sampling, and the later posts from the doctor are different in tone from the early stuff. He starts off talking about universal harmony and gradually gets more and more strident. And here's something I thought you'd want to see."

Wolfe scrolled down, then clicked on a link. Horatio's eyes narrowed as he scanned through it. " 'Nature itself will pass judgment on those who deride us,' " he read out loud. " 'Justice may take its time, but when it arrives it will hit like a bolt from the blue.' Posted two days ago . . ."

"I tracked down those cell phone records you asked for, too. Guess who the last person our vic got a call from was?" Wolfe punched up the information.

Horatio nodded. "The good doctor himself. And if our time of death is accurate, it looks like Mister Mulrooney may have even been talking to him when the lightning struck."

"That seems like—" Wolfe stopped, then shook his head. "I don't know what it seems like. A pretty unlikely coincidence, at the least."

"Oh, I don't believe it's a coincidence at all," Horatio said. "Any more than I believe Doctor Sinhurma has a direct line to the Almighty."

"So what *do* you believe, H?"

"I believe," Horatio said, "in the evidence. And right now, it's telling me to take a very close, hard look at the methods of Doctor Kirpal Sinhurma. . . ."

The place was called the Mental Freedom Foundation, and despite the lofty title it was only a small office on the third floor of a run-down building in Little Haiti. Horatio had found it online, and booked an appointment over the phone.

The neighborhood was colorful, to say the least. Horatio parked in front of a gigantic mural depicting some sort of voodoo ritual, was greeted by loud *compas* music blaring from the open door of a nearby music shop and nearly stepped on a chicken fleeing from a wildly barking yellow dog. The smell of frying pork mingled with that of rotting garbage, coming respectively from a restaurant and a heap of trash bags piled up a few steps from the entrance. Horatio found the address, a brick building that looked like it had weathered its share of hurricanes, and went inside.

The elevator wasn't working, so he took the stairs to the third floor. In a small, sparsely decorated foyer with a wheezing air conditioner, he found a man with thinning brown hair sitting behind a desk and talking rapidly on the phone, scribbling notes at the same time. He didn't stop talking or writing when Horatio came in, just nodded and pointed at the door to the inner office. "Uh-huh, uh-huh," he said. "That's terrible. Yes, I know. Uh-huh."

Horatio went in. The room was an untidy mess, filing cabinets lining two walls with stacks of papers and books piled atop them. The desk in the back held more stacks and had a small Asian woman seated behind it, framed by a large window. Outside, white clouds piled up against each other on the horizon like an immense field of mutant cauliflower.

She got up and extended her hand across the desk. "Lieutenant Caine? Sun-Li Murayaki."

Her grip was strong and quick, no more than a brief squeeze and yank. She wore a black business suit with a white blouse, her black hair long and straight and her smile professional.

"What's the problem, Lieutenant?" she said, sitting back down and motioning for Horatio to do the same.

"It's Horatio," he said. "And my problem is lack of information."

"I can't discuss any of the cases I handle," she said. "Nor can I disclose the whereabouts of any clients that may be currently undergoing exit counseling."

"Exit counseling? You mean deprogramming?"

"If you like. I understand you're just doing your job, Lieutenant, but waving a kidnapping charge at me won't impress me. I take what I do *very* seriously—"

"Whoa!" he said. "Slow down, Ms. Murayaki. I'm not here to charge you with anything—this has nothing to do with any of your clients. I'm here because I was hoping I could tap your expertise."

She studied him for a moment. "I apologize, Horatio. Unfortunately, most of my dealings with law enforcement tend to be adversarial. It's not that I have any antagonism towards the police—quite the opposite, in fact—it's just the nature of my business. Usually when I get a visit from an officer it's because some demagogue is accusing me of holding one of his drones hostage. What exactly would you like to know?"

"Anything you could tell me about cult methodology."

She frowned. "That's a pretty big area. Can you narrow it down a bit?"

"Okay. What about recruiting?"

"They like the college crowd, especially freshmen. There's a common perception that only stupid people join cults, but that's not accurate. They target people who are vulnerable emotionally, not intellectually—someone in late adolescence, away from home for the first time, is just about perfect."

"So a person with self-esteem issues would fit that description as well."

"Sure—anyone with a big void in their life is prime. People who've recently lost a job or had someone close to them die are often in the crosshairs. They prefer people with money or access to money, but slave labor is valuable too." She shrugged. "Really, they'll take anyone they can get. To them, followers are like livestock; young and strong is always best. Breeding is important too."

"Breeding? How so?"

"Several reasons. The more attractive the recruit, the better he or she will be at attracting *more* recruits.

The better the family, the more likely they have access to money. If they can't get money, there's always the 'worldly goods are evil' approach. Convince them to hock the jewelry, the car, even the clothes, and donate the proceeds to the organization." She sighed. "Nobody ever seems to complain when the Glorious Leader owns a dozen Bentleys, though."

Horatio nodded. "Of course not. So how does a cult go about converting someone with a brain into someone who follows orders without question?"

"Love bombing."

Horatio's eyebrows went up.

"It's a technique where everything the target does is met with unconditional love—at first. No judgment, just acceptance. I had a former cult member describe it as sort of like being swarmed by golden retrievers. You cheat on your girlfriend? Not your fault. You have a drug problem? We don't care. You steal from your family? They were asking for it. No matter how irrational, that kind of positive reinforcement is addictive. And they don't let up, either; once a cult targets a potential member they stick with him every hour they can. They'll show up where he works, where he hangs out, where he lives."

"So the recruit does whatever he's asked because he's loved?"

"It's not that simple. Once the target is hooked, the love becomes *very* conditional. It's withheld as punishment for breaking any of the rules of the cult. Those break down into two main categories: the standard ones, like 'no unauthorized contact with strangers,' 'no questioning the decisions of the leader,' 'only the cult loves you'; and the ones specific to a particular group, which can be pragmatic—'no sex,' or bizarre— 'You must never say the word "yellow".' Breaking any of these results in the love being cut off, sending the addict into emotional withdrawal."

"Or to put it another way, they gorge on approval then get put on a diet," Horatio said. "Leaving them literally starving for affection."

"Splurge and purge?" Murayaki said. "That's as good a metaphor as any. Emotional bulemia—except it's your mind being ravaged, not your body."

"So they prey on the unloved," Horatio said. "Who else?"

"The idealistic. A lot of cults masquerade as volunteer organizations, doing community work for free. Idealists," she said flatly, "tend to be naïve."

"I sense that doesn't apply to you," Horatio said drily.

"Oh, I've elevated cynicism to an art form," she said. "Anyway, once the cult has them working it doesn't let up. Someone who's busy and exhausted doesn't have time to think. And of course, the 'community project' always winds up being something directly beneficial to the cult.

"Those are general approaches, but cult recruiters can be a lot more focused. They're salesmen—they have a whole bag of tricks, and they pull out whatever seems appropriate for a particular subject. If you're a complainer, they'll give you an outlet for your grievances. If you're socially conscious, they'll talk about politics. They don't just put together a profile of you—they put together a profile of what the

ideal friend for you would be, and then they manufacture that identity. Sometimes it's the recruiter
themselves, sometimes they assign someone else in
the cult to become that person. Either way, that person's job is to put you in a position to be receptive to
the cult's ideas."

Horatio had been studying Murayaki while she
spoke. She was obviously passionate about what she
did, but there was a cold, objective intelligence at
work too.

"And sometimes," Horatio said, "the recruiter is an
attractive member of the opposite sex."

"Absolutely. But so far, all we've talked about is
bait—how they get potential members interested. The
techniques they use once they have your attention
are far more sophisticated."

"Such as?"

"Hurt and Rescue, for one. Put the potential recruit
into a dangerous or uncomfortable situation, then
'rescue' them. Properly done, you can even get the recruit to ask for help. Gratitude leads to trust, which
leads to manipulation. Or you can involve the recruit
in a trust exchange, where you do something for
them without asking, and they feel obligated to do
something for you in return, building an artificial
bond which can then be played upon."

"Don't all these games become transparent after a
while?"

She leaned back, picked up a letter opener shaped
like a tiny Japanese sword and began toying with it.
"You have to remember that at this stage, nothing
that questionable has happened. You've made some

new friends. They pay a lot of attention to you. They do nice things for you. They seem to share the same values you do . . . and all they're asking for is a little bit of your time."

She made her eyes go big and her voice soft. "Just come to a meeting, okay? Really, it would mean a lot to me. . . ."

He grinned. "Okay, I get it. And once you agree to go to said meeting—"

"—it often turns out to be in a remote or isolated place. An evening can quickly become a weekend. Little or no sleep, food with no protein, lots of group activities like singing or chanting. No privacy—a member of the cult is always there, talking to you, touching you. When they think you're ready, they start the last stage."

She paused, her eyes distant, then took a deep breath and continued. "It's called breaking. Basically, they destroy your personality in order to build a new one—one that will do whatever the cult says. They've already laid the groundwork; by this point the recruit believes the cult's values parallel his own, and the leader of the cult has been portrayed as the living embodiment of those values. A more perfect version of the recruit has been created in his mind, the kind of person that he *could* be if he wanted to."

"A more *popular* person?" Horatio ventured.

"Never heard it put that way before—but yeah, sure. More popular, more attractive, happier—just better in every way. That's the carrot . . . and then they hit you with the stick.

"It starts with confessions. Everyone's feeling emotional, so it's not hard to get the recruit to admit to something. Then the accusations start—you shouldn't have done that, you have no ethics, you're a terrible person. It's the last thing the recruit expects; having been pushed up this emotional ladder, they suddenly have their support yanked away."

"It sounds brutal."

"You have no idea. It's like having your emotions gang-raped. People that have carefully portrayed themselves as trustworthy are now calling you garbage. Reducing the recruit to tears isn't enough; they won't stop until the subject is curled up in a fetal ball on the floor. At that point, the subject is filled with such self-loathing they'll do anything to escape . . . but it's not as simple as just running away. Aside from the fact that they're probably in the middle of nowhere, it's not that easy to get away from *yourself*."

"Except," Horatio said, "to become a different person."

"Exactly. A senior member of the cult—someone the recruit has come to respect—comes forward and embraces them. They offer forgiveness, redemption. All the recruit has to do is reject the person they used to be—which, at that moment, is all they want to do anyway. They seize the opportunity to become a new person—and the cult has another member.

"Even then, it's not over. The new recruit is in his most malleable state, and they capitalize on that. This is when the false front the cult has put up vanishes and their real ideology comes out. The new personality soaks it up like a sponge—having rejected his old values, he needs something to replace them. The new structure is kept in place and reinforced by keeping the member busy, exhausted and overloaded with supercharged emotion. Disobey or question the smallest rule, and the love is immediately replaced by intense disapproval. To someone in the cultist's state of mind, it feels like being rejected by God himself."

"Which is the point," Horatio said. "You know, I get the feeling none of this is purely academic for you."

"What?" She looked taken aback.

"I just mean that you seem to be drawing to a certain degree on firsthand experience—"

Now she looked unbelieving. "Excuse me? Are you trying to say I'm some sort of unbalanced ex-cult member myself?"

"No, no, I—"

"Because that is a *very* hurtful thing to say." She looked on the verge of tears—and then, abruptly, her voice and face settled into an easy, blank expression. "Hurt and Rescue," she said. "See how easy it is to yank somebody's chain? I had you on the verge of apologizing for doing your job. Another few minutes and you'd be thinking what a swell person I was for forgiving you so quickly."

Horatio shook his head ruefully. "I suppose you're going to tell me you learned how to do that from talking to clients."

"No, I learned how to do that by apprenticing to a master. He taught me how get inside anyone's head and push their buttons, without ever feeling a flicker of remorse or guilt about it. I used to think of nonbelievers as machines; they looked like people, but they didn't really have souls. It was my job to get the machine to the workshop, where it could be *given* a soul. Anything I did or said to get the machine there was justifiable."

"You were a recruiter?"

She nodded. "One of the best. I belonged to the Divine Order of Enlightened Thought and Wisdom, headed by a woman who called herself Boddhisatva Gaia. Her real name was Irene Caldwell."

"I wasn't aware there were cults with female leaders."

She snorted. "What, you think only men have charisma? Women play the game just as well. If I hadn't been physically taken away, I'd still be working for them."

"And now you perform that service for others?"

She looked at him blankly, and said nothing.

"Right, you can't discuss that," he said, smiling. "No problem."

She hesitated, then said, "Do you understand the concept of retroactive consent?"

"I think so. Usually applied to mentally disturbed people who've stopped taking their meds, correct? The argument being that you can force someone who can't make rational decisions into treatment that returns their ability to choose."

"Right. That's the principle we work on—the person may disagree violently with what we do initially, but afterward they're very grateful."

"That," Horatio said, "is a very slippery slope, Ms. Murayaki."

"That it is, Lieutenant Caine. But after all the people I've pushed down it, I feel somewhat obligated to try and haul a few people the other way."

Horatio stood. "I can appreciate that. I hope they do, too."

"So far, I have a recidivism rate of less than five percent. Not perfect, but—" She shrugged. "I'm only mortal, right?"

"Aren't we all?" Horatio said.

The Vitality Method Clinic was at the edge of Northwest Miami, out where suburbia shifted to swampland and local residents had gotten used to finding the occasional alligator in their swimming pool. The Hummer's big tires crunched their way up a driveway of pulverized white seashell, through wrought-iron gates set into stone walls painted a soothing shade of blue. A security camera tracked Horatio as he drove in.

He parked in the center of the turnaround in front of the main building, a sprawling structure that looked more like a mansion than a clinic. Horatio got out, took off his sunglasses and looked around. Late-afternoon sunlight shone down on a well-tended expanse of lawn and thick hedges bracketing the house. The driveway branched off and around the building on the right.

The man that came out to greet him looked like his natural environment was poolside, his natural activity handing out towels. He wore neoprene sandals, white pants and a T-shirt the same aquamarine as his eyes. He was young, tanned and muscular, with wavy, shoulder-length black hair and a broad white smile

that reminded Horatio of a gleeful time-share salesman.

"I'm sorry, you can't park that there," he said, his
smile turning apologetic.

"Sure I can," Horatio said with a smile of his own.
"It's an official police vehicle *and* a Hummer. I can
park pretty much anywhere . . . and you are?"

The man's eyebrows went up, but his smile didn't
falter. "Randolph. Is there anything I can help you
with?"

Horatio resisted the urge to ask him for a towel.
"Yes, you can," he said. "I'd like to see Doctor Sinhurma."

"I'll see if he's available," Randolph said. "Follow
me."

Horatio let himself be led inside, through an immense, double-paneled door that would have looked
more at home on a courthouse. *Or a church*, Horatio
thought.

The foyer reinforced his first impression; a stained-
glass skylight painted the marble floor with stripes of
crimson and deep purple, while the high, polished
wood island in the center of the room seemed almost
like a cross between a sergeant's booking desk and a
pulpit.

The blond woman behind it wore a T-shirt and
smile that matched his guide's. "Hi!" she said brightly.
"Welcome to the Vitality Method Clinic!"

Horatio stopped, returned her smile with one of
considerably less wattage and put his hands on his
hips, casually pushing aside his jacket to show the
badge clipped to his belt. "Hi yourself," he said.

"Marcie, can you tell Doctor Sinhurma a police officer is here to see him?" Randolph said.

"Sure," Marcie said. "Just a second." She picked up a phone.

Horatio took in details while he waited. Two more security cameras, in either corner of the roof. Motion detectors over the door. Large windows with almost-abstract patterns of iron rebar overlaying them, armor disguised as art.

Randolph stood beside the desk, large hands clasped in front of him. His smile was at parade rest, plainly ready to spring into action if some sudden pleasantness broke out.

Marcie put down the phone. "Okay, Randolph, can you show him in? Doctor Sinhurma's in room C."

"Follow me, please."

Randolph led him through a plain white door—metal, Horatio noted—and down a hallway carpeted with an intricately woven Persian rug the same colors as the stained glass in the lobby. They walked past two doors—rooms A and B, Horatio supposed—and Randolph knocked on the third.

"Come in, come in," a hearty voice said.

Randolph opened the door and motioned Horatio in. The interior wasn't what he expected—it was more like a lounge than an examining room, with a couch on the far wall, a few comfortable-looking armchairs and a low-slung glass-and-chrome coffee table.

There were two men in the room, one seated on the couch, the other already striding forward to meet him. Brown-skinned, slender, dressed in sandals, a pair of white pants and an aquamarine silk shirt, the man put his hand out and said, "It's a pleasure to meet you!"

Horatio hesitated, then shook his hand. Doctor Sinhurma looked to be in his fifties, his black hair streaked with silver at the temples and throughout his bushy sideburns. He met Horatio's eyes with a steady, warm gaze of his own, and held Horatio's hand for just a second longer than was necessary.

"Lieutenant Caine," Horatio said. "Miami-Dade police. I was wondering if I could ask you a few questions."

"Absolutely, Lieutenant," Sinhurma said, beaming. "Oh, this is my assistant, Mister Kim," he said, indicating the man on the couch. "You don't mind if he's present as well, do you?" Kim was an Asian man in his twenties, also dressed in the ubiquitous white pants and blue T-shirt. He nodded at Horatio but said nothing.

"That's fine," Horatio said.

Sinhurma sat down in one of the armchairs and motioned for Horatio to sit as well.

Horatio smiled, and stayed on his feet. "It's about one of your patients—Phillip Mulrooney."

The smile vanished like the sun behind a cloud. "Ah, yes, Phillip," Sinhurma said. "Very sad, very tragic."

"Not to mention unusual."

"Life is abundant with surprises," Sinhurma said. His voice was solemn, but the smile was creeping back into his eyes.

"It most certainly is . . . tell me, when was the last time you talked to Phillip?"

"We were speaking at the moment of his death," Sinhurma said calmly.

"I see. What about?"

"He was undergoing a spiritual crisis. I was trying to help him clarify his thoughts."

"Can you be more specific?"

"Not without violating doctor-patient confidentiality, I'm afraid."

"Oh? I thought the discussion was spiritual, not medical." Horatio studied the doctor's body language; the man seemed totally relaxed and at ease.

"In my practice, the two are frequently one and the same. In any case, I can tell you that I was unsuccessful."

"Was that because the conversation was cut short?" There was an abstract watercolor hanging on the wall behind the doctor; it looked to Horatio like it had been painted by the same artist that had done the ones in the restaurant.

"No. It was because he'd made an erroneous choice."

Horatio brought his gaze back to Sinhurma. "And what would that be?"

"Again—I really cannot say."

"Uh-huh. So you had an unspecified disagreement, and then he died. Is that accurate?"

"So it appears."

"How long was Mister Mulrooney a patient of yours?"

"Approximately eighteen months." Sinhurma raised a hand and scratched absently at one bushy sideburn.

"And how long had he worked at the restaurant?"

"That was more recent—three weeks or so."

"Is it normal for you to employ people you're treating?" Horatio glanced at Kim, but the man was staring straight ahead, stone-faced.

"My relationship with my patients involves all parts of their lives. I sometimes recommend working in a hands-on environment as part of their food reconditioning."

"So working in your restaurant is part of their therapy. Do they pay you for the privilege as well?"

Sinhurma laughed. "Life is therapy, Lieutenant. I simply point out which parts should be concentrated on and which should be ignored."

"Of course. Tell me, was Mister Mulrooney involved in anything he shouldn't have been?"

"You mean illegal activities? No, not that I'm aware of." Sinhurma's voice was bland, with just a hint of boredom.

Horatio could have pushed him, but he knew he wouldn't get anything further. He smiled and extended his hand instead. "Thank you for your time, Doctor. Would you mind if I took a look around? I'd like to get a sense of the place."

"Not at all," Sinhurma said, shaking Horatio's hand just as thoroughly as before. "I'm rather busy, but I'll get someone to show you around." He reached for a phone on the wall.

The young woman that showed up a minute later was dressed the same as the previous two staff members, with striking green eyes and brown hair braided into two short pigtails.

"Lieutenant Caine, this is Ruth," Sinhurma said. "Ruth, I'd like you to show the lieutenant our facilities. Give him the full tour."

"Okay," Ruth said. Her smile was a little more hesitant, but just as friendly. "Are you thinking of signing up?"

"You never can tell," Horatio said. "Life is abundant with surprises. . . ."

3

THE DINER ACROSS THE STREET from the Miami-Dade crime lab had been around a long time; it had weathered hurricanes, economic downturns and even brief periods of trendiness. Wolfe couldn't tell if the neon flamingos that shone over the lunch counter were art-deco retro from the eighties or the real thing from further back.

The place was called Auntie Bellum's, and it was Calleigh's favorite breakfast joint—not to mention a regular hangout for lab techs and off-duty cops. She and Wolfe were grabbing a quick bite in the middle of their shift.

"Thank you," Calleigh said to the waitress, a woman that looked like she'd been pouring coffee since the Cuban missile crisis. The waitress nodded as she set down two plates full of food.

"Grits," Wolfe said, shaking his head. "How can you eat that stuff?"

"With a fork and a great deal of appreciation," Calleigh said. "I've been eating grits since I was a little girl, and I don't see any reason to stop now."

Wolfe dug into his serving of scrambled eggs, bacon

and toast. "Yeah? Well, my mom used to serve me fried Spam sandwiches, and I don't eat those anymore. . . ."

"Ugh. I already get more spam than I need via e-mail, thank you very much." She poured some more grapefruit juice from a carafe into her glass. "So, H is out talking to the diet doctor?"

"Yeah. I know I haven't worked with him that long, but he seemed pretty . . . intense."

"Horatio? Oh, he's just a big old pussycat."

"Sure. Like a hungry tiger, maybe."

She gave him a wide, dimpled smile, then forked a sizeable amount of grits into it. "Mmm—bliss," she mumbled. " 'Scuse me—shouldn't talk with my mouth full." She swallowed, then answered. "When I was a kid, we used to have this cat, a gray tabby by the name of Tina. Tina was a mouser, and she had this very specific way of catching mice. She would find a spot where she was sure there were mice—a hole in the baseboard, something like that—and she would hunker down. And then she'd wait. And wait. And wait . . . for hours, sometimes. Totally alert, totally patient. And sooner or later, that mouse would stick his head out—and Tina would nail him."

She drank some juice, put down the glass and said, "That's who Horatio reminds me of. He never gives up, never loses his focus. He watches, and he waits."

"So the intensity—that's just the way he is, huh?"

"Oh, that varies. His lowest setting is somewhere around 'simmer,' I think."

"And his highest?"

Calleigh's smile faded. "That can be a little scary. Kinda like standing next to a volcano about to blow."

Wolfe took a sip of coffee. "You ever seen that happen?"

Calleigh's smile came back. "Nope. Don't think I ever will, either. Unless . . ." She broke off, took another mouthful of grits.

"Unless what?" Wolfe prodded.

"Well . . . the only time I've ever seen Horatio come close to losing it is when kids are involved. Not that he ever has," she added quickly. "Those sort of cases are hard on everyone, but H always seems to take them personally."

"Kids," Wolfe said. "Yeah, that's got to be tough. . . ."

Wolfe trailed off. Calleigh drank some more juice.

"Better get used to it, Ryan," she said. "Some of the things you're going to be dealing with are not pleasant. There was a case I read about where a serial killer threw the bodies of prostitutes into a wood chipper and fed the results to his pigs. They had to ID the victims by DNA from bone chips in fecal matter—and by the time they caught the guy, a lot of those pigs had already been slaughtered and the meat sold commercially."

Wolfe looked at her. He blinked, once. She calmly took another forkful of food, chewed and swallowed.

"And this is why you invited me out to eat?" he said finally.

"No, I invited you out because I thought you looked hungry," she said. "Of course, you *always* look sort of hungry . . . anyway, I just thought I'd take the opportunity to bring a few things up. So to speak."

Wolfe looked down at his food. He picked up a piece of bacon, studied it for a second, then put it in his mouth and began to chew.

Calleigh smiled, and signaled the waitress for more coffee.

The grounds, it turned out, were even more extensive than Horatio had thought. Behind the main house were a large pool, an archery range and a gym. Paths lined with white seashell fragments led from one area to the next. As they walked along, Horatio listened attentively to Ruth's spiel, which sounded as well-rehearsed as any tour guide's.

". . . and in the back of the clinic we have the dorm rooms," she said. "Doctor Sinhurma converted some of his own living space to make room for more patients. There's room for around two dozen at the moment, but we're going to be expanding soon. Doctor Sinhurma plans on eventually having space for at least two hundred."

"Ambitious," Horatio said. "But then, I understand the Vitality Method is very popular."

"Oh, yes . . . we have a long waiting list. And Doctor Sinhurma treats every patient personally, so it's not like there's a standard length of time a patient stays."

"How does that work?"

Ruth waved at a couple walking by on another path, and they waved back. One of them, Horatio noted, he'd seen before—usually hitting three-pointers for the Miami Heat.

"Every patient is different," she continued. "Depending on how toxic their body is and what their lifestyle habits are, they might be here for two weeks or six months. Maybe even longer."

"I see . . . and what exactly does the detoxification process entail?"

"Well, a strictly vegan diet, for one—no meat, no eggs, no dairy, not even honey. You have to have been on that diet for at least six months before Doctor Sinhurma will even see you. Once you're admitted, you'll be put on a purification diet of brown rice and water for a few days. Group exercise every morning at dawn, personal exercise after lunch and dinner. Encouragement sessions every evening and vitamin therapy before bed."

"Encouragement sessions?"

"That's when Doctor Sinhurma addresses us as a group. We share our experiences, get advice on what we're doing right or wrong. It probably sounds boring, but it can get pretty emotional; he has this talent of getting you to just open up."

I'll bet he does, Horatio thought. "You ever have sing-alongs?" he asked.

She gave him a puzzled smile. "Sometimes—they're always lots of fun. How did you know?"

He shrugged and didn't meet her eyes. "Archery, swimming, dorms . . . seems a lot like summer camp to me. It was either that or telling ghost stories around a campfire."

"Well, we don't do that—but there is a spiritual component to the encouragement sessions too. Doctor Sinhurma is a very wise man." To Horatio, she sounded vaguely defensive.

"What happens after they leave here?"

"Well, they stay on the diet, and he does encouragement sessions online. Plus they come back for weekly checkups."

"And how long have you been here, Ruth?" he asked.

"Just over a year. But you have to understand—the longer you're here, the more you want to stay. That's why I volunteered to work for the clinic."

"I understand Phillip Mulrooney was here even longer than that."

Her smile wavered. "Oh. Yes, he's been—he had been with the doctor even before the dorms were added. He was one of the original staff of the clinic."

Horatio stopped. "I'm sorry. Did you know him well?"

"It's okay." She glanced down at the ground, then back up. "We were friends. When I heard what happened, I couldn't believe it."

"Doctor Sinhurma didn't seem to have any problem."

Her smile was gone now. "He—he and Phillip were having a difference of opinion."

"Is that why Phillip was working in the restaurant instead of the clinic? Was he being punished for something?"

She didn't answer, but Horatio could see how much she wanted to talk. He put a hand on her shoulder, gently. "Hey," he said softly. "I know you don't want to get Doctor Sinhurma in trouble. But if he didn't have anything to do with Phillip's death, then any information you can give me will help clear him."

"But—but I thought Phillip was killed by lightning.

I mean, you can't be saying—oh, God. I don't know. I don't know what to do." Her chin quivered and tears spilled down her cheeks.

"It's all right," Horatio said. He reached into his jacket pocket, pulled out a handkerchief and handed it to her.

She took it and wiped her eyes. "Thank you," she sniffled. "I just . . . I'm just kind of confused right now. See, Phillip used to be really close to Doctor Sinhurma. He had his own room in the main house even before the dorms got built. But a few weeks ago, things changed. Phillip came to me one night and said he'd seen Doctor Sinhurma have some kind of breakdown, raving like a crazy man about gods and devils and the Garden of Eden. It really shook Phillip up. After that, he moved out of his room and into one of the dorms."

"Ruth, listen to me. I know you have a great deal of respect for Doctor Sinhurma, but maybe staying here isn't the best idea right now."

She stared at him, her eyes still glistening. "Maybe you're right. A while ago, Doctor Sinhurma asked me to do something—something I didn't feel right about. I didn't think there was anything wrong at the time, but it's been bothering me ever since."

"Forgive me for asking—but was it sexual? If so, he's broken the law—"

"No, no, it wasn't like that—not exactly. I'd rather not say, all right? But he didn't come on to me." She paused, took a deep breath and let it out. "I really believe in him. Before I came here, I was overweight and ugly, you know? He changed all that."

"Overweight, maybe," Horatio said. "But I can't believe you were ever ugly."

The smile that crossed her face was only a flicker of what was there before, but it was genuine. "That's very kind. Though I could show you some pictures that might change your mind."

"I very much doubt that," Horatio said. "But then, I'm a skeptic by nature. Ruth, I'd like you to promise me something."

"What?"

Horatio took a card out of his pocket and handed it to her. "I want you to promise me that if you feel your safety is being threatened, you'll get out of here—and that you'll call me. Is there anywhere else you can stay? Relatives or friends?"

She took the card and shook her head. "Not really—I came down from Tampa to get into the program. Everyone I know is part of the clinic."

"Check yourself into a motel if you have to, okay?"

She tucked the card into her pocket and nodded. "Okay. Do you really think Doctor Sinhurma had something to do with Phil's death?"

"That's what I intend to find out. . . ."

Calleigh was studying a printout when Horatio walked into the layout room, her face lit by the glow of the light table. "Hey, Horatio," she said brightly. "How'd it go at the clinic? See anyone famous?"

"Just a pro athlete who should have stuck to Gatorade. What do you have?"

She handed over the printout. "This just came in.

Mass spec readings on the substance you found on the roof of the restaurant."

Horatio looked it over. "Fifty-eight percent potassium nitrate, thirty-two percent dextrose, ten percent ammonium perchlorate. Well, that explains the sweet smell—almost a third of it was sugar."

"What is it, H? Some kind of accelerant?"

"That's exactly what it is. Usually designed to accelerate rockets, in fact—these are all components of solid-fuel model rocket engines."

"So someone launched a rocket off the roof?"

"It's starting to look that way."

"Well, what goes up has to come down, right?"

Ryan Wolfe picked that moment to walk in. "Anything I can help with?" he asked.

Horatio and Calleigh glanced at each other.

"You know, Ryan," Calleigh said sweetly, "there is. . . ."

Before becoming a CSI, Ryan Wolfe had been a beat cop. He was no stranger to canvassing neighborhoods or knocking on doors . . . but that didn't mean he had to like it.

He sighed as he walked up to his twenty-third door. It wasn't that he regarded the work as demeaning, or even boring; processing evidence often meant hours spent poring over data or repeating the same task over and over again. That didn't bother him in the least.

But talking to witnesses drove him crazy.

He could deal with the ones that lied—at least that meant he was getting somewhere. But most people's stories were incomplete or contradictory or just plain wrong. It was deeply frustrating to the scientist in him, and it didn't make the obsessive-compulsive part terribly happy either.

He knocked on the door. There was a Spanish-accented shout of "Just a minute!" from inside, accompanied by a frenzied barking.

The door opened and a balding, heavyset Cuban man with a thick black mustache stared blankly at him. He was dressed in a short frilly robe that ended at mid-thigh and had a poodle standing between his legs.

"Jes?" he said. The dog growled balefully.

"Miami-Dade police," Wolfe said, holding up his badge. "I'm looking for a piece of evidence in a crime investigation that might have turned up in this neighborhood. Can I ask you a few questions?"

The man stared at him. "Hokay."

"What I'm trying to find is a model rocket. It would look like a long tube with fins and a conical head, probably made out of cardboard. It may have come down in a tree or on top of a roof."

The man considered this. The poodle continued to glare, trembling with indignation. "Ha tube?" the man asked.

"Yes."

"Habout thees long?" He held his arms apart and his robe fell open, revealing more than Wolfe cared to see.

"It could be," Wolfe said, keeping his eyes on the man's face.

"Weeth feens?"

"Yes. With fins."

The man's brow furrowed. He reached into one pocket of the robe and drew out a cigar, then pulled a lighter out of the other. He lit up, then favored Wolfe with a thoughtful look.

"I do not theenk," he said carefully, "that I have ever seen such a theeng."

The dog barked, and Wolfe made the mistake of looking down. He quickly looked back up again. "Would you mind if I took a look around your backyard? I won't be . . . long."

The man took a long, slow drag on his cigar. "You may do thees theeng," he said, "but be careful of the doggie poo-poo." He closed the door.

"Great," Wolfe said. "I'll do that."

Around the Miami-Dade crime lab, "What have you got?" was heard so often it was almost a standard greeting; but unlike being asked "How's it going?" it usually generated more than an automatic response. When Yelina spotted Horatio waiting for an elevator at the lab, it was the first thing she said to him.

"A very bad feeling," he answered.

"About?"

"Doctor Kirpal Sinhurma. I've been out to his compound—excuse me, 'clinic'—and what I saw did not fill me with religious awe. More like a nasty case of *déjà vu.*"

"Oh? He remind of you someone?"

"Several someones. David Koresh, Jim Jones, Reverend Moon . . ."

"You think he's running a cult?"

"According to the expert I talked to, the techniques he's using are textbook. He deprives his followers of food and sleep, puts them in a controlled environment and bombards them with his message. Group activities like exercise and sing-alongs to keep them exhausted and emotional and break down their sense of individuality. He's even got them working for free, under the guise of 'therapy.' "

He almost spat the last word out. Yelina looked skeptical. "Are you sure, Horatio? The man has A-list celebrities lined up for his treatment. I mean, it's just a diet, isn't it?"

"That's just it," Horatio said grimly. "He's managed to slip in under the radar by selling his philosophy as a fitness trend. You buy his book, you listen to the current hot actor talking about how the diet changed his life, you get a sprinkling of New Age ideas from the Web site. Nothing too extreme, nothing too controversial. But once you're at the clinic . . . that's when you get the hard sell."

"Still—even if he is operating a cult, it doesn't make him a killer. Aren't you the one that's always going on about letting the evidence decide?"

Horatio paused as the elevator doors slid open. "And I will," he said as they got on. "Actually, I'm sure he has a pretty good alibi for the crime itself. But that's like saying a mob boss is innocent because he was somewhere else when the trigger was pulled. I'm telling you, Yelina, I talked to this guy. I looked him in the eye."

"Yeah? He come across like a psycho?"

"Just the opposite. Warm, personable, completely at ease. Charisma to burn."

"Well then," Yelina said drily, "by all means, let's lock him up."

Horatio smiled despite himself. "I couldn't shake him. You remember Seth Lockland?" Lockland was a serial killer and rapist Horatio had helped convict five years ago. Both Horatio and Yelina had been present when the needle had gone into Lockland's arm, and the last look they'd seen on his face was a grin and a wink.

"I remember him," Yelina said. "Little bastard lived in his own world."

"Exactly. That's the kind of relaxed arrogance this guy projects, Yelina. His attitude wasn't 'You have the wrong guy,' it was 'You'll never understand.' Sinhurma practically told me God struck Mulrooney dead on his say-so . . . and made sure his second-in-command *heard* him tell me, no doubt so the word will get spread to the faithful. He thinks he's untouchable."

The doors opened and they walked out. "And I suppose you're going to prove him wrong?" Yelina asked.

"I'm going to prove what I always prove," Horatio said. "The truth."

Atmosphere Research Technologies was in South Dade, just outside of Homestead. They specialized in studying lightning and its effects, and were known as one of the best such facilities in the world; it made perfect sense they were located in Florida, who along with Texas annually racked up the highest number of lightning-related injuries in the country.

Horatio pushed open the thick glass door and stepped inside. A south-facing glass wall let plenty of light into a spacious reception area, with a low-slung, curving wooden desk against the back. A hallway led off to the left and a large, blown-up photo of a lightning strike over Miami took up most of the far wall. A round-faced woman in her fifties with short gray hair, wearing a white sweatshirt that read ALL CHARGED UP! ZAPCON 92 was working at a computer behind the desk. She looked up when he came in and smiled. "Hello?" There was something Eastern European in her voice, but Horatio couldn't quite place the country.

"Hello, yes," Horatio said. "I have an appointment with Doctor Wendall. Horatio Caine."

"I'll tell him you're here." *Czech? Polish? Maybe Croatian . . .*

The man that bustled out a moment later was in his forties, completely bald, and wore a blue lab smock over a Miami Dolphins T-shirt, a pair of blue jeans and white sneakers. He had a wide, impish grin and eyebrows so thick and black it looked like they'd been put on with a Magic Marker. "Hi! You must be Lieutenant Caine!" He put out his hand and Horatio shook it.

"Please, call me Horatio."

"Come on back to the lab—I'm just in the middle of something." He led Horatio down the hall, past numerous doors and into one labeled LAB 4. The room held several workstations, a long table covered with disassembled electronic equipment and what looked like an aquarium full of murky, whitish liquid.

Doctor Wendall pulled a plastic chair from beside one of the workstations and offered it to Horatio, then took one himself and sat down. "I'm just crunching some data," he said cheerfully, motioning to a screen where numbers and figures were scrolling past too fast to read. "But I'm happy to help out, if I can. You mentioned something about a lightning-related homicide on the phone?"

"That's right. I was wondering if you could shed a little light on the subject."

Doctor Wendall chuckled. "Well, I have to admit, it's not too often I hear the words 'lightning' and 'homicide' in the same sentence. For one thing, most people survive lightning strikes—less than a third are fatal. It seems an unlikely murder weapon."

Horatio smiled. "In my experience, murder weapons are sometimes chosen exactly for that reason. And I have reason to believe that this particular suspect might find a thunderbolt from the heavens to be an irresistible choice."

"Well—even assuming you don't have Thor or Zeus in a jail cell downtown—I would have to say it's possible. Lightning does kill about a hundred people a year in the U.S.; the question is, how do you persuade your victim to be one of them? Did you find him tied to a lightning rod on top of a building?"

"Not exactly . . ." Horatio explained where the body was found.

"A toilet? Well, it's where they found Elvis, so I

guess he's in good company. And you say he was talking on a phone at the time?"

"A cell phone, yes."

"Hmm. Well, a number of people do get hit by lightning every year while on the phone—but usually through a landline, which makes an excellent conductor. There was a story going around for a while about cell phones attracting lightning strikes, but it was only an urban legend—cell phones operate at an omnidirectional radio frequency of around six hundred milliwatts, which is not going to make any difference to ground potential. Were his eardrums intact?"

"As far as I know."

"If it had come through the phone, it probably would have damaged at least one." Wendall glanced over at the numbers scrolling down the screen, then back to Horatio. "Still, lightning's hardly predictable. There was a case in Denmark where a bolt came in through a window, broke every other plate on a shelf, shattered sixty panes of glass and every mirror in the house, then jumped outside and killed a pig and a cat."

"I think I can safely say," Horatio said, "that there was a definite lack of livestock on the premises. There was, however, something on the roof . . . we found evidence that a model rocket had been fired."

Wendall's reaction was immediate; his eyes popped wide open with astonishment. "You're *kidding*," he said slowly.

"I'm afraid I am not."

Wendall shook his head. "Okay, that changes

everything . . . now I see how it could be done, sure. But really, you're talking to the wrong guy."

"Oh?" Horatio leaned forward intently. "And who would the right guy be, then?"

"His name's McKinley—Jason McKinley. And I can tell you exactly where he is, too. . . ."

4

CALLEIGH WALKED INTO THE LAB and wrinkled her nose. "Why is it every time I see you lately I smell cooking meat?"

Delko grinned. "Are you sure?" He was stirring the contents of a small metal pan over a Bunsen burner.

Calleigh set her folder down on the lab table. "You know, if H catches you using lab equipment to make lunch, you're gonna be in big trouble."

Delko turned off the burner. "This isn't lunch, it's more along the lines of a comparison." He took a small spoon and measured out a few scoops of the lumpy, gray material in the pan onto a small plate. A very similar pile of gray lumps was heaped onto a second plate beside it.

"I got to thinking about what was found in the vic's stomach," Delko said. "Hamburger, only partially digested. He had to have eaten it recently."

"Maybe he went out for lunch on his break," Calleigh pointed out.

"I checked all the restaurants in easy walking distance—none serve chili. We didn't find any evidence that he brought a lunch with him, which suggests the chili came from the restaurant itself. The empty package of hamburger I found in their Dumpster supports that."

"That doesn't make any sense. They don't serve meat, and I can't believe they'd let him use the kitchen to fry up his own."

Delko nodded. "Yeah, most vegans are pretty hard-core—they won't even use the same cookware meat is prepared in. Then I thought, what if he didn't *know* he was eating meat?"

Delko pointed to the first plate. "This is regular hamburger. And this," he said, indicating the other, "is TVP."

"Ah," Calleigh said, understanding Delko's point. "Textured Vegetable Protein. *Fake* meat."

"Right. TVP is often used in vegetarian recipes as a substitute for hamburger—look pretty similar, don't they? I got this package from The Earthly Garden— they use it in some of their dishes. Guess what was listed as the daily special the day Mulrooney was killed?"

"Vegetarian chili?"

"Add some beans, some tomatoes, a big whack of spices . . . even a vegan might not notice he was eating something that used to have four legs."

"So somebody slipped him a meat Mickey? Why?"

"I was wondering about that myself. I did a little research and found that many vegans claim to get violently ill if they eat meat accidentally—even if they're unaware of what they've consumed at the time. Because animal proteins are digested at a lower PH than plant proteins, eating meat produces higher levels of stomach acid—so I had the vic's stomach contents analyzed for their PH level." He picked up a piece of paper and handed it to Calleigh.

She glanced at it and nodded. "One point one? That's awfully low."

"And awfully acidic. Maybe even enough to make him sick."

"Putting him inside the bathroom, either on or hugging the toilet. Okay—so who fed it to him?"

"I thought you'd never ask. I lifted a print off the plastic wrap around that empty package of hamburger and our winner is . . . Shanique Cooperville, one of the wait staff."

"Does Horatio know?"

"Already called him. He's having her brought in for questioning, but H says there's something else he has to confirm first. How's your stuff going?"

She leaned up against the wall, crossed her arms and sighed. "Hard to say. I've been going over that section of pipe I pulled out of the wall, but copper's a soft metal; it's got so many tool marks it's hard to say what's plumbing-related and what isn't. The burn mark where the lightning went through gave me a nice outline of something, but I haven't been able to positively identify it. Thought it was a clamp at first, but I haven't been able to get a match."

"Any prints?"

"Yeah, a couple of latents. Nothing from AFIS, but I thought I'd compare them to what you pulled from the hamburger." She picked up her folder from the table and took a sheet out.

"Hand 'em over," Delko said, reaching for his own

stack of paper. He grabbed a magnifier, lined the sheets up in front of him, and peered through it, one after the other. "Nope. Sorry."

"Well, that would have been too easy, wouldn't it?" She took the sheet back, put it away in the folder. "I tracked down the contractor that did the work on the pipe. I'll see if it matches anyone in his shop."

"Guess I'll start processing that blender and the knives H found."

"Well, aren't you just three steps ahead of the rest of us," Calleigh said.

"Hey, I just caught a lucky break with that print," Delko said. "If it had been a bullet, I'm sure you'd be the one—"

"—with the big, goofy grin on my face. Right," Calleigh said. "Oh, well. Making chili is such a guy thing, anyway. . . ."

Boys and their toys, Horatio thought. *Some things we never seem to outgrow . . . like the desire to throw things at the sky. Or maybe it's just the need to play with explosives.*

He squinted up at a tower of wooden scaffolding three stories high, built on a concrete apron in the middle of a grassy field surrounded by low scrub. The only other structure in sight was a small trailer at the edge of the field, a white shoebox of a building with a single door and no windows.

"Jason McKinley?" Horatio called out.

A head appeared over the railing that lined the top floor of the tower. "Yeah?"

"Miami-Dade police. I was wondering if I could ask you a few questions."

There was a pause. "Sure, come on up." The head disappeared again.

A wooden staircase zigzagged up the outside of the structure, ending at a simple platform on top. A man with short, stubbly black hair, dressed in baggy khaki shorts, hiking boots and a faded orange T-shirt, was kneeling in front of a gray metal box the size and shape of a large trunk. A cluster of a dozen or so yard-long tubes grew from the top and several thick cables snaked away from the base and through a hole in the floor. The man had an access panel open and was fiddling with something in the interior.

"Sorry to bother you," Horatio said, "but Doctor Wendall says you're the man to talk to about RTL."

McKinley stopped what he was doing and looked back at Horatio. He was in his mid-twenties, with a large, bucktoothed mouth and acne-scarred cheeks. A wispy goatee curled off his chin. "Rocket-triggered lightning? Well, I could deny it . . . but considering what I'm doing, I don't think I'd have a lot of credibility."

Horatio smiled. "I'm Horatio Caine, Mister McKinley. I hope you don't mind if I pick your brains for a few minutes?"

"Well, *I* sure didn't pick 'em, but I wound up with 'em anyways. And call me Jason. What do you want to know?"

"I was wondering about the mechanics of the process. . . . How exactly does it work?"

Jason fished a stick of gum out of his pocket and unwrapped it as he spoke. "Basically, we stick a rocket up a thunderstorm's ass. Not surprisingly, this irritates the thunderstorm, and it retaliates by trying to blow the shit out of the rocket. It doesn't realize that a bunch of clever monkeys on the ground have attached a really long wire to the rocket, and in fact can channel the lightning bolt right down to the ground—more specifically, to our instruments." He popped the gum in his mouth and started to chew.

Horatio's smile turned into a grin. "Okay . . . it's not that I don't appreciate the laymen's version, Jason, but I was hoping for something a little more technical. Despite the badge, I do know a thing or two about science. You can use big words around me—I'm something of a clever monkey myself."

Jason didn't look embarrassed at all; instead, he laughed. "Really? All right then, I'm gonna turn off all my 'normal society' filters and just talk like the science geek I am. But I warn you, it's not pretty."

"I think I can handle it," Horatio said.

"The first thing we do is use electric field meters to look for an appropriate field in a *cumulus congestus* cloud. Usually, a negative charge tends to build up at the base of the cloud while positive charge tends to build at the top of the cloud. If a charge—negative or positive—starts growing at the base, an opposite charge shows up on our equipment."

"How strong a charge do you need?"

"We don't launch unless we've got a reading of eleven kilovolts per meter or higher. Even so, we only trigger a strike about half the time. We use a rocket with a one stage J-class motor, send it up around two thousand feet. It trails a Kevlar-sheathed copper wire off an attached spool, which feeds the charge down to this baby right *here* . . ."—he thumped the box beside him with his fist—". . . and we monitor the whole process from over *there*." He pointed in the general direction of the windowless trailer.

"And who pays your bills?"

"You mean, who does ART sell the research to? All sorts of places: power company, airplane manufacturers, NASA. We get some grant money, too—SFU students work for us on special projects sometimes. That's how I wound up here."

Horatio nodded. "Pretty interesting work, sounds like."

"Most of the time, yeah. I get to tell people I yell 'Shazam!' for a living—unfortunately, it seems the more attractive the person I'm talking to, the less likely they are to get the reference."

"I always preferred Batman to Captain Marvel, myself."

"Me too! You know, between Adam West camping it up and Michael Keaton in a rubber suit, people forget he's the World's Greatest Detective. The Batcave has to have the best crime lab on the *planet*."

"Well, we can't all be playboy billionaires. . . ." Horatio peered at the equipment Jason had been working on. "So this is where you launch from. Nice setup."

"Oh? You a rocketeer yourself?"

"I fooled around with it a bit when I was a kid. And I used to work in a related field. . . ."

"Aerospace?" Jason reached into another pocket

and pulled out a folding multitool. He snapped it into its pliers configuration with a practiced flair and squatted down next to the open access panel again.

"Bomb squad. You'd be surprised how often model rocket components turn up in homemade explosive devices."

"That why you're here?" Jason reached into the hatch with the multitool and started poking around. "Somebody leave a pipe-bomb lying around with a rocket igniter for a detonator or something?"

"No. I think someone used a rocket to trigger a lightning strike that killed someone."

Jason frowned and considered that. "Well, I guess it could be done. Don't waste time looking for the wire, though."

"Why's that?"

"Because the charge vaporizes it. Zap, pfft, gone. The rocket usually survives, though—that what you found?"

"Not yet. But we're looking. . . ."

Wolfe had searched alleys. He had searched backyards. He had found the highest building in the area and surveyed as many rooftops as he could see, and climbed onto the rooftops of every building he couldn't. He had checked treetops, playgrounds, balconies and awnings. He had talked to anyone in the neighborhood who might have seen or found a model rocket, and so far he had come up with nothing.

He had no intention of giving up. He stood on the corner, ran a hand through his unruly brown hair and thought about it. Presumably, the person who fired the rocket didn't want it found. That meant it was probably painted in such a way as to not stand out. It could even have been rigged to explode after its job was done, which would mean he was looking for fragments, not a whole rocket. If it was made of cardboard, like many rockets, the rain would have turned the remnants into waterlogged scraps.

"So," he said to himself, "nondescript, soggy scraps of cardboard. Sure. No problem."

He looked up, trying to imagine the rocket blazing into the stormy sky. A flash as the lightning hit, and then—what?

He studied the street. A fair amount of traffic, but not too busy. It was just off the part of the Gables known as the Miracle Mile, a commercial district full of chain outlets: big stores like Old Navy or the Gap, smaller ones like Starbucks. A bus pulled past him, then stopped halfway down the block, letting on an Asian woman with a bag of groceries.

Wolfe pulled out his cell phone, called the lab and got put through to Calleigh.

"Hello?"

"Calleigh, can you check something for me real quick?"

"What do you need, Ryan?"

"Transit information. I'm in Coral Gables and I need to know when the bus comes by a particular corner."

"Isn't there a phone number you can call for that?"

"Sure, if you want to wait ten minutes to talk to an automated system. I'd rather talk to you."

"Aw, that's sweet. Give me the location."

After he did, she said, "Okay, I'm looking it up online. . . . You're in luck—there's a listing for that very stop. Starts at six forty-five A.M. and runs every half hour until six forty-five P.M. After that, it's once an hour until eleven."

"That's just what I wanted to hear."

"Gonna catch a bus?"

"Nope. A rocket."

He thanked her and hung up, then called directory information to get the number for the transit dispatch office. He supposed he could have gotten Calleigh to look that up too, but he knew she had more important things to do.

Twenty minutes later, he was showing his badge to a bus driver. The driver, an olive-skinned woman with her hair pulled back in a French braid, stared at it as if it were a forged transit pass.

"Excuse me," Wolfe said. "Were you driving this route yesterday?"

"That's right," the woman said suspiciously. "What, did that drunk I kicked off complain?"

"Nothing like that. Is this the same bus you drove yesterday too?"

The woman's frown deepened. "Yeah, I think so. Why?"

"Did you hear something like a bang or a thump on the roof at this stop, around two forty-five?"

"Driving this route I hear all sorts of bangs and thumps. Long as it's not a flat or a gunshot I don't pay much attention."

"I'm going to have to ask you to wait here for a second."

An elderly black woman seated in the front asked anxiously, "Is it gonna be long? I got an appointment."

Wolfe smiled reassuringly. "Not long at all, I promise."

The bus was articulated, sixty or so feet long with a flexible join in the middle. Wolfe walked to the back door, where a series of oval-shaped metal rings on hinges were mounted up the side. He snapped each rung into place, then used them to climb up and onto the roof.

Sure enough, he found what he was looking for caught between the corrugated folds of the flexible accordion section: a cardboard tube almost three feet long with a finned base and a tapered nose, painted a flat, matte black and singed even darker at one end.

"Houston, we have solved our problem," Wolfe murmured.

"Hello? Lieutenant Caine?" The voice on the other end of the line sounded female, nervous, and familiar.

"Can I help you?" Horatio said. He was in the Hummer, on his way back to the lab.

"It's Ruth, Ruth Carrell. I—I need to talk to you. In person."

"What's wrong?" he asked immediately. "Are you all right?"

"Yes, I'm okay. I just—there's a few things I'd like to tell you, and I didn't feel right saying anything at the clinic."

"Is that where you are now?"

"No, I'm in Miami Beach. Lummus Park, across from the Starlite Hotel."

"I can be there in twenty minutes," Horatio said.

"Okay. I'll wait."

Lummus Park was in South Beach, right on Ocean Drive. He took the MacArthur Causeway to Miami Beach, through Watson Island. A seaplane buzzed overhead, trailing water from its pontoons, on its way to the Caribbean or Key West or maybe just a quick tour over Miami itself. He drove across the glittering blue bay, past Dodge and Lummus Islands with the immense white bulk of their cruise ships, and then onto Fifth Street to Ocean.

Ocean Drive was what most people thought of when they thought of Miami, ten blocks of neon-splashed art-deco extravagance, all of it looking out over a white sand beach and the deep blue of the Atlantic. Horatio was used to it, but it was always interesting.

Parking in SoBe was slightly less difficult than getting in some of the clubs there—which is to say, almost impossible. For Horatio, of course, it wasn't a problem. Lummus Park was frequented by many an in-line skater, and thus had plenty of flat concrete surfaces to park on . . . as long as you were willing to ignore little things like sidewalks in order to get there. Although Horatio was always unfailingly polite when doing so—excuse me, large tanklike vehicle coming through, thank you *so* much—he always got a secret kick out of doing it.

Well. Maybe not *that* secret.

He found Ruth Carrell sitting on a bench under a little thatched roof, looking out over the Atlantic. Rolling black thunderheads were gathering on the horizon, but the sky overhead was still bright and blue.

Horatio sat down beside her and took off his sunglasses. Instead of the usual blue T-shirt, she was wearing sandals, a pair of jeans and a white tank top, her brown hair pulled back in a ponytail. She held a small fabric purse in her hands, and looked troubled.

"Ruth?" Horatio said. "Hi. How are you doing?"

"Lieutenant Caine—"

"Call me Horatio."

"Horatio. I'm . . . I'm confused." She stopped and looked down at her hands.

"About what?"

"Doctor Sinhurma. I know he's a good man, but . . ." she trailed off.

This, Horatio knew, was the delicate part. She obviously wanted to talk, but she didn't want to betray a man she saw as her saviour. If Horatio played it wrong, she'd only get defensive and angry.

"This is hard, I know," Horatio said. "And I understand, I do. Doctor Sinhurma clearly has the best of intentions, and I can see that he's done a lot of good. It's not my intention to persecute him—I only want to get to the truth. Doctor Sinhurma believes in the truth, doesn't he?"

"Yes, yes, of course. It's just—he has such a better *understanding* of the truth than I do. I mean, who am I to second-guess him—"

"Ruth. There is only one truth, and it's there for anyone that wants to see it."

She glanced up at him. "I guess that's your job, isn't it? Seeing the truth."

"I suppose it is."

"Is it always that simple? Things are or aren't? People are innocent or guilty?"

"Not always, no." Horatio looked away, over the rippling gleam of the ocean. "My job is to establish the facts. What happened, how it happened, where and when and who it happened to."

"What about why?"

He smiled. "That's the tricky one. The first five are science, the last one's often human nature. But you can find truth there, too. For instance—do you know why the ocean off Miami Beach is that particular color?"

"No, why?" She shaded her eyes with her hand and stared at the waves shushing in.

"A scarcity of plankton. Colder water holds more dissolved CO-two and oxygen, which is better for the growth of phytoplankton and zooplankton. The more plankton in the water, the murkier it looks. Florida seawater is warm; therefore fewer gases, fewer plankton . . . and crystal-clear, blue water. That's the science."

He paused, then said, " 'When beholding the tranquil beauty and brilliancy of the ocean's skin, one forgets the tiger heart that pants beneath it; and would not willingly remember that this velvet paw but conceals a remorseless fang.' "

"Shakespeare?"

"Herman Melville—*Moby Dick.* It's easy to describe the sea in scientific terms . . . but he understood it on another level. He looked out over the same ocean I do, but saw it a different way. He saw a different part of the same truth."

"Yeah. Doctor Sinhurma's like that. He sees parts of the truth that just go right over my head."

"I see. And the things he understands and you don't have started to worry you?"

She didn't answer at first, and he thought he might have rushed it. Then, in a hesitant voice, she said, "A little."

He waited.

"It's just that—well, you know that thing I mentioned? That Doctor Sinhurma asked me to do?"

"I remember."

"I've been thinking about it a lot. At first I thought it was no big deal, but then the more I thought about it the wronger it felt. And I really need to talk to someone, and I *can't* talk to anyone at the clinic or to Doctor Sinhurma, and, and—"

She put her hands over her mouth and started crying, her shoulders heaving. Horatio wanted to comfort her, but this was a negotiation and now was the time for him to make a demand. He leaned forward, offering her the hope of solace but not the guarantee, and said softly, "Ruth. What did he ask you to do?"

She blinked at him with watery red eyes and said, "He asked me to be nice to someone."

"But not in a sexual way?" Horatio asked, recalling their previous talk.

"No. Not exactly. Doctor Sinhurma invited me to his study one evening for a long talk. We talked about the Vitality Method and how important it was to change people's lives, and how those people go on to affect other people, and how you can wind up affecting the whole world by changing just one person."

She pulled out a handkerchief—the one he'd given her previously, Horatio noted—and blew her nose. "And it takes a very special sort of person to find the *right* people to change, because if you change the right people it affects *more* of the right people, and—oh, I'm not explaining this very well, am I?"

"You're doing fine."

"Anyway, even though he didn't say so, I knew that Doctor Sinhurma was one of those people who were good at finding the right people to change. And it's such a huge *responsibility*, you know? He tried to hide it, but I could tell how hard it was for him, sometimes."

"You wanted to help," Horatio said.

"Yes! Because some people just *can't* or *won't* see how amazing Doctor Sinhurma's methods are. And we were eating these pastries, these fantastic almond tarts he gives out sometimes as a special treat, and he says he's going to tell me a secret—it turns out that actually they're really *healthy*, they're made with whole wheat flour and almost no fat or sugar, and then we started talking about how it was okay to offer somebody something they *thought* was decadent when it was actually *good* for them."

"Because ultimately, they would benefit," Horatio said, nodding.

"Yeah. And it turns out there was this—person— who Doctor Sinhurma thought would really benefit from the Vitality Method. A person who was one of those *right* people, you know? And he asked if I would talk to this person. Talk to them and . . ." She stopped, wiped her eyes and blew her nose again.

"Offer them an almond tart?" Horatio prompted.

She gave him a wan smile. "More or less. He didn't ask me to do anything inappropriate, he just wanted me to make them feel welcome."

"And did you?"

She sighed. "Yeah, I did." She glanced at Horatio, then away. "*Really* welcome, if you know what I mean."

"Who was this person, Ruth?"

"I—I'd rather not say, okay? I don't want to get them in trouble—it's not like *they* did anything wrong. I just wanted to talk to someone about it."

Horatio nodded. He knew what she wanted to hear: that she'd done the right thing, that everything was fine and she was overreacting.

But that was just on the surface. The fact that she wanted to hear those reassurances from Horatio instead of someone at the clinic meant she had serious misgivings.

And now was not the time for Horatio to be kind.

"Let me ask you a question," Horatio said. "Would you have had physical relations with this person if Doctor Sinhurma's opinion wasn't involved?"

She thought about it. "No, I guess not," she said quietly.

"Would you have done what you did if Sinhurma hadn't had that long talk with you?"

She looked over at him, and now he heard just a trace of anger in her voice. "Probably not."

"I know you'd like to paint yourself as a martyr in all this, Ruth, but that's just not true. You didn't sacrifice your honor to prove your dedication to a cause; you were manipulated into prostituting yourself—"

She stood up abruptly. "I thought you would understand," she said, her voice quivering. "But you don't. It wasn't *like* that—"

"It's not your fault, Ruth. You can't blame yourself for what you did—"

"Doctor Sinhurma says that ultimate responsibility and ultimate acceptance are the same thing," she said flatly. "I accept what I did and take full responsibility for my actions."

Horatio could see he was losing her; she couldn't face the possibility that her benefactor didn't have her best interests at heart. "So," Horatio said evenly, "you're prepared to do it again?"

The look on her face was as if he'd slapped her. "I—he *wouldn't*—"

Horatio stood up. "It's not about what he would do anymore," he said. "It's about what *you're* willing to live with. Think about that . . . and when you reach a conclusion, give me a call."

He slipped on his sunglasses and left her there, staring out at the ocean. Still clutching his handkerchief.

Shanique Cooperville wore three-inch heels, a tight pair of white satin pants, a midriff-baring pink top, and a glare. Horatio met her eyes across the table of the interview room calmly and said, "Shanique. Thanks for coming down."

"No problem." Her tone suggested the exact opposite.

Detective Salas, standing beside the table, said nothing. She crossed her arms and favored Shanique with a look that could be described as tolerant. "You've been on the Vitality Method for what, eight months now, right?" Horatio asked. "How's that working out for you?"

"Fine."

"Good, good. Still, it can't be easy—giving up all those tastes forever. No more steak, no more omelettes, no more shrimp cocktails or eggs Benedict or barbecued chicken—"

"What, are you trying to make me sick? I don't miss any of that stuff," she snapped.

"Oh?" Salas asked. "You mean you don't cheat? Maybe have a little side of bacon with your granola and soy milk now and then?"

Shanique rolled her eyes. "You don't get it. Giving up animal products isn't like quitting smoking or drinking or trying to lose weight—it's a shift in how you think, in what you *are*. I don't think of those things as food anymore; just the idea of putting any of that in my body disgusts me."

"I see," Horatio said. "So handling something like—I don't know, a package of raw hamburger—you'd find extremely distasteful."

She narrowed her eyes. "Yes."

"Then could you please explain how your fingerprints wound up on such a package in the Dumpster of The Earthly Garden?"

Her glare faltered. "I—I don't know."

"I do," Horatio said. "You brought it to the restaurant so you could slip it into the vegetarian chili that was on special that day. Not to the stuff being served to the public, though—just the bowl that Phillip Mulrooney had for lunch. And I can prove it."

She didn't reply, but Horatio could see she was rapidly losing her confidence. He pushed a little harder. "Mulrooney, a known vegan, had meat in his stomach. We found a dirty bowl with his fingerprints and traces of the doctored chili in a buspan, and *your* prints on the package of ground round."

She tried to regain a little of her former bluster. "So? Even if I did, what's the charge? It wasn't like I poisoned him."

"The charge," Horatio said, "is accessory to murder. Right now I can link you to a very questionable crime scene . . . questions that I *will* get the answers to. At the very least, I can arrest you for assault—and if Mulrooney's death was *not* an accident, the fact that your actions put him in that bathroom puts *you* in a very bad place. . . ."

Her resolve cracked, then crumbled, replaced by resignation in her eyes and voice. "I just wanted to show him he was wrong."

"About what?" Salas prodded.

"About Doctor Sinhurma. About the Vitality Method. About—about us."

Horatio nodded. "You had a relationship with Phillip Mulrooney?"

"We were sleeping together, yes. Until he started having doubts."

"Doubts about you?" Horatio asked.

"Doubts about Doctor Sinhurma. Phil started questioning his methods, even his intentions. I tried to reason with him, but he wouldn't listen."

Horatio leaned forward, his elbows on the table. "What sort of things was he saying?"

"Crazy, paranoid things. That the Vitality Method was brainwashing, that Doctor Sinhurma was running a cult. He stopped taking the shots."

Horatio frowned. "What shots?"

"Vitamin shots. We get them every night at the clinic."

"And when he discontinued the shots, the doctor moved him to the restaurant?"

"Well, Doctor Sinhurma wasn't going to lock him up and *make* him take his vitamins, was he? He's a nutritionist, not Charles Manson."

"So you two argued," Salas said. She leaned on the table with both hands. "The hamburger was a little payback."

"No! I just figured . . . I could tell he was thinking about leaving the clinic. Sooner or later, he would have dropped the diet, too. I thought if I made him sick, he'd see how *poisonous* meat is, how bad it was for his body."

"Like making a kid smoke a whole pack when you catch him with a cigarette, is that it?" Horatio asked.

"I thought it would make him realize. I thought it would make him *understand*, like he did when we first got together. It was so special, so golden. . . . Doctor Sinhurma, we have so much to thank him for. And when Phil stopped seeing that, it just—it just *hurt* me."

"So you hurt him."

"It was for his own good."

"Well, going meat-free may be good for you," Horatio said, getting to his feet, "but high voltage definitely is not."

"Am I under arrest?"

"Not at the moment," Horatio said. "But don't plan any long Caribbean vacations."

5

CALLEIGH WALKED THROUGH the open doorway into a room dimly lit by sunshine slanting through a battered set of blinds over the front window. The faded sign on the door read LEAKYMAN PLUMBING in bright orange, red, and green letters. She could hear reggae music playing from somewhere in the back—old Bob Marley, it sounded like. "Hello?" she called out.

She could hear someone moving around in an adjacent room, but heard no reply. She surveyed the room: black plastic pipes of varying sizes and thicknesses leaned into one jumbled corner, while a row of white toilets stood against a wall like squat albino gnomes. A wooden counter took up most of another wall, and was piled high with tools, fixtures and stacks of paper. A calendar five years out of date tacked up behind it displayed a topless blonde with an improbable physique demonstrating a unique way to hold a plunger.

"More like Dustyman," Calleigh murmured, running a finger along the counter.

"Hey, out there—just a sec, mon," a voice called back. "I be right out." A bearded black man, his hair in dreads, appeared a moment later through a door-way behind the counter. He wore a tie-dyed purple T-shirt and round, orange-tinted sunglasses.

"What you need?" he asked. His voice held a distinctive Jamaican lilt, burred by a smoker's rough undertones. "If it flushes, flows, or fountains, we can fix you up."

"That's a catchy slogan," Calleigh said. "I need to ask you some questions about something in the 'flushes' category."

"Sure t'ing. What you wanna know?"

"I understand you did some work for a restaurant called The Earthly Garden?"

"Ah, they recommend me, huh? Yes, I put a new toilet in for them. Did a good job, they were very happy."

"This was how long ago?"

"Oh, quite a while. Six months or so ago."

"Really?" Calleigh frowned and pulled a notepad from the pocket of her black blazer. The jacket shifted, revealing the holster riding on her hip and the badge right beside it, and did so in a fashion that looked entirely accidental. "My information says it was only put in last week."

The man's smile remained in place, but his eyes hardened. "Oh, yes. My mistake. The toilet is new—it was the sink we put in six months ago."

Calleigh smiled back. "Look, you don't have to impress me with the quality of your work and how long it lasts. I just want some facts to help out with a criminal investigation, and then I'll get out of your hair. Okay?"

"Sure, sure," the man said, shrugging. He picked a pack of cigarettes up from beside the till and shook one out. "Ask away."

"What was the reason the new toilet was installed?"

The man lit his cigarette with a small butane torch before answering. "It was old. Old and cracked, with a bad seal. They wanted a new one."

"Uh-huh. And why did you choose a stainless steel version and copper piping, as opposed to porcelain and PVC?"

The man took a long drag and blew it out through his nose. "Hey, I give them what they ask for. They want stainless, they get stainless. They want copper . . ." He paused, and gave a pointed glance at her badge. ". . . they get *copper*."

She ignored the look and continued. "And who, exactly, asked for those things?"

"I don't recall—*exactly*," he said. His sunny tone of voice had begun to cool.

"I understand—it being a whole seven days ago and all," she said. "You know, workplace toxins can have serious neurological consequences. Maybe you have something lying around that's affecting your short-term memory?" Her voice maintained its Southern hospitality, but her eyes met his and didn't blink. "Something you'd rather not be found by a person with a search warrant?"

He chuckled—and looked away. "Okay, okay," he said. "I just like to give my customers their privacy, you know?"

"How commendable. I had no idea the concept of

confidentiality had spread from doctors and lawyers to plumbers . . . now, who was it that ordered the work done?"

"Humboldt. Albert Humboldt. He told me he wanted something *primo*—I think he was trying to impress his boss, you know?"

"I think I do," Calleigh said. "And you know what? I think *my* boss is going to be impressed, too."

Horatio joined Wolfe in the layout room. The rocket lay on the light table, looking like the remains of a cheap special effect for some Z-grade science fiction movie. "Found it on top of a bus, huh?" Horatio said. "Good work."

"Thanks," Wolfe said. "No prints, though. Trace is running a mass spec comparison on chemical residue, seeing if we can get a match to what you found on the roof."

"Good, good. How about identifying marks on the rocket itself?"

"No serial number, but I have managed to pin down the make: an Estes Cometmaster. Widespread commercial availability, unfortunately."

"How about the technical specs? What sort of altitude is it rated for?"

"Sixteen hundred feet if you stick to the recommended guidelines."

Horatio grabbed a white lab coat and slipped it on over his suit jacket. "I'm guessing this one was customized to go a little higher than that—the fuel mixture is probably a custom blend, too." He picked up a magnifier and held it over one of the fins. "And take a look at this . . . hand me a pair of tweezers, will you?" Horatio carefully picked a tiny sliver of material from where the fins met the body of the rocket. He held it up and examined it closely. "This model is from a kit, right? Not preassembled?"

"That's right. You think it's transfer?"

Horatio put the sliver in a small envelope and handed it to Wolfe.

"Could be. When the rocket was put together something may have been trapped between two of the pieces."

"Or it could have gotten wedged in there after hitting the bus."

"Depends on what it is, doesn't it . . . what else do we know?"

"I can tell you it was launched using a rail system, probably mounted on a tripod," Wolfe said. He pointed to two small circular projections that jutted from the side of the rocket, one near the base and one about halfway up. "These are called launch buttons. They slide into a groove on the rail—keeps the rocket vertical when it takes off."

"How about the shard we found in the burn pattern?"

"Trace identified it as a fragment of ceramic tile. Rocketeers sometimes use tiles as blast deflectors, but they can shatter—that's why the burn was in a fractured pattern."

"So they took the launch rail and the broken deflector with them, but missed a piece. . . ."

Horatio's cell phone rang. "Caine," he answered.

"Horatio," Yelina said. "We've got another DB connected to the Mulrooney case."

"Connected how?"

"She was also one of Sinhurma's patients. Name is Ruth Carrell."

Ruth Carrell's body lay in a wooded lot, just off the Tamiami Trail. She wore the same clothes she'd worn the first time Horatio had talked to her, and lay sprawled on her back, her blue shirt turned a blood-soaked dark purple. Yellow-finned star fruit, brown-pelted kiwis and bumpy green *atemoyas* clustered around her, spilled from two cloth bags she had obviously been carrying.

Alexx examined the body while Horatio looked on. Her combination of compassion and professionalism never failed to impress him; she never lost sight of the fact that she was looking at a person, someone with hopes and dreams and a history, even while she was calmly inspecting the most grisly wound.

"Puncture wound in the chest," Alexx said. "Thin blade, double-edged. No hilt mark."

Horatio looked down. "Muddy out here. No other tracks but hers. How'd the killer get close enough to stab her without leaving footprints?"

"He didn't," Alexx said. She grabbed the body by one shoulder and rolled it partially over, exposing an equally bloodstained back. "He shot her from a distance. See the exit wound?"

Horatio frowned. "An arrow?"

"Went right through her heart, looks like." She

shook her head. "Honey, this is not the way to meet Cupid."

Horatio pulled out a pair of tweezers and carefully extracted a small item from the sole of the body's right shoe. He held it up and studied it. "Plant matter. Doesn't fit with the rest of the vegetation here, or what I saw at the compound."

Calleigh was walking the perimeter of the lot. She called out, "Horatio? Can you tell which way she was facing?"

"From the way the body's lying and the tracks, I'd say she was standing looking toward that edge of the lot," Horatio replied, pointing.

"Which means our arrow should be over here, on the opposite side," Calleigh said, heading for a small stand of brush. "Assuming the killer didn't retrieve it."

"And our archer would have been standing somewhere in this area," Horatio said, heading in the opposite direction. There was a small stand of trees and the rusting corpse of a washing machine that looked like it had been cleaning clothes back when Eisenhower was in the White House.

Calleigh peered into the brush. "Brambles," she said. "Terrific!"

Alexx walked up behind her. "If I was the one who had to get in there and search," the ME said, "I wouldn't be too happy, either."

"Hmm?" Calleigh said, "Oh, no, Alexx—I wasn't being sarcastic. I really did mean 'terrific'—because if our Robin Hood did try and retrieve his arrow, there's a good chance he left some transfer on some of these stickers. If we're *really* lucky, maybe even some blood. . . ."

She pulled out a spray bottle of orthotolidine and misted it over the branches. She preferred ortho over Luminol in situations like this for two reasons: Luminol, while usually reliable, required darkness to show up properly, and it also reacted to certain kinds of plants—horseradish and potatoes in particular. Orthotolidine produced a bright blue color in the presence of hemoglobin or myoglobin, which stood out sharply in daylight—or at least it did when there was any blood to detect.

"No luck, darn it," she muttered. No blood, no fibers that she could see; it looked like the killer hadn't braved the brambles after all. Still, that meant the arrow had to be there, somewhere—and if she couldn't find a bullet, Calleigh would gladly settle for an arrow.

Horatio inspected the site where the arrow must have been launched from. The ground here was grassy, not muddy; there were no clear footprints he could see.

After satisfying himself that the killer hadn't left any obvious traces, he looked around. The road beside the lot was fairly busy, but his view of traffic was obscured by waist-high scrub. He could see the back of a large, beat-up panel truck, though; its owners were the ones who'd discovered the body. They'd been selling produce out of the rear of the vehicle and Ruth had stopped to do some shopping. After making her purchases, she had started to walk back to her car—parked a short distance away—when something must have caught her attention in the lot. She had walked in, and never returned. One of the produce vendors, looking for a bush to stand behind and relieve himself, had noticed the body around twenty minutes later. Yelina was still talking to him, but apparently he hadn't seen or heard anything else.

Calleigh was already burrowing into the brush on her hands and knees. Horatio discreetly looked the other way.

"Horatio?" Alexx said. "I noticed something else on the body, too. She belonged to the same group that Phillip Mulrooney did, right?"

"That's right."

"Well, she has needle tracks on her upper thigh, just like he did."

"I'm not surprised," Horatio said. "Apparently the vitamin part of the Vitality Method is administered through nightly injections. Mulrooney had recently stopped getting his."

"That explains why they were intramuscular," Alexx said. "Absorbs into the body at a slower, steadier rate."

"But hers are still fresh, right?"

"I'd say so."

"Good. Hopefully the tox screen will tell us exactly what she was being given. . . ."

"Got it!" Calleigh cried. She emerged from the bushes, wisps of hair straggling away from her head where the brambles had pulled at them, bits of leaf and twigs clinging to her clothes. She held an arrow with a wide, bloodstained head triumphantly in one gloved hand. "It was in there pretty far, but it hit a branch and stuck."

"Nice work," Horatio said. "Let's get that to the lab."

"And let's get *you* inside," Alexx said.

She wasn't, Horatio knew, talking to him.

"Hello, Randolph," Horatio said.

"Uh, my name is Mark—," the handsome but confused-looking man in the blue T-shirt said.

"Mark, Randolph—you all sort of look the same to me," Horatio said. "Follow me, Eric." He led Delko around the main building, Mark trailing behind.

"Doctor Sinhurma isn't here right now," Mark tried again. "He told me that if the police stopped by I was supposed to help in any way I could—"

"Really? That's very kind of you, Mark. Did Doctor Sinhurma say where he was going?"

"Uh, no."

They crunched along the path, Delko doing his best not to stare as they passed the pool.

"That's all right, Mark. I'm not here to talk to Doctor Sinhurma, anyway." Horatio stopped before a small outbuilding with an extended, peaked-roof porch jutting from one side that was easily five times longer than the building itself, held up by posts every six feet. Fifty yards away, a row of bull's-eye targets stood on the green lawn, in front of a wall of stacked hay bales.

"This is where you store the archery equipment?" Horatio asked.

"Yes, but I don't have the key—"

"Then get it," Horatio said pleasantly. He handed a folded piece of paper to Mark. "This is a warrant to search for and confiscate any and all archery-related items on the premises."

Mark told him the key was in the main house, and trotted off to retrieve it.

"Not that I'm criticizing, H," Delko said, pulling on a pair of gloves, "but even if we find the bow, how are we going to match it to the arrow?"

"That, my friend, we will leave in the capable hands of Ms. Duquesne. . . ."

The first thing Calleigh did was identify the arrow. It was a kind commonly referred to as a broadhead, with a wide, double-edged, diamond-shaped tip. Two triangular vents were cut into the center, one on each side of the shaft, to help airflow and prevent a phenomenon known as planing, where the flat surface of the arrowhead acted like the wings of an aircraft. Calleigh had an uncle who was an avid bow hunter, and he'd taken her on the occasional hunting trip when she was a teenager—though she soon learned she preferred the kick of a firearm to the snap of a bowstring. Still, he'd taught her a lot about the sport, and she remembered it all.

Blood on the arrowhead was being checked against the DB, but Calleigh didn't expect any surprises there. She was more interested in what the rest of the arrow could tell her.

The shaft was made of wood, painted dark green. There were cracks in the paint, especially where the head met the shaft. There were three five-inch vanes of white feathers, and she could tell they were hand-fletched; the vanes were attached by thread, wrapped around the quill of the feathers at the front and back and sealed with some sort of clear varnish. She scraped off a bit of the varnish and took a sample of the thread. The nock of the arrow was plastic and worn, with a chip missing from one edge.

She examined the tips of the vanes under a microscope, and took pictures of the images. Looking through a database, she identified the model of arrowhead—a Magnus two-bladed Broadhead, with a 125-grain weight.

She sent the varnish and thread off to be analyzed, then made herself a cup of tea and waited for Horatio.

On the drive back from the Vitality Method compound, the back of the Hummer full of confiscated gear, Delko turned to Horatio and said, "I don't get it, H."

"What's not to get, Eric?"

"The cult thing. I mean, people giving up control of their lives like that? Being told what to do, what to eat, what to think? Don't these people have brains?"

Horatio kept his eyes on the road. "We're not talking about rational behavior, Eric. Cults prey on emotional weakness, not intellectual. Most cult recruits are well-educated and from middle-class backgrounds; the one thing they all have in common is they're unhappy. They think their unhappiness has a specific cause and a specific solution, and the cult offers them that on a plate. Sinhurma's just found a way to modernize the whole process—the Internet's a great place to target lost, lonely people looking for answers. . . ."

"And he can recruit worldwide."

"Sure. Use the Web site to find prospective members. Draw them in with promises of youth and beauty and celebrity. Get them in an environment where Sinhurma controls all the variables."

Delko's brow furrowed. "That sounds awfully familiar."

"Yes it does," Horatio said softly. "Trolling, seduction, capture. Three out of six for the stages a serial killer goes through."

"Leaving out what? The first one and last two, right?"

"The aura phase is first, but it doesn't show up in every serial. Hallucinations, heightened senses, intense fantasies. Of course, if what Ruth Carrell told me about Sinhurma ranting and raving to Mulrooney is true, he may be manifesting that one as well."

"After capture comes trophy-taking," Delko said. "How's that fit?"

Horatio glanced over at the young CSI. "Taking a trophy is a way for the killer to relive the act later, once the high has faded. Sinhurma doesn't have to relive anything; his control is ongoing, twenty-four/seven. In a sense, every one of his patients is a trophy. . . ."

"So the last phase, depression, never kicks in—since he's always in control and always has new patients coming in, he can just keep the high going forever."

"Highs never last, Eric. That's why serials escalate.

Just like a junkie, they need more and more to maintain the level of intensity they're used to. If Sinhurma was responsible for Phillip Mulrooney and Ruth Carrell, he's exercised the ultimate control twice. You know what that means."

Delko nodded soberly. "He's got a taste for it. You really think he's a serial?"

"I think he's a sociopath. I think he got that degree in psychology to fine-tune his ability to manipulate people, and the degree in nutrition to launch his scam."

"And Mulrooney threatened his control."

"Mulrooney was having doubts. When I talked to Ruth, she seemed to be having doubts as well. To someone in Sinhurma's position, those are cracks in the foundation his whole movement is built on; there's no way he could allow them to spread. He may have even killed Ruth Carrell to stop them."

"Or had her killed by another cult member?" Delko suggested.

"If so, it would have to be someone he trusted implicitly. Maybe even someone with a vested interest in keeping the cult going . . . which means we should take a close look at his second-in-command."

"Mister Kim, right? I'll get on it when we get back to the lab."

"See if you can get a subpoena for the phone records of the clinic and the restaurant while you're at it. I want to know who Sinhurma was talking to and when. . . ."

"You mean you're just going to dump this whole

Sherwood Forest yard sale on Calleigh?" Delko's tone was mock-serious.

Horatio smiled. "Something tells me she won't need any help, Eric. . . ."

"So Albert Humboldt had new plumbing installed," Yelina said. She and Horatio were sitting in one of the interview rooms that was currently empty, sipping coffee and comparing notes. Hazy golden sunlight shone through the honeycomb grid that covered the windows; it always made Horatio feel like he was conducting interrogations in a beehive.

"But did he do it on his own," Yelina said, "or was he told to?"

"Well, the plumber thought he was ingratiating himself to someone," Horatio said. "Which doesn't tell us much . . . except something doesn't quite add up."

"What do you mean?"

"Sinhurma's ego demands the best, and he can afford it. From Calleigh's description, the plumbing shop was something of a dive."

"Maybe Humboldt was acting on his own, and it was all he could afford."

"That doesn't scan, either. You don't get into Sinhurma's clinic unless you're young, pretty or rich—and since Humboldt is neither young nor pretty, he must have money. If he was trying to impress Sinhurma, he wouldn't go cut-rate."

"So—a personal connection, then? Humboldt and the plumber know each other?"

Horatio nodded and took a sip of his coffee. "That

could explain why he was reluctant to cooperate with Calleigh. Even when she explained he wasn't a suspect, she practically had to twist his arm to get his fingerprints."

Yelina flashed a grin. "But she got them?"

Horatio grinned back. "What do you think?"

"I think Ms. Duquesne can be very persuasive when she wants to be."

"Well, she can certainly make evidence stand up and talk. . . . I've got her processing the archery equipment from the Vitality Method compound right now."

Yelina finished her coffee and stood up, brushing her long hair back with one hand. "You think she can match the arrow to a bow? It's not like there's any rifling marks to compare it to."

Horatio stared at the honeycombed window; a black-and-white patrol car pulled slowly past outside, its driver an anonymous blur. "If anybody can," he said quietly, "she can."

"Now this," Delko said, "is interesting."

"Hmm," Wolfe said. "Yeah. Yeah, that is interesting."

Delko was examining the pair of blackened knives Horatio had found. "At first I thought they were charred from the lightning. But it looks more like they were heated over and over again, over a direct flame."

"Did you find something like a large bottle with the bottom cut off, or maybe a hole in the side near the base?" Wolfe asked.

Delko looked puzzled. "No. Nothing like that. Why?"

"Because this looks like hot knifing equipment to me."

"Which would be?"

"It's a technique used for smoking hashish. They carve tiny chunks—smaller than a matchhead, usually—off a larger block with a razor blade. A pair of butter knives are heated—sometimes over a propane torch, sometimes stuck between the coils of the heating element of an electric stove—until the tips glow red to white-hot. The chunk of hash is tapped lightly with one of the knives, causing it to stick to the hot surface. The two knives are held slightly apart, and the person taking the hit holds the bottle with the bottom cut off over them, like an inverted funnel. When the knives are brought together, the drug is instantly incinerated; the resulting puff of smoke fills the bottle, flows up into the neck and gets inhaled through its open mouth."

Delko looked impressed—then skeptical. "And how does a clean-cut science geek like yourself know about this kind of stuff?"

"Believe it or not, it's a Canadian thing," Wolfe said. "There's this house over on Ninth Street we used to bust on a regular basis—every spring break it would fill up with university students from Ontario, looking to party somewhere they didn't have to wear a parka. We'd always find this stuff in the kitchen."

"I thought all snowbirds were in their sixties and drove RVs," Delko said, grinning.

"Apparently, some of them prefer to fly," Wolfe replied absently. He was studying the blade of the knife with a magnifier. "Have you compared this to the pattern you found on the wall outlet?"

"Yeah—no match," Delko said glumly. "The melted pattern is much thinner and squared off. It's starting to look like those knives were stashed for an entirely different reason than the one we thought."

"It may not be the crime we were looking for," Wolfe admitted, "but it's still evidence. We should follow it up, see where it leads."

"I'll check the records, see if any of our suspects has ever been arrested for drugs," Delko said. "How about you? How's the rocket investigation going?"

"Waiting to hear back from Trace," Wolfe said.

Horatio stuck his head in the door. "Mister Wolfe— do you have a minute?'

"Sure thing, H."

Horatio motioned him to follow with a tilt of his head and led him down the hall to another lab. "I'd like your opinion on something," Horatio said. He indicated a microscope. "Take a look at this."

Wolfe bent over the eyepiece. "Hmm. This the material you found on the rocket?"

"That's right. Trace identified it as Kevlar . . . which, according to my information, is what coats the outside of the wire used in rocket-triggered lightning. I think this scrap came off prior to the wire being attached— maybe when the end was trimmed."

"The end definitely looks cut," Wolfe said.

"Run out to the restaurant and grab anything that looks like it might be a match," Horatio said. "Wire cutters would be ideal, but it could be anything with an edge."

"Like a razor blade," Wolfe said. He told Horatio what he'd told Delko about the hot knives.

"So we have a possible drug connection," Horatio mused. "Okay, let's take a closer look at Sinhurma's past. He's from India, and a lot of hashish gets produced in that particular neighborhood."

"Delko's on it," Wolfe said.

"Good," Horatio said. "While you're at the restaurant, look for a bottle like the one you described—Eric might have missed it if he didn't know what he was looking at. Check the Dumpster the blender was found in too. I'm heading over to talk to Alexx—give me a call if you find anything."

"Will do."

"Well, she'd definitely lost a lot of weight recently," Alexx said. "See? Stretch marks on the belly." She looked down at the body on her autopsy table and shook her head. " 'Such a pretty face—if only you could drop a few pounds.' Bet you got tired of hearing that, didn't you, sweetie?"

Horatio stood next to the table, studying the mortal remains of the woman he had talked to such a short time ago. Others in Horatio's position would have preferred the distance of the observation gallery, would have used the impersonality of the cameras and monitors to reduce Ruth Carrell to no more than evidence. Horatio refused to allow himself that luxury. Ruth Carrell had been a living, breathing human being— one he had extended an offer of protection to—and someone had ended her life with a weapon commonly used to kill deer.

Not that he would waste any time blaming himself. Horatio had long ago perfected a very efficient mechanism for dealing with guilt: he swallowed it whole and processed it as cold rage. "Guilt is good," he'd said once. "It makes us stronger." In Horatio's case, that strength fed his determination and focused his will; for him, taking a case personally didn't get in his way at all. It just meant he would never, ever give up. . . .

"Cause of death was cardiac arrest, brought on by the pericardium being punctured," Alexx said. "Entrance wound is one point five inches in diameter, exit wound is the same. Passed clean through her."

"Can you tell me anything more, Alexx?"

She reached down and pulled the body's mouth open, using both hands. "Thick, yellowish coating on the tongue," she said. "Means she was probably fasting—it's a common side effect. That fruit she was buying wasn't for her."

"So she was grocery-shopping for the compound. That means someone sent her to that produce stand . . . someone who'd scouted out the location beforehand and knew they could lure her into position to be shot. What else?"

Alexx lifted one of the corpse's hands. "Well, she was doing hard physical labor. Calluses on her palms and fingers."

"Probably more 'work therapy,' " Horatio said. "Although I didn't see anything at the compound that would correspond to this. . . . Thanks, Alexx."

"I'll know more when the tox screen gets back," Alexx said.

"Let me know as soon as it comes in," Horatio said.

His next stop was the firing range they used for ballistics tests. Calleigh was there, but for once she wasn't wearing a pair of yellow-tinted shooting goggles and padded ear protectors. Instead, she had a bow in her gloved hand.

"Hey, H," she said. "I've been test-firing the bows you brought me. This is the last one."

"Don't let me stop you," he said.

She nocked an arrow, fitting the grooved end of the shaft to the bowstring. "I'm using arrowheads of the same style and weight as the one that killed Ruth Carrell," she said, bringing the bow up and pulling the arrow back. About three-quarters of the way down the range stood a target dummy. "The dummy's twenty yards away, approximately how far Ruth Carrell was from the shooter. The dummy also simulates the same amount of resistance a human breastbone, musculature and internal organs would."

She released the arrow. It hit the dummy in the chest and passed through it, clattering to the floor on the other side.

"Didn't go much farther, did it. . . . " Horatio said, frowning.

"No. The arrow I found was at least another twenty yards away, and still traveling at a fairly flat trajectory. This bow is a recurve, with a pull weight of fifty-five pounds; the others are all in the same range. I don't think any of them could have fired the arrow that killed Ruth."

"So we're looking for a heavier bow."

"Probably a compound. I'm going to do some more tests, but I'm guessing the pull weight we're looking for is closer to eighty or ninety pounds."

"What about the arrow?"

"The arrow I found is hand-fletched, with a green-painted wooden shaft and a hunting tip. All the arrows from the compound have carbon graphite shafts, factory fletching and target heads."

"So, no match."

"No, but the news isn't all bad. The paint on our arrow is quite worn, so there's a chance of transfer from the arrow to the bow. If the shooter has more arrows of the same type, we may be able to link them to the one we have."

"All we have to do is find the bow. . . ."

"Well, we're looking for a hunter's bow, as opposed to target shooting," Calleigh said. "And in Florida—"

"—all bow hunters have to be licensed," Horatio finished. "Good thought. I'll check the state database. You know, when we nail this guy, people might start calling you 'Arrow Girl' instead of 'Bullet Girl.' "

"As long as our killer gets the shaft," Calleigh said.

"Well, well, well," Horatio murmured, satisfaction in his voice. He hit a button and scrolled a little farther down the screen.

"Find something, H?" Delko said. He was at a workstation on the other side of the lab, doing some research of his own.

"I believe I have. A bow-hunting license issued to a Mister Julio Ferra of Hialeah."

"One of the waiters. Maybe he was the one keeping tabs on Mulrooney for Sinhurma—I've got the phone records for the restaurant right here, and someone made a call to the compound at two forty-three."

"Just before Mulrooney was killed."

"Right. Whoever made the call saw Mulrooney bolt for the bathroom, called Sinhurma and let him know the sacrifice was on the altar—"

"So to speak—"

"—letting Sinhurma call Mulrooney. But why bother? What did Sinhurma have to say that was so important?"

"It wasn't what he said, Eric; it was probably some overblown, melodramatic statement along the lines of 'You have failed me and now you're going to die.' No, the important thing for Sinhurma was that his voice was the last thing on earth Phillip Mulrooney heard . . . and that Mulrooney knew it."

"So what's our next move?"

"We get a search warrant for Ferra's place. See if we can link him to the bow."

"He doesn't live at the compound?"

"Maybe he does now, but he listed a different address the first time we talked to him. Part of him still thinks of that place as home . . . and that's the most likely place he'd go to hide something."

The address Ferra had given was his parents' house in Hialeah, a stone's throw from the famous racetrack. The neighborhood was primarily Cuban, the street filled with modest, red-tile-roofed suburban houses. Ferra's parents, a short Cuban man with a well-groomed mustache and a stout woman with thick, tinted glasses, were indignant in the extreme when Horatio showed up with a patrol car and a warrant. The entire time he was searching, he could hear a steady torrent of outraged Spanish from outside; Horatio felt sorry for the patrolman who had to stand there patiently and endure it.

The house was middle-class, homey, almost touchingly kitschy. The Ferras, it seemed, took their American citizenship very seriously; the roof sported a large flag and there was another in the front hall, plus an entire wall devoted to commemorative plates of U.S. Presidents. *The Franklin Mint*, Horatio thought, *must love these people*.

He started with Julio Ferra's bedroom. It had that distinctive look a child's room gets when the occupant is in transition between teenager and adult: somewhere between abandoned and anticipatory, as if the room was holding its breath and afraid to exhale. A poster of the Miami Dolphins cheerleading squad and pennants from various sports teams adorned the walls; a *Star Wars* Millennium Falcon hung from a hook in the ceiling by a length of fishing line.

That was Julio's. The neatly made bed, the pictures of Julio carefully arranged on his spotless dresser—those were the parents'. *Half discarded chrysalis, half shrine*, Horatio thought. *The Museum of the Empty Nest*. Julio Ferra was in his early twenties, but it appeared as if his parents hadn't quite let go yet.

Oddly enough, this part of his job bothered Horatio more than dealing with bodies. It was his job to collect evidence, but any search of a residence, no matter how specific, wound up revealing much more about the person who lived there than you were after; Horatio had found more caches of pornography than he could count.

Occasionally this was helpful—he'd nailed a child molester or two in just that way—but usually made him feel vaguely embarrassed, like he'd walked in on someone using the bathroom. Still, any piece of information might prove valuable, and so you collected as many of them as you could.

He learned quite a lot about Julio Ferra. He learned that he collected baseball cards. He learned that he'd been a chubby child and a bigger teen. He learned that he'd won first place in an archery contest in summer camp when he was eleven, and that a girl named Marcia Spring had a crush on him his junior year of high school. He learned that he'd had a bow-hunting license since he turned nineteen, and that he liked to go hunting with his father.

In the garage, he hit the jackpot.

An old fiberglass recurve—probably from his summer camp days—and two compound bows hung on the wall from pegs. A quiver full of arrows was propped up in the corner. Horatio examined it critically without touching it; the arrows all appeared to be hand-fletched.

"Bull's-eye," Horatio said.

If anyone connected to the Vitality Method had ever done drugs, they'd never been arrested for it—not as far as Delko could find. The waiters, the cook, the dishwasher—none had ever been charged with anything related to narcotics. Albert Humboldt had a drunk-and-disorderly and Shanique Cooperville had been arrested once for shoplifting; the others, including Sinhurma himself, had no criminal record at all. If

Sinhurma was connected to the drug trade, there was no evidence of it in his past.

And then Delko remembered the plumber Calleigh had talked to. From what she'd said, he'd been pretty reluctant to give up his prints. . . .

He ran them through AFIS and got an immediate hit. Samuel Templeton Lucent, arrested for possession of a Schedule One drug: hashish.

"Now we're getting somewhere," he muttered. He gave Horatio a call on his cell. "Got a possible break in the Mulrooney case," he told him. "The plumber that installed the new pipes was busted once for hash."

"Which connects him to the person at the restaurant who hid the knives, and the crime scene itself. Good. I'm coming in with some promising evidence myself. See you in a few."

Something else was nagging at Delko, but he couldn't quite put his finger on it. He stared into space and drummed his fingers on the desktop, then picked up his cell and made another call.

"What's up, Eric?" Wolfe answered.

Delko briefly wondered if caller ID would eventually kill the word "hello." "Where are you?"

"On my way back to the lab from the restaurant. Got a box full of cutting implements to test for tool marks."

"The stove there—it runs on natural gas, right?"

"I think so. It's not electric, anyway."

"But it could be propane?"

"I guess it's possible. Why?"

"You said hot-knifers sometimes use propane

torches to heat the knives. Like the kind plumbers use for soldering pipes." Delko filled Wolfe in on what he'd found on Samuel Lucent. "I'm going to scrape a little bit of the char off those knives and do a mass spec. It'll tell us whether they were heated using propane or natural gas."

"Which means you want me to go back and check on the type of fuel the stove at the restaurant uses."

"Well, you're closer than I am. . . ."

"You couldn't have had this brainstorm fifteen minutes ago?" Wolfe sighed. "Okay, okay. I'll double back."

Delko thanked him and hung up. He dug out the knives, scraped off a sample and sent it to Trace, then sat down in front of the computer.

Delko, as he would freely admit, was more than a little competitive. He liked to push himself, both physically and intellectually—the challenge of figuring out what the evidence meant and how it fit together was one of the things that drove him and kept him interested in the job. He couldn't help but see Wolfe as competition; Horatio certainly seemed to be taking the new CSI under his wing.

So though there was no personal antagonism there it had irked him when Wolfe had known details about hot-knifing that Delko hadn't. The fact that he might have missed a crucial piece of evidence as a result bothered him even more.

So he did what he usually did when something bothered him—he got busy with research.

He had shelves at home that were crammed floor to ceiling with reference material. Every time he moved to a new place, his friends all swore it was the last time they'd help unless he hauled all the damn books and magazines himself. "What," they'd say, "you never heard of the Internet? You want to know something, just Google it."

It wasn't that simple, of course—not everything was on the net, and even with his police clearance there were databases he couldn't get into. But despite all the hard copy Delko owned, despite his rep as a hands-on, physical kind of guy, the Web was still one of his favorite CSI tools.

Eric Delko was a certified police diver, the guy they called when they needed a body retrieved from a canal or a car hauled out of Biscayne Bay. He loved his work, even though there was a certain grisly aspect to it that couldn't be avoided—floaters were never pretty, and predation by everything from crabs to sharks always made things worse.

But there was a silent beauty to being underwater that never went away. The rippling quality of light in the shallows when the sun was high and bright; the somber, green-hued mystery of the deeps, where anything could be just out of range of your vision. He'd been diving once off of West Palm Beach, checking out some coral, and turned around in time to see a humpback whale glide past no more than ten feet away. It was like being snuck up on by a Greyhound bus.

There was something about surfing for data on the Web that reminded him of diving, something about the feeling of isolation and possibility. He always turned the sound down on any workstation he was using; he didn't want to hear chimes and beeps and bursts of tinny music when he jumped from site to site, file to file. He preferred the feeling of quiet solitude, of floating alone in a sea of pure, weightless information, inhabited only by flickering schools of thought.

Also, the next time the subject of hashish came up he intended to kick Wolfe's butt.

6

"MISTER FERRA," Detective Salas said. "Take a seat."

Julio Ferra sat down across from Horatio. He was in his early twenties, well-built, with dark hollows under his eyes and a prominent nose. His black hair was cut fashionably short, and he wore a small metal hoop in each earlobe—not earrings, disks with a hole punched in the center, like little steel doughnuts embedded in his flesh. When he turned his head the right way, light from the window would cast a tiny dot of illumination right through and onto his neck, giving the impression that a sniper was about to put a bullet through Ferra's jugular. He wore the same blue shirt the rest of the Vitality Method patients did, at least while working—they'd pulled Ferra in from the clinic itself.

He was also, Horatio noted, twitchy. Despite his obvious effort to appear relaxed, he had all the classic symptoms of someone with something to hide: he wouldn't meet Horatio's eyes, his body posture was tight and closed off, and his hands moved up to rub his chin or scratch his nose every time he answered a question. Salas had picked up on it too; she stood to one side and behind him, just out of his sight, trying to keep him off-balance. It was a technique Horatio had seen her use before—but then, they had questioned many a suspect together. It was always a subtle dance, a matter of cues and signals and intuition, not so much good cop/bad cop as an interrogation tango.

"I understand you're quite the archer," Horatio said.

"I used to be," Julio said noncommittally.

"Oh?" Salas said. She leaned in close and said, just a little too loudly, "You don't shoot anymore?"

"I don't hunt, no. Killing animals for sport or food pollutes your karma." His response had the ritual flavor of dogma, and Horatio knew he'd have to shake him off that track if he wanted anything but rote answers.

"How about killing human beings? That okay with you?" he shot back.

"What? No, of course not—"

"Well, it's funny, Julio. Two people you worked with have died in a very short period of time, and one of them was killed with an arrow fired by a compound bow. At this very minute, my investigators are examining a compound bow and some arrows we took from your parents' garage . . . and what do you think they're going to find?"

Julio met his eyes and refused to look away— something many liars did, not realizing that overcompensation was just as telling. "You'll find I used it recently," he said, defiantly. "I still target shoot sometimes, at the clinic's archery range. But that's all."

"Sure," Salas said. She'd moved, without making a

sound, to his other side. "And where were you today at ten A.M.?"

"I was at the clinic, doing some laps around the pool."

"You by yourself?" she asked.

Julio glanced back at her and smiled. For just a second, Horatio could see the plump, happy kid in his parents' collection of photos. "No. You watch television?"

It was an odd question, but Horatio had a sinking feeling he knew why Julio had asked it.

"Not a lot, no," Salas answered.

"Then you should pick up a copy of *TV Guide*," Julio said. "At ten o'clock I was hanging out with the guy on this week's cover. And his girlfriend. She's in this month's *Vogue*, or maybe it was last month's—I forget."

"I'll check on that," Horatio said mildly. He already knew Julio was telling the truth. "But even if that's so, it doesn't mean we're done."

"What do you mean?"

"Doctor Sinhurma's methods really worked for you—you used to tip the scales on the other side of two-fifty. That about right?"

"I'm one seventy-five now. I do a hundred laps every day." He sounded more wounded than defensive, but Horatio knew he had to get under his skin.

"Sure, I can see that. You hang out with celebrities, you look good, you're surrounded by people who appreciate you—it's a shame that all has to end."

"You don't have anything to charge me with," Julio said, sounding a little confused.

"That's not what I mean. I'm talking about the clinic. It's a shame, really—I can see that Doctor Sinhurma's doing good work. But you have to understand, Julio, that there are certain people who don't want that work to succeed."

Horatio paused, and shot Salas a meaningful look. The expression on her face told him she had no idea where he was going, but looked forward to finding out. Julio couldn't see her response, but a spark of suspicion kindled in his eyes. "What people?"

"People I answer to, Julio. This is Miami; you know how it works. One hand washes another, favors get done and then repaid. A man in my position . . . well, let's just say I owe a lot of favors." Horatio dropped his voice, ever so slightly. "So believe me when I say: Sinhurma is through. His message is just too threatening. I've been told to shut him down, and I'm afraid that's what I'm going to do." He put the barest note of regret into his voice.

Cults, as Horatio knew, relied on emotional manipulation to instill a particular set of values into their members. There were several themes that were almost always used: that the leader of the cult possessed mystical knowledge he could pass on to his followers and it would make them happy forever; that the members of the cult were special people, and only the cult had the wisdom to recognize that; that dark forces in high places hated the cult and wanted to tear it apart, and only through the utmost loyalty of its members could it survive.

Emotional manipulation worked both ways, though . . . and Horatio intended to play Julio's artificially instilled paranoia against him for all it was worth.

"You can't do that," Julio said. He sounded disbelieving, but what Horatio wanted was shock.

"Waco," Horatio said softly. He met Julio's eyes, willed him to believe it, tried to project sincerity and just a touch of sadness. "Ruby Ridge . . ."

"The Branch Davidians," Salas added.

"No!" Julio said, and Horatio knew he had him.

"That's crazy!" Julio blurted. "Those places were cults! The Vitality Method is a medical clinic—"

"Cut the crap, Julio," Horatio snapped. "Just a clinic? Do you think we're all *idiots*? Did you really think the *power* of what Sinhurma's saying wouldn't get noticed? *Did* you?"

Julio's eyes had the wide, trapped look of an animal that doesn't know which way to run, but Horatio couldn't afford the luxury of feeling sorry for him. "*I* know, and *you* know, about what's really going on out there. *Transformation.*" Horatio paused and leaned forward, ever so slightly. "You're not the same person you were when you first arrived there. That's obvious. And that kind of radical, transformative change is exactly what certain people don't want. . . ."

Julio's nod looked a lot like a nervous twitch, but Horatio could see he agreed. "But—but we're not a cult," he tried again. "We have people—*famous* people—who come there for treatment. There's no way—"

"Those people are being warned right now," Horatio said. "Do you really think they'll put their lives on the line? They're not like you, Julio; they're already rich and attractive and popular. How many of them actually live at the compound like you do?"

"None of them," he admitted.

"That's right. They don't have the level of commitment you do—they don't really *understand*." Horatio got up, walked over to the window and stared out through the grid of hexagons. He waited.

"There's—there's got to be something you can do."

"I wish there was," Horatio sighed. "I really do. But two people have died, Julio; that's not the kind of thing that gets swept under the carpet. If I could just give them the murderer, they might be satisfied; you'd get a lot of bad press, but that's better than being annihilated by a SWAT team armed with riot shotguns. . . ."

"I—I don't know anything about the murder. My bow was at the clinic for—for a while. Anyone could have borrowed it."

And right after the murder it went straight back to your parents' garage? went through Horatio's mind, but he let it stay there. *Okay, so he won't give up the killer— doubted if he would anyway. Let's see if I can pry something else out instead.*

"I know what's going through your mind," Horatio said, turning around. "You're thinking about sacrificing yourself. That's commendable, but it won't work. You've got an airtight alibi, remember?"

The flash of guilt on Julio's face told Horatio that hadn't been exactly what he was thinking . . . which was good. The better the kid's instinct of self-preservation, the better Horatio's chances of making a deal.

"It's too bad," Horatio said. "The feeling that I got from the higher-ups is that they'd settle for a good scandal. I think the Vitality Method's strong enough to survive a little bad publicity myself, but I'm not the one calling the shots."

"What about . . . what about drugs?" Julio asked slowly.

Aha.

"What about them?" Salas said.

"Would a drug scandal be enough?" Julio asked, hope in his voice.

"It might," Horatio said. "What kind of drugs are we talking about, Julio?"

"Hash. Black hash."

"You're not going to pull a martyr act, are you, Julio?" Horatio said. He put his hands on the table and leaned forward, right into Ferra's face. He put a hard, cold edge into his voice. "Try and take the fall yourself to save everyone else? Because I'm not stupid, and neither are my bosses. Anything you give me better not waste my time, because I will check out each and every piece of information you give me and I will do it very, *very* thoroughly."

"No. I mean, no, I'm not trying to do that. This is about someone else."

"Who?"

"Albert Humboldt."

"Humboldt the dishwasher." Horatio straightened up, but stayed in Ferra's personal space.

"He wasn't always a dishwasher. When he worked at the clinic, he was one of Sinhurma's assistants. He has a degree in nursing."

"And he was involved in drugs."

"He used to smoke hash in a little pipe in his room. He got caught once and Doctor Sinhurma was very angry—he doesn't believe in abusing drugs of any kind."

Horatio wondered how that policy went over with some of his celebrity clients, but kept it to himself. "Were you the one who caught him, Julio?"

"No. It was Ruth."

"And what was Mister Humboldt's reaction to this?"

"Well, he was put on dishwashing duty at the restaurant, and he wasn't too happy with that."

"Did he ever threaten Ruth? Say he'd get even?"

"No! He was upset, but he was more sorry than anything else. He knew he shouldn't have been doing what he was doing. He was trying to make up for his . . . mistake."

Almost said "sin," didn't you . . . "What about the plumber, the one that worked on the bathroom at the restaurant? Do he and Albert know each other?"

"Yeah. Yeah, they do. He comes to eat in the restaurant now and then, and they always talk."

"What about?"

"I don't know, I never paid attention. But—" Julio hesitated, then went on. "I think I saw the plumber pass Albert something once. It was really small and wrapped in tinfoil."

Horatio considered this. Finally he said, "I'll be honest with you, Julio. I don't know if this is enough to forestall the inevitable . . . but . . ."

"We'll do our best," Salas said.

"Okay," Julio said. "Can I go?"

"Not just yet. I told you I was going to check out your story, and that's exactly what I'm going to do. . . ."

"The compound bow," Calleigh said to Horatio, holding up the latest piece of evidence. It looked much like a regular bow except that the bowstring was doubled through two wheels, mounted at each tip. "A fine piece of technology. Basically, it works on a pulley system. Recurve bows store energy as the tips bend toward the archer when the string is pulled taut. The compound uses a different system to store energy: the tips of the bow are pulled toward each other instead of back."

She demonstrated, pulling on the bowstring. "When you draw a compound, you turn the wheels— they're called eccentric cams. An eccentric cam is really just a pair of levers, one extending from the cam harness to the axle at the tip of the bow and the other extending from the string to the axle. The cam's like a scale with two unequal weights moving in toward the fulcrum and out toward the end at the same time.

"As you can see, it's not that hard to hold in place. When the harness is right next to the axle, the bowstring has maximum leverage; one weight sits at the end of the scale while balancing a heavier weight next to the fulcrum."

She let the bowstring snap back into place. "When you let go, the energy is released all at once. The formula for how much kinetic energy you're actually throwing at your target is arrow weight in grains, divided by 450,800, multiplied by arrow speed in feet-per-second squared."

"More than enough to punch through Ruth Carrell's heart," Horatio said. "What about the arrows?"

"They're pretty old—the ferrules are glued on, whereas most modern arrows are screw-ons. I think the arrowhead that killed Ruth was added recently to an older shaft—but so far, I can't tell if the shaft of the killer arrow matches the ones you found in Ferra's garage."

"How about the paint?"

"The other arrows were painted too—but none of them green. I was hoping to match the green paint to transfer on the bow, but look at this." She held the bow out and pointed to a small mounting hole near the handle. "Fresh scratches—it looks like our shooter mounted an arrow rest on the bow and took it off afterward. Any transfer from the arrow would be on it."

"So either our shooter knew exactly what he was doing," Horatio said thoughtfully, "or he was nervous enough to need a little technological assistance and had a friend who was savvy enough to help him out."

"Maybe not savvy enough. I took a good look at the spot where the arrows would normally rest, and sure enough, there were traces of paint. Still no green, but I got a match for black and brown. It's not much, but I can prove the arrows we confiscated were fired by this bow."

"Every piece counts."

"I also ran samples of the varnish and the thread through Trace. They both match the Ferra arrows—

but they're both extremely common, too. The thread
was broken by hand, not cut, so no tool marks, either.
Nothing a jury's gonna convict on."

"What about the feathers?"

She sighed. "Unfortunately, you can't do DNA
fingerprinting from old feathers—they're mainly keratin, just like hair. Hair shafts are hollow and sometimes have DNA inside, but the corresponding
structure of the feather—the base of the quill—has
been trimmed. Sorry, H."

"Don't worry about it," he told her. "We have the
weapon, which is a step in the right direction. Nailing
the shooter is just a matter of time . . . and thanks to
you, we now have another angle to work." He told
her about the plumber and what Ferra had said.

"So Humboldt and Lucent were drug buddies,"
Calleigh said. "And Ruth was responsible for Hum-
boldt's being demoted to scrubbing pots and pans.
Think that's enough for him to kill her?"

"It's hard to say. We're dealing with people who
have been pushed to a variety of emotional extremes,
including paranoia; you add drugs to the mix—"

"—and there's no telling what one of them might
do," she finished. "True enough. What's next? Bring
in Lucent for questioning?"

"Not quite yet. I'd like to have a little more leverage when we do . . . did you see anything in the
plumbing shop that might get us a search warrant?"

"Nothing probative—unless you want to bust him
for raising dust bunnies without a license."

"I was thinking more along the lines of
possession—"

"I think I can help you out there, H," Delko cut in, walking up with a clipboard in his hand. "Mass spec on the knives confirms that they had traces of both burnt natural gas and MAPP gas on them."

"MAPP gas?" Calleigh asked.

"It's a combination of methylacetyline-propadiene and liquid petroleum. It's a flammable, nontoxic gas used for—"

"Let me guess," Horatio said with a smile. "Soldering metal pipes, right?"

"You got it, H. Used for soldering and brazing—especially by plumbers."

"And that, boys and girls," Horatio said, "is enough to get us a warrant to inspect *all* the pipes in the possession of Leakyman Plumbing."

"You think some of those pipes may show traces of being used for other than their intended purpose?" Calleigh asked, making her eyes go all wide and innocent.

"I wouldn't be at all surprised," Horatio said.

Leakyman Plumbing was right on the Miami Canal; as Horatio pulled up in his Hummer, he could see a rickety boathouse attached to the back of the shop.

"Think we'll get lucky, H?" Delko asked as they got out.

"No such thing," Horatio said, taking his sunglasses off and slipping them in a breast pocket. "Just preparation and opportunity."

Samuel Lucent sat on a beat-up folding chair behind the counter, eating a pungent-smelling curry from a wooden bowl. He looked up as they entered, put down his spoon and stood up. "Yes? What can I do for you fine officers?"

"Good cop radar, huh?" Horatio said. He pulled out the search warrant and showed it to Lucent, who leaned over to peer at it. "We're here to search the premises, Mister Lucent."

A loud buzz sounded from another room. "Sure, sure," Lucent said. "Just a second, I have to get that." He turned and ambled toward the back.

"Sir? I'll have to ask you to stay here—"

Lucent bolted.

Horatio was over the counter in an instant, gun already out. "Eric! Cover the back!" he yelled.

A door slammed shut with a sound far too solid for Horatio's liking. *Damn! Should have brought a patrol car with us*, Horatio thought as he edged forward, his Glock aimed straight ahead. *Looks like Sammy has something to hide, after all.*

"Samuel Lucent!" he called out. "Open the door and come out, *now*!"

The door was just inside the other room, and Horatio could see that it hung in a heavy steel frame by industrial-strength hinges. He grabbed the radio from his hip and got backup with a battering ram on the way, but he knew that by the time it arrived Lucent might have destroyed valuable evidence.

The room was filled with junk; a dismantled Jet Ski took up a large chunk of floor, and a steel, eight-foot-high framework on wheels dominated the rest, a thick, greasy chain-and-pulley dangling from a heavy strut across the frame's top. Horatio recognized it as a portable engine-puller, designed to lift motors out of cars. It gave him an idea.

A waist-high, rusted oxyacetylene bottle stood in one corner. Moving quickly, Horatio holstered his gun, then tilted the bottle and rolled it over to the engine-puller. It only took a few seconds to wrap the chain around the bottle and hoist it up to waist height, lengthwise like a torpedo.

He rolled the engine-puller over to the door, with the base of the welding tank forward. He pulled the steel bottle back as far as he could, then swung it forward with all his strength.

The impact sounded like someone taking a sledge-hammer to a mailbox. A huge dent appeared in the metal of the door. Horatio hauled back and let fly again.

THOOM!

THOOM!

THOO—CRACK!

On the fourth hit, the lock broke and the door gave way, slamming inward. Horatio whipped his gun back out and cautiously edged ahead.

Inside the room, he had a brief impression of a row of white buckets along one wall, several cube-like metal machines no higher than his knee, a battered white fridge, a table covered in a plastic sheet with kitchen equipment and some sort of long trays stacked on it. There was also another door, which stood open—Lucent had obviously gone through it.

The roar of a Jet Ski powering up came at the same second Horatio heard Delko shout, "Hold it!" He ran through the door and into the boathouse just in time to see Lucent take off down the canal, a black garbage bag clutched in one hand, the Jet Ski's rooster tail spraying a veil of water between Horatio and his target.

Horatio sighted down the barrel of the Glock, drew a bead and fired. Once, twice, three times. The Jet Ski sputtered and died, coasting to a stop in the middle of the canal. Lucent dove into the water and tried to make it to the far side, but Delko was already in the water and halfway across, swimming with a strong, even stroke.

"When you get to the other side, Mister Lucent," Horatio called out, "please put your hands on your head and wait for my partner. Otherwise, my next shot is going to do more than ruin your noisy toy. . . ."

Lucent did as he was told. As it turned out, he didn't have to wait at all; Delko beat him to the shore. A few seconds later, Lucent was wearing handcuffs.

Now, Horatio thought, *let's take a closer look at what's in that room. . . .*

"The bag was full of marijuana," Delko said. He and Horatio were in Lucent's once-secure room; Lucent himself was locked in the back of a patrol car outside. "Pretty high-grade, too, by the smell."

"Obviously, our friend Samuel is more interested in botany than plumbing," Horatio said, surveying the room with hands on hips. "Or maybe that should be chemistry. . . ."

"Actually, it's more like what a miller does," Delko said. He bent down, picked up a single fleck of green from the floor and held it out to Horatio. "See those little white hairs all over the leaf, makes it look like it's covered in frost? You stick that under a microscope, you'd see mushroom-shaped glands called trichomes. They're loaded with tetrahydrocannabinol, the psychoactive ingredient in pot. It's present in most parts of the plant, but you get the highest concentrations in the flowering parts of the female."

"The proverbial forbidden fruit," Horatio murmured.

"I guess," Delko said with a grin. "Anyway, hashish is basically a concentrated form of the drug, made of bits of resinous stalk and leaf processed and pressed together—sort of like particleboard."

"Using different parts of the hemp plant instead of glue and sawdust."

"Right. Used to be made for the same reason, too—using leftover materials to generate out a cheap product, squeeze out a few more dollars worth of profit. Workers harvesting plants would get sticky hands, covered in resin and bits of leaf; they'd rub their fingers together and produce little balls of black goo."

Delko walked over to the table and picked up one of the trays. It was just a rectangular wooden frame with what looked like shiny yellow cloth stretched across it, stained with long streaks of green.

"Then, of course, technology got into the picture," Delko said. "People figured out that if you could separate the trichomes from the rest of stuff, and just press *that*, you'd have a product with a lot more punch. Looks like Lucent couldn't make up his mind which process he wanted to use; he's got several on the go in here."

"Is that silk?" Horatio asked.

"Yeah. They rub the leftovers—called skuff— against it; the trichomes are small enough to break off and pass through the weave, but nothing else is. Sometimes they use steel mesh instead. It generates this fine dust, which they collect and press into little bricks—using that." Delko put down the screen and pointed out something that looked like a vise with a fire extinguisher attached. "Hydraulic press."

"Uh-huh. And this device here?" He nodded at the metal cube.

"Same idea, only mechanized. It's called a drum machine—it's got a drum inside that revolves, with a built-in screen. Basically, it works just like a clothes dryer."

"Except you can get high off the lint it collects . . . what about the kitchen equipment?" Horatio indicated several blenders and mixers on the table.

"Well, the blenders use a different principle, which is that the trichome glands are heavier than water, while the rest of the skuff isn't. They add ice and water to the skuff, which makes the glands brittle, then agitate the mix to break them off."

"Sounds like a marijuana margarita."

"Looks like one, too. The slush gets strained through a metal mesh, then put in a fridge to separate. After a half hour or so, the trichomes settle out, sinking to the bottom. They skim off the stuff floating on top and throw it away, then filter the remainder through these." Delko picked up a stack of crinkle-edged paper cones. "Ordinary coffee filters. What's left is dried out and then pressed into bricks."

"Okay. Last of all, we have all these five-gallon plastic buckets. Professor Delko?"

"I did a little research, all right?" Delko said, sounding half-embarrassed and half-proud. "Anyway, these combine the ice-water and screen techniques. They use a hand-mixer to agitate a mix of ice, water and skuff, let it settle, then filter it through these." Delko picked up what looked like a small blue cloth sack with the number 220 on the side. "Technology again. The mesh weave is only two hundred twenty microns in diameter; that's for the first filter. After that, they use a series of bags nested inside each other, each one with a successively smaller weave—the last one being around twenty-five microns or so. Fewer and fewer contaminants make it through the weave, so the residue left in the last bag is the purest and strongest; it's sometimes called 'bubble hash' because it's so pure it bubbles when exposed to flame."

Horatio walked over to the fridge, opened it and looked inside. Jars of greenish water with white sediment at the bottom filled the upper shelves, while square black bricks were stacked up on the lower ones.

"Mixers, blenders, coffee filters and dryers," Horatio murmured. "Very domestic. The one thing I don't see, though, is a large quantity of source material—an operation like this must go through a lot, and the bag Lucent was carrying couldn't be more than a pound or so."

"He must get regular deliveries," Delko said. "Looks like we caught him at the end of the week."

"Right. The question is, who's supplying him . . . and how is this connected to the deaths of Ruth Carrell and Phillip Mulrooney?"

Horatio slipped his sunglasses back on. "Come on— let's go see what our little homemaker has to tell us. . . ."

7

"MISTER LUCENT," Horatio said pleasantly. "That's quite the operation you had going."

Samuel Lucent glared across the interview table at Horatio with undisguised hostility.

"Thank you, mon," he said sarcastically.

"The problem, of course, is that no matter how you process it, the psychoactive ingredient remains the same—at least in a legal sense. Considering the quantity you had in your possession, you're looking at a felony conviction and up to five years in prison."

"Tell me something I don't know," Lucent said.

Horatio gave him an indulgent, fatherly look. "I intend to. What you don't know is how lucky you are that *I* nailed you instead of the DEA . . . see, those guys confiscate everything they can get their hands on—cash, cars, property, jewelry—and sell it at auction. And you know where all that money goes?"

"I do," Lucent said sullenly. "Right back into their very own budget."

"That's right. So if I were a DEA agent, I'd be kind of unhappy that you forced me to put holes in that shiny new Jet Ski you tried to escape in. It wouldn't look good on my bottom line. But—lucky you—I don't give half a damn about that. Actually, I don't much care about the stack of homemade bricks piled up in your refrigerator, either."

Horatio could see he had the man's attention. "And why would that be?" he asked suspiciously.

"Because I have other concerns. Two people have died and it's my job to catch who's responsible. That's a job I take *very* seriously . . . whereas putting away a middle-management lab rat like yourself barely shows up on my radar."

"What are you trying to tell me, mon?"

"I'm saying that, as far as I know, nobody's ever died from smoking hashish. And while it's true you did run, you didn't take a shot at me—which, in my book, goes a long way toward establishing you as a salvageable human being. If you cooperate, I could talk to the judge and ask for leniency."

Lucent considered this. "I don't know nothing about any killings," he said finally. "And I'm not gonna rat anybody else out—"

"I'm not interested in going after your supplier or your customers," Horatio said. "Unless one or the other is involved in murder. Is that the case?"

"I told you, I don't know about no murders—"

"Okay, then. How about Albert Humboldt?"

"What about him?"

"You know him, then?"

Lucent shifted in his chair uneasily. "I suppose I do. We hang together, by and by."

"That a euphemism for getting high?"

"Hey, I did not say—"

Horatio put his hand up. "Don't bother. I already know you dealt a little hash to Humboldt. I don't care. What did Humboldt tell you about the toilet you installed at the restaurant he worked at?"

"The *what*?" He sounded completely baffled.

Horatio sighed. "The *toilet*, Samuel," he said. "For The Earthly Garden. Stainless steel bowl, connecting copper pipe?"

"Uh—sure, yes. Al was very specific about what he wanted. Had to special-order it and everything."

"He tell you why?"

Lucent frowned. "He kept making little jokes. Something about a hot seat, I think, which makes no sense—steel is chilly, you know? But then, Al is a strange one, I think."

"Oh? How so?"

"The whole Vitality Method thing. Very, very strange, it seem to me. He seem to think it will make him happy and popular, but I think it just make him dumb and stupid. He scrubbing dishes for nothing, you know? All because the big doctor say it good for his soul."

Horatio sat down in a chair opposite Lucent. "And how does the doctor feel about his patients using drugs?"

"Oh, he don't like it one bit," Lucent said with a chuckle. "Al, he get in plenty of trouble when he get caught. But he still like to smoke, you know."

"I see. How about any of the other people at the restaurant? Any of them like to smoke?"

Lucent eyed him speculatively. "I think maybe yes. Never with me, you know, but from the way Al talk, I think now and then somebody there might like a little puff too."

"It seems like Doctor Sinhurma doesn't run a very tight ship. . . ."

Lucent laughed. "Maybe not, but he got some pretty fine women, you know?"

Horatio smiled. "So you've been out to the clinic?"

"Just the one time. Beautiful people everywhere! But it all too much for me—I like my sleep, you know? Those crazy mothers, they up at the crack of dawn doing push-ups, don't eat nothing but rice. Not for me, I think."

"I can see how you might find that limiting," Horatio said. "So nobody else involved with Sinhurma has ever been in your little drug kitchen?"

"No way."

"You better not be lying to me," Horatio said mildly. "Because my people are going over every square inch of that place even as we have this conversation. And if you're being less than honest, the words I put in that judge's ear will be less than flattering."

"I *swear*, mon," Lucent said.

Ryan Wolfe had the light table in the layout room covered with knives, cleavers, and blades of various sizes and shapes. He had a short length of Kevlar-coated wire that approximated the scrap Horatio had found on the rocket, and he methodically used each and every tool to carve a small chunk off the wire. He then used the comparison microscope to examine each sample side by side with the first, looking for a match.

He didn't find one.

It didn't mean he was out of options, though. Delko's linking of the knives to the plumber through gas residue gave him an idea; if the fuel mixture for the rocket was, as Horatio had theorized, a custom blend, then maybe he could find the person who mixed it.

He hit the web, then made some phone calls. Ryan himself had never done any rocketry, but some of his friends from school had been just as geeky as himself; it didn't take long to find one with contacts in the local amateur rocketry scene. He told Ryan he'd send a few e-mails and get back to him.

Ten minutes later there was a message in his in-box giving him a time and place. He jotted it down on a piece of paper, then headed out to pick up some Diet Coke and Cheetos. Regardless of whether they were playing D&D, tinkering with computers or building model rockets, there were some things a gathering of geeks always required; by bringing an offering of such goods, Wolfe hoped that his status as a cop would be less of an issue.

It probably didn't matter, though. Even though many geeks identified themselves as rebels, few of them could resist the lure of esoteric technical knowledge, and as a CSI, Wolfe had plenty of that coin of the realm.

He just hoped they wouldn't ask to play with his gun.

"Okay, first of all," the overweight man with the bushy orange beard said, "we're not into *model* rocketry. We're into *amateur* rocketry."

Wolfe sat on the edge of a beat-up green recliner, both of its arms patched with gray duct tape. Across from him was a couch in even worse condition, completely upholstered in some god-awful tartan fabric except for its middle cushion, which was covered with dark brown leather and somehow gave the impression that the sofa was missing a tooth.

At the moment, there were three men sitting on it, all of them clutching plastic Big Gulp containers filled with approximately enough Cola product to carbonate and caffeinate a fish tank. The men at either end of the couch were both recognizable as archetypal geeks to Wolfe; heavyset, bearded, eyeglassed, wearing baggy shorts and T-shirts that proclaimed allegiance to a brand of software and a science fiction franchise respectively. One had frizzy orange hair that stuck up, the other had black hair pulled back in a ponytail; other than that, they could have been brothers.

The one between was as thin as the other two were fat, as if by sitting in the middle he had lost half his mass to either side through osmosis. He had a bony face, a shiny cranium fringed with white hair, and a nose road-mapped by red veins. He wore a checked sweater vest over a short-sleeved pale blue shirt, stained brown corduroy pants and sandals with black socks.

"What's the difference?" Wolfe asked.

The one with the ponytail—Mark—rolled his eyes. Eye-rolling was as common a trait in geekdom, Wolfe had noted, as high-fiving was amongst jocks.

"*Model* rocketry is basically for kids," Mark said. "You buy the rocket and the motor commercially, it's all very safe. *Amateur* rocketry is about innovation—coming up with your own designs, your own fuel mixes, your own payloads. Half the time our stuff explodes on the pad or in midair."

"I don't think that's really fair?" the one in the middle—Bruno—said. He had the kind of Southern accent that turned every statement into a question. "I mean, I think our ratio of successful missions to CATOs is closer to seventy/thirty?"

"CATO?"

"Catastrophic Take-Off," the redhead—Gordon—answered. "It's how we refer to a rocket that blows up."

"So you guys make your own rockets."

"Mostly," Gordon said. He took a long, meditative pull on the thick blue straw stuck in his Big Gulp. "We mess around sometimes with adapting commercial designs, seeing how big a motor we can put in, that kinda thing."

"Excuse me?" Bruno said. "I also don't think it's fair to say that model rocketry is just for kids? Some model rockets are really quite powerful?"

"So what?" Mark said. "It's all just preassembled, commercial crap. It's like thinking that buying an SUV makes you some kind of outdoorsman. Any idiot with the money can walk into a hobby shop, buy a sport scale, slap on some flashy decals and stick a G motor in it. That doesn't make him a *rocketeer*."

Gordon laughed. "Mark doesn't think anyone's a rocketeer, unless they've built the airframe out of PVC pipe, mixed the fuel on their own stove, hand-painted the thing and then launched it using an ignition system made of old strobe-light parts."

"Don't mock the Space Condor," Mark said. "It was a creature of nobility and grace."

"It flew twenty feet sideways and set your neighbor's doghouse on fire," Gordon said. "With the dog in it."

"Science requires sacrifice," Mark said.

"Uh, so this is the whole club?" Wolfe asked. Another identifying characteristic of geeks was that when you got them in a group, any conversation had the tendency to abruptly veer off on a bizarre tangent, then keep changing direction as it ricocheted off puns, anecdotes, technical information, pop culture quotes and the occasional non sequitur. You had to keep a firm grip on the narrative rudder or you'd wind up mired in a discussion of the engineering specs of Seven of Nine's underwear.

"Nah, we got here early to talk to you," Gordon said. "The rest are coming in half an hour or so for the cooking party."

"Um. Uh. Erm," Bruno said, suddenly looking intensely uncomfortable.

"Oh, take a pill—a red one," Gordon told him. "Roger vouched for him, okay? Besides, cooking parties aren't illegal—you really think we'd invite him if we'd get into trouble?"

"Oh, yeah, yeah," Wolfe said. "Don't worry about that. Gordon already showed me your storage facilities. You guys are fine."

Cooking parties, as Wolfe's friend Roger had explained to him, were social events where rocket enthusiasts got together to mix fuel. Ammonium perchlorate composite propellant, one of the trace elements found in the residue of the rocket launched from The Earthly Garden, had been classified by the Safe Explosives Act of 2002 as a low explosive; though rocket-builders had been using it for years, in order to purchase it now they were required to be fingerprinted, have their backgrounds checked and have their propellant storage be available at any time for inspection by local and federal authorities. To get around this, rocketeers invoked a law allowing low explosives to be manufactured for personal use; originally designed to let farmers mix fuel oil and fertilizer to blast irrigation ditches, it also worked just fine when applied to brewing up model rocket fuel.

"Really, I appreciate you sitting down with me like this," Wolfe said. "I just want the benefit of your expertise for a few moments."

"What do you want to know?" Mark asked.

"Well, I'm trying to figure out the origin of a particular blend of rocket fuel. It was used to send a rocket to a height of two thousand feet and had this chemical composition." He handed Gordon a sheet with the mass spec figures on it.

"Hmmm. Candy rocket," Gordon said. Bruno and Mark were both leaning over, trying to read the paper at the same time.

"With an APCP kicker?" Bruno added.

"Gotta be at least an I class," Mark muttered.

"My boss says it was probably a J motor," Wolfe said.

"I said *at least* an I class," Mark retorted. "*Probably* a J, or even a K."

"Anything over a G requires certification," Gordon said. "A G motor is one defined as capable of generating an impulse of eighty-eight Newton-seconds but not exceeding a hundred sixty Newton-seconds."

"But if he mixed the fuel himself, he wouldn't have to worry about that," Mark pointed out. "APCP is only regulated above sixty-two and a half grams. He obviously didn't use that much."

"And this rocket was used to commit a crime?" Bruno asked—at least, Wolfe thought it was an actual question.

"It's part of the evidence of a crime scene, yes," Wolfe said. "I can't say too much, I'm sorry."

"I bet it was drugs," Mark said. "Somebody stuffed a rocket full of crack and it blew up all over a playground or something."

"Why would they do that?" Bruno said.

"Smuggling," Mark said.

"What, smuggling a few hundred yards?" Gordon scoffed. "That doesn't make any sense. I bet it was some crack house or something, and some tweaker came up with the idea of keeping his stash in a rocket pointed out the window, just in case of a raid—"

"Might work if you could dump it in the ocean," Mark said. "You could even have a second stage that went off when it hit the water, turn it into a torpedo so it would be almost impossible to find—"

"Ha!" Gordon exclaimed. "I can just see a bunch of DEA guys busting down the door, and then this crackhead hits the ignitor and fires this thing out the window—"

"And the police? Would probably think it was a *mortar* or something?"

"Oh, man," Gordon chortled. "That would wind up being *such* a bad idea—"

"Guys?" Wolfe interjected. "It had nothing to do with drugs, okay?" Which wasn't strictly true, but he had to try and get them back on track before they started designing a narcotic-loaded air-to-sea missile. "What I need to know is, do any of you recognize this particular fuel mix?"

"People don't generally dope candy rockets with ammonium perchlorate," Mark said. "Iron oxide or charcoal, maybe, to increase the burn rate."

"I don't think I've seen this, either?"

"Sorry, man," Gordon said. "But people are experimenting with mixes all the time. You could check who's registered to buy APCP, I guess—but a lot of rocketeers aren't going to be on it. We have a problem with the idea that a fed or a cop could search our premises at any time, without a warrant, just because we have a hobby that involves firing little tubes into the air. That's why we have cooking parties in the first place."

"Firing little tubes in the air is a pretty good description of how to shoot down an airplane," Wolfe said quietly.

"Sure, if you have a sophisticated guidance system to make sure you actually hit the thing, and something a lot more volatile than APCP," Mark said. "The stuff is less explosive than *gasoline*, for Christ's sake!

And even if you manage to document every molecule in the country, any terrorist that really wanted to make his own rocket would just do exactly what your guy did—he'd use sugar! What's the government going to do, outlaw *candy*?"

"I . . . see your point," Wolfe conceded. "But it's not really as simple as that—"

"Well, no, the actual fuel-making process is a little more complicated," Mark said, missing Wolfe's point entirely. "You need an oxidizer, of course. Your guy used potassium nitrate—saltpeter—which is pretty standard and easy to get. It's used in fertilizer, preserving meat, even toothpaste. You have to bind it with the fuel, in this case dextrose—"

"Which is also interesting, actually," Gordon put in. "Most candy rockets use sucrose. Dextrose is a good choice, though—lower melting point and less caramelization."

"True," Mark said. "That's important when you're mixing the slurry."

"Slurry?" Wolfe said.

"The blend of oxidizer and fuel. First, though, you have to grind both up into a fine powder. Then you can heat them together or mix them dry. You gotta be careful if you do it dry, though—the mix is really combustible at that point."

"So it's safer to mix by heating it up?" Wolfe asked.

"Long as you're careful, yeah," Mark said. He shifted on the couch, wedging his Big Gulp between his thighs. "I use an electric deep fryer for that kinda thing—no exposed heating element, and you can control the temperature exactly. Anyway, you let the finished product cool and mold it into shape—that's basically it. Stick it in an airframe, jam a couple Nichrome-tipped wires in it and hook the other end to a battery, you got yourself a rocket."

Wolfe nodded. "So whoever mixed this up knew what he was doing. He was an experienced rocketeer."

"Definitely," Gordon said. The other two nodded in agreement.

"In that case," Wolfe said reluctantly, "I'm going to need a copy of your membership list."

There was a sudden silence. Gordon looked amazed, Bruno looked stunned and Mark looked like he'd been expecting it all along.

"You want our fingerprints, too?" Mark said sarcastically.

"That won't be necessary," Wolfe said.

Working a crime scene was, Horatio thought, much like writing a novel. The common perception was that it was a linear process: fact A led to fact B, which led to conclusion C and so on. A nice straight line, starting at the beginning and running to the end.

In practice, though, it was—like life itself—essentially fractal. Just as every twist of the plot led the imagination of the author to explore another possibility, every piece of evidence branched off in a different direction, each leading down a different path.

Fiction, though, contained endless possibilities, endless choices. Fortunately for Horatio, evidence did not; sooner or later it would lead him either to what he was looking for or to a dead end. The image of a tree with infinite, extending branches was often in his mind when the details of a case began to spread into increasingly wider territory.

The limb he was currently out on had to do with his conversation with Samuel Lucent. Horatio had told him he wasn't interested in prosecuting him or getting him to roll over on his supplier, but that had simply been to get Lucent to talk. In fact, Horatio was very much interested in where the pot Lucent was turning into hash was coming from, and who was bringing it to him; there was obviously a lot of money involved in an operation like this, and you never ignored money when investigating a murder.

Still, he thought he had played it right. He could always turn the heat up on Lucent later.

He went down to the lab to see Calleigh, who was processing the equipment they'd pulled out of Lucent's place. She was dusting the handle of one of the blenders for prints when he walked in.

"How's it going?" he asked her.

"Oh, a woman's work is never done," she said. "From power tools to kitchen appliances—you trying to tell me something, H?"

"I was hoping you could tell me instead."

"Well, so far Lucent seems to be telling the truth—the only prints I've gotten have been his. I haven't done the drum machine yet, though."

Horatio took a good look at the blender she was working on. "Is this the same model that we pulled out of the Dumpster?"

"I don't know. Let me check. . . . Hmmm. Not exactly. Same brand, different model."

Horatio moved farther down the table and examined a hand-mixer. "Which is the same as these—maybe there's a connection here. Find out which restaurant supply company The Earthly Garden gets their equipment from and check them out."

"I'm on it."

"Where's Eric? I thought he was going to help out with all this."

"He's in the computer lab—said he was going to work up a simulation."

Which is exactly what Horatio found Delko doing, sitting back and staring at a screen with his arms crossed. "Eric? What's up?"

"Oh, hi, H. I thought I'd try to reconstruct the scene from start to finish, give us a clearer picture of what happened."

"Good thinking. How far are you?"

"Let me show you." Delko reached forward and tapped a key. The screen lit up with a simple wirework graphic, showing the restaurant in a gridded outline. The bathroom was represented inside the frame in blue, the kitchen in red. There was a small digital time readout at the bottom of the screen.

"Okay, the action starts at approximately two o'clock." The counter showed 2:00. "Shanique Cooperville, trying to show Phil Mulrooney the error of his ways, serves him a helping of meat-laced chili. At two-fifteen, Albert Humboldt takes his lunch break. By two-thirty, Mulrooney starts to feel a little queasy. At two-forty, he makes a dash for the bathroom."

Delko hit another key. A little wireframe rocket appeared on the roof. "At two forty-three, Doctor Sinhurma calls Phil Mulrooney's cell phone."

"But how does he know Mulrooney is in the bathroom?" Horatio mused.

"Somebody could have phoned and tipped him off," Delko suggested. "I'll check the phone records for the restaurant and the clinic, see what I can find."

"Good idea. So at this point, we know where Sinhurma is—miles from the crime scene, giving him an alibi."

"Right. At approximately two forty-four, someone hits the igniter switch, launching the rocket from the roof."

Horatio was no longer watching the screen. He was seeing it in his mind's eye: the spark of electricity traveling down the length of wire to the rocket, the flare of heat and light as the motor ignited.

"The rocket launches. It pulls a thin, Kevlar-coated wire with it—"

The spool, attached to some kind of base, spinning wildly as it feeds a thin copper line into the heavens . . .

"—going two thousand feet, straight up, and trailing a charged leader of electrical particles behind it. A stepped leader heading toward the ground hits the rocket. The bolt travels down the wire, vaporizing it at the same time—"

The bolt smashes into the rocket and roars earthward, consuming the copper and Kevlar like an angry shark devouring a fishing line. . . .

"It travels down the copper pipe in the wall, through the steel toilet bowl and into Phil Mulrooney. From the position of the body, it probably entered through his left hand—his right was holding his cell phone. It went down the arm, down the torso and legs and out through his knees—"

The charge skates across the skin like mercury on glass, too fast to burn but turning sweat to steam in an instant. Some of it makes it through the barrier and races down nerves, veins, bones. It slams through the muscle of the heart, shocking it into silence. . . .

"The bolt hits the puddle of water on the floor, follows it down to the metal drain, and grounds out. Except—"

"Except somewhere along the way, it intersects with a wall outlet, burning out a blender," Horatio finished.

"Yeah. Via whatever was wedged between the wall and that plug."

Horatio rubbed his forehead. "But there's another problem. According to the autopsy, Mulrooney displayed signs of being hit by lightning *and* being electrocuted by house current."

"So—more than one method, more than one killer?"

"Maybe . . . or maybe just a belt-and-suspenders approach. From what I've found out, lightning doesn't seem to be the most reliable of weapons; it's frequently nonlethal, and even using a rocket to trigger it only has a fifty percent success rate."

Delko nodded. "So somebody was trying to hedge their bets. Take out a little thunderstorm insurance."

"Possibly . . . we're missing two pieces of physical evidence here. One, the ignition system and launch pad for the rocket. Two, whatever connected the wall outlet to Phil Mulrooney."

"There's also the rocket fuel—if it was a custom blend, it had to be cooked up somewhere."

"Wolfe's following up on that right now," Horatio said.

"How about the Carrell murder? Any luck with the arrow?"

"I'm afraid not. We can prove the arrows we found were fired by the bow they were stored with, but that's it."

"So what's next, H?"

Horatio's cell phone rang. He held up one finger while he answered it.

"Horatio Caine." He listened intently, said, "Really. Good job, Mister Wolfe. I'll have him brought in."

He snapped the phone shut and said to Delko, "Well, it seems as if we have somebody we can talk to after all. . . ."

8

DETECTIVE SALAS STARED across the table. Light threw six-sided shadows across her subject's face. "Caesar," she said. "That's an unusual first name. Your parents have high ambitions for you?"

Sinhurma's second-in-command stared back stonily. "Mister Kim is fine, thank you. I don't really feel we're on a first-name basis."

Horatio, sitting at Salas's right hand, favored Kim with a smile. "Certainly, Mister Kim . . . we appreciate you coming in. Your name popped up in connection with part of our investigation and I was wondering if you could clear up a few things."

"I'll do what I can." Kim's back was straight as a board, his voice inflectionless.

"Tell me a little about yourself, Mister Kim."

"Can you be more specific?'

"When the mood strikes me." Horatio waited. He enjoyed it when a suspect tried to outwait him; it was a contest he always won. He'd sat and stared at a man once for thirty-seven minutes without saying a word—the man finally broke when Horatio got up, left for two minutes to use the bathroom, then came back and sat down again with a smile.

Salas's face was as impassive as stone. She hated waiting, but if that was how Horatio wanted to play it, she'd sit there like a statue until he indicated otherwise . . . then chew him out for it later.

Kim apparently didn't need that long to figure the situation out. "What," he said frostily, "would you like to know?"

"Oh, you know, the usual things: your favorite color, what kind of food you like to eat—wait, I already know that—any hobbies you might have?"

"I prefer the color green. And as for hobbies, I have none." He smiled, ever so slightly. "Not even archery."

"Oh, I wasn't thinking of archery. I mean, someone as repressed as you evidently are would choose *something* phallic to express himself, and archery does have that whole penetrating shaft aspect to it . . . but somehow it seems a little too hands-on for you. No, you'd go for something grander, I think. I see you . . ."

Here Horatio leaned forward, his hands steepled together, and said, ". . . as a *rocket* man."

Kim blinked, very slowly and deliberately. "Rocketry is a science, not a hobby," he said.

"Ah. Then you do count it among your interests?"

"I suppose I do," Kim said.

"Hmmm. Which would explain your name on a membership list for the Florida Model Rocketry Association, I assume?"

"That seems self-evident."

Horatio leaned back, picking up a folder from the table as he did so. He flipped it open and pretended to study it. "Mmm-hm. A number of things are becoming self-evident, Mister Kim. For instance, these financial disclosure statements my staff dug up. You're quite heavily invested in The Earthly Garden restaurant chain, aren't you?"

"It's a matter of public record," Kim answered calmly.

"Indeed it is. It also means that you have a rather vested interest in the Vitality Method as an entity continuing to do well."

"Is there a point to this?"

"Funny thing about public records," Salas said. "Some records are more public than others. For instance, phone records show that a call was placed just minutes before Phillip Mulrooney died, from The Earthly Garden to Doctor Sinhurma's private line."

"I wouldn't know anything about that."

"Of course not," Horatio said. "Your area of expertise is rocketry, not telephonics."

"I wouldn't say I'm an expert—"

"Just someone with an interest," Salas said.

"That's right."

Horatio studied the man for a moment. He thought he had Kim pegged now; the less emotional affect the man showed, the more likely it was he was hiding something. Horatio thought he knew what it was.

"Tell me, Mister Kim—what's the basic unit of measurement for a rocket's thrust?"

The blink, this time, was noticeably faster. "I don't see how that's relevant."

"Humor me."

Kim stared at him impassively—but the blankness

of his gaze was that of a turtle retreating into its shell. Horatio paused just long enough for it to get uncomfortable, then said, "Or what about the recommended minimum launch speed to keep a model rocket stable in flight?"

"I—I don't recall at the moment—"

"No? How about a really, really easy one? Something even a grade-school kid would know after his first launch. Like . . . what's the most powerful rocket motor you can buy without certification?"

Silence.

"The answers—of course—are: Newton-seconds, forty-four feet per second, and 'G'," Horatio said. "Very cagey of you to deny knowing any of this. Unless . . . it couldn't be that you're actually *unaware* of these facts, could it?"

"I suppose," Kim said, giving him the barest trace of a smile, "that I'm a bit rusty. Hardly a crime."

"Hardly," Horatio agreed. "But it does mean that you're not exactly being truthful with us, Mister Kim. I also notice that you don't seem to find a discussion of model rocketry in the context of a homicide investigation at all unusual."

"I simply assumed you were building to some sort of metaphor."

"I prefer the real thing to symbolism, Mister Kim. And the rocket that I'm talking about, as I'm sure you're aware, is very much an actual object . . . an object in the possession of the Miami-Dade crime lab. We know it was launched from the roof of The Earthly Garden and used to trigger a lightning strike,

and we know that strike was intended to kill Phillip
Mulrooney."

"That sounds rather bizarre," Kim said. "As I'm
sure any jury would agree."

Horatio smiled. "You know how you make the
bizarre commonplace, Mister Kim? With evidence.
You explain it, step by step, fact by fact. And in my experience, sooner or later the jury *does* agree. . . ."

There was an antechamber outside the Miami-Dade
crime lab, an oddly shaped foyer of sorts. It had a
long, low, padded bench against one black wall, facing
a window that slanted up from the floor to the roof at
a forty-five-degree angle. It always made Horatio feel
as if he were inside some pyramidal tomb, a waiting
room for the dead.

Right now it was empty. He sat by himself, looking
at the angled window but not really seeing it. He was
seeing something else: a face with a startling pair of
green eyes.

Ruth Carrell.

She'd come down from Tampa, she'd told him. Just
another overweight girl who wanted the dream: to be
thin, to be pretty, to be popular. To be accepted.

And Doctor Kirpal Sinhurma had seen her potential through the baby fat and decided she was worth
recruiting. She didn't have much money, but she was
young and insecure and willing, and that was perfect
material for a foot soldier. Before you could bilk the
headliners for endorsements and fat donations you
had to have your success stories all lined up and ready

for inspection; you had to fill the front lines with taut bodies and gleaming smiles, all charged up with unswerving dedication and fervor. You basked in the glow of their admiration, and that reflected light made you seem even larger and more impressive than ever.

And when that loyalty flickered, even for a second, you threw the cause away like a bad bulb in a string of Christmas lights. Because doubt was one luxury you could not afford . . . and young, insecure girls were as cheap and plentiful as citrus fruit.

That insecurity had let Sinhurma shape the direction of Ruth's thoughts, let him guide her into thinking that what he wanted her to do was actually her own idea. And what he'd wanted, obviously, was to bring someone else into the fold—someone who would be vulnerable to the attention of a young, attractive girl. But who? And why did Sinhurma want them?

He'd misjudged the doctor. He'd been thinking Sinhurma was only a sociopath—devoid of any real compassion or human connection, but no worse than many businessmen or politicians Horatio had dealt with.

But he might be wrong. If Sinhurma was responsible, then he was a delusional sociopath—a psychopath. Which meant that killing two or twenty people meant much the same to him.

If he was responsible.

Any cop on the street would tell you to trust your gut first. Any scientist would tell you to ignore personal bias and let the evidence speak for itself. Horatio was both, which meant he was continually trying to find the balance between the two. Right now, his gut told him that Sinhurma was about as far from the straight and narrow as a monk was from a crack den . . . but the evidence was strictly circumstantial.

Which was why Horatio was out in the waiting room, all by himself, doing some hard thinking. He was, unfortunately, not convinced that Sinhurma was guilty of murder. Manipulation, yes—but if that was illegal, there'd be a lot of salesmen behind bars. Any of the members of his organization might have become unhinged enough to kill in his name, under the impression they were protecting his great endeavor; that didn't mean Sinhurma was directly responsible.

But even indirect responsibility had its price. In Horatio's case, it was the nagging memory of the last words he'd said to a girl with only hours left of her life.

Prostituting yourself. That was what he'd said. He'd meant to shock her into seeing what she'd done, how she'd been used, but maybe he'd gone too far. Maybe Ruth Carrell had died thinking of him as a hard-assed, judgmental cop, one who didn't care about her or her feelings. It was possible . . . but he'd never know.

Some cops would have shrugged and said it didn't matter; she was dead and it was Horatio's job to catch the killer. Others would have obsessed over it and let it eat away at them until the day they died. But Horatio wasn't either of those sorts of cop. He didn't run from guilt, nor did he wallow in it. He embraced it, analyzed it, learned from it. He accepted emotional pain the way an athlete accepted the physical kind, and used it to make himself stronger.

Who needs steroids, he thought, *when you have death?*

Which brought him back to the case, and the drug angle. If someone at the Vitality Method was involved in trafficking, Ruth Carrell or Phillip Mulrooney might have been killed because they learned something they shouldn't. Again, Sinhurma might be involved, or he might not.

Calleigh walked around the corner. "Horatio? Got a minute?"

"Sure. What's up?"

"I could ask you the same." She arched an eyebrow. "You want to be alone?"

Horatio smiled. "No, that's all right. Just going over the case in my mind."

She came over and sat down beside him. "Yeah, it's a strange one. Still, this is Florida—figures that sooner or later somebody would try to kill someone using a rocket or a thunderstorm. But at the same time?"

"I'm sure being shot with an arrow wasn't high on Ruth Carrell's list of possible endings, either."

She sighed. "Arrows, lightning—haven't these people ever heard of *guns*?"

It was Horatio's turn to lift an eyebrow.

She colored slightly. "Sorry, H. I'm just venting. Not being able to positively match that arrow to the bow is really bugging me. Give me a plain old shell casing any day."

"On the bright side, at least no bystanders got shot."

"That's true. One thing about bows and launch pads—they both have notoriously low rates of fire."

"Maybe we should try to convince people to switch."

"Well, concealed weapons would become a thing of the past. And visiting Cape Canaveral would take on an entirely different flavor." She gave him a patented Calleigh Duquesne wide-eyed smile, and he chuckled despite himself.

"Of course, people *would* keep shooting each other," Calleigh added. "That's the problem with any kind of gun control—it's not the *guns* that need controlling."

"Guns don't kill people?" he asked, knowing the answer.

"Of course not," she said primly. "*Bullets* kill people. I should know."

Horatio just grinned and shook his head.

"Seriously, though," she said, "we both know it's human nature that makes people into killers, not guns. If you took the guns away, they'd just find other ways to kill each other."

"Less convenient ways, one would assume . . ."

"Granted, shooting someone is awfully easy," she admitted. "I have a friend who refers to shootings as computer crimes—point-and-click, you know? But that's not the reason guns are always gonna be with us."

"Oh? What is?"

"If there's one thing people find harder to give up than anything, it's control. Owning a gun gives you control over life and death; once someone's tasted that—not killed someone, just truly understood that they *could*—it's hard to give up. Keeping someone from having a gun is a lot easier than letting him have one and then trying to take it away."

Horatio nodded. "It all comes down to power,

doesn't it? You threaten someone's control, you threaten to take away their power. And at that point, they don't react rationally, do they?"

"Not in my experience. I hate to boil life down to a bumper sticker, but the most honest statement I ever saw concerning gun control was 'YOU CAN HAVE MY GUN WHEN YOU PRY IT FROM MY COLD, DEAD FINGERS.' Not really a sentiment I agree with—especially considering how many times I've had to do just that—but it really cuts through all the rationalizations about home defense and target shooting and ethical hunting to one simple fact: people don't want to give up the power owning a gun gives them."

"Emotional reason, emotional reaction," Horatio said. "And people acting emotionally make mistakes. . . ."

"You haven't made any mistakes on this case, Horatio," she said quietly. "Not that I've seen."

"Thank you," he said, "but in truth, you've got me thinking more about our friend Doctor Sinhurma. Maybe a threat to his own power would shake him up a little."

"Make him react emotionally, hope he makes a mistake?"

"Exactly. The question is, what do I use for ammo?"

"Wish I could help," Calleigh said, getting up. "I just came out here to tell you I'm finished processing the Lucent stuff. No prints except his—I'm gonna tackle the appliances next, see if they came from the same source."

"Okay."

Calleigh went back to the lab. Horatio sat and thought. Eventually, he got up and went to pay Alexx a visit.

Calleigh traced the hand-mixers and blenders back to a company in California. They didn't do much business in Florida, but had sold a bunch of equipment to a restaurant in Georgia that had gone belly-up two years ago. They, in turn, had disposed of most of their hardware through a liquidator called Charette and Sons, a place that bought up equipment and fixtures from businesses that failed and resold them.

C and S's warehouse was in an industrial area of Opa-Locka, a neighborhood that had seen better times. Built in the twenties by a developer named Glenn Curtiss, it was intended to one-up the Mediterranean style of Coral Gables by borrowing from a little farther east—the Middle East, to be exact. While its city hall, with its Moorish domes and minarets, was certainly unusual, the city itself had faded over the decades to a place largely housing lower-income families. And there was something distinctly odd, Calleigh had always thought, about eating at a McDonald's on Ali Baba Way.

Charette and Sons' showroom was considerably cleaner than Leakyman Plumbing's. It featured a large, well-lit room, one wall lined by industrial-size stoves and sinks, one with floor-to-ceiling shelves holding various kitchen appliances, and another with a long glass display case that doubled as a countertop with a computer sitting on it. Inside the case were rows of gleaming knives, cleavers and other utensils.

A pear-shaped man in a short-sleeved white shirt, with a round, jowly face and a flushed pink complexion bustled up to her. "Hi! Lookin' for anything 'n particular?" His accent was Southern, and deeper than Calleigh's by about two Kentucky valleys.

"Well, I sure hope so," she said, flashing him a brilliant smile. She shifted her own voice a few more degrees away from North almost automatically; people always felt more comfortable dealing with one of their own, or at least someone they perceived as belonging to the same group. "I was hoping I could ask you a few questions about some of your customers." She showed him her badge, almost apologetically.

"Well, I don't see why not," the man said, returning her smile. "What would y'all like to know?"

"Have you sold equipment to a restaurant called The Earthly Garden?"

"I'd have t'check mah records," the man said. He walked up to the counter and swiveled the computer around to face him, then frowned. He reached out with one thick finger, pressed a key, then raised his hand. He added a squint to his frown, moved the finger over another key, then changed his mind. His hand moved over the keyboard from one side to the other, as slow and hesitant as a chubby hummingbird on a diet.

"Excuse me, Mister—"

"Charlessly, Oscar Charlessly. Call me Oscar." The man beamed at her, then turned his attention back to the computer and immediately sank into a pit of despair. "Oh, Lordy," he muttered. "I'm really not much of a computer person. Kari usually takes carra this sorta thing, but she's off sick t'day."

"Do you mind if I have a look?"

"Help y'self," he said, stepping back and waving her forward. "It's all geek t'me."

It only took her a few seconds to figure out the filing system, but as soon as she tried to access a list of accounts it asked her for a password.

"Would you like to type it in?" she asked him.

"Sure—if I knew what it was," he said cheerfully. "Like I said, Kari usually takes carra this stuff. Me, I just sell equipment. I c'n tellya 'bout some great deals we got on toaster ovens, but the accountin's a little over mah head."

"What about the owner? Is Mister Charette around?"

"Nah, he's kinda retired. Comes in now and then and pokes around, but he kinda lost interest after his sons quit the biz. Guess they didn't wanna spend their lives sellin' used grease traps and old freezers."

"I see. When will this Kari be back?'

"Oh, she sounded pretty sick on the phone—nasty flu bug, ah think. Might be gone the resta the week." He shrugged apologetically. "Sorry 'bout that."

"Well, I suppose it can't be helped. Maybe *you* can help me, though—salesman like yourself, I'll bet you remember all your customers."

He laughed heartily. "Well, I do mah best. Who were you lookin' for, again?"

"Actually, it would be either of three businesses: Leakyman Plumbing, a restaurant called The Earthly Garden, or a clinic called the Vitality Method."

A look of mild confusion crossed Charlessly's pudgy face. "Well, I guess the restaurant's a possibility, but we don't do much business with doctors or plumbers. And I can't rightly say I remember this Garden place buyin' from us, neither."

"Do you think you could call this Kari? Maybe get the password from her?"

"I could—but she told me she was gonna turn her ringer off, take a bunch of cold medicine and hit the sack. I doubt we could raise her."

"All right, then," Calleigh said with a sigh. "Guess I'll try again later. Thanks for your help, Oscar."

"I regret I could not be of more assistance," he said solemnly, then added a grin. "Y'all come back, anytime."

Doctor Alexx Woods believed in many things. She believed in family, she believed in friendship, she believed in giving back to the community. She believed that every life was precious and that individuals could make a difference; she saw it every day in the people she worked with, and she was proud of every one of them.

She also believed in the dead.

"Dead men tell no tales?" she sometimes said. "Honey, my entire professional career wouldn't exist if that were true." The dead had much to teach; all you had to do was pay attention. Alexx had gotten very good at hearing what they had to say—sometimes she swore a corpse *wanted* her to notice something.

Today, the corpse of Ruth Carrell had told her something important.

"You wanted motive?" Alexx said, handing Horatio a sheet of paper. "You got it. Tox screen on Ruth Carrell just came back."

Horatio scanned the sheet—and whistled. "Alexx, is this right? This reads like a pharmacy's shopping list."

"Tell me about it. Antidepressants, hypnotics, stimulants—this is the weirdest goddamn cocktail I *ever* saw. No wonder Sinhurma's patients are so ecstatic: those shots he's giving them keep them in a permanent state of chemical rapture."

"And he's passing them off as vitamin supplements. His patients are so light-headed from lack of sleep and fasting they don't even question a little more euphoria . . . this must be why Phil Mulrooney was killed. He'd stopped taking the shots and his head was starting to clear. Once he figured out what was going on it was only a matter of time before he exposed the whole scam."

"Proving it's another matter," Alexx said. "Giving people these drugs isn't technically illegal—he does have a medical license. Lying about it is enough to get his license revoked, but our only witnesses are people so brainwashed they'll do whatever he tells them to. We can't even prove Sinhurma was the one who injected Ruth Carrell."

"This may not be proof, Alexx, but it certainly qualifies as something else," Horatio said.

"And what would that be?"

"Ammunition . . ."

"Doctor," Horatio said pleasantly. "Nice of you to see me."

Doctor Sinhurma sat cross-legged on a small pedestal in the center of a Japanese garden. Stands of bamboo around the perimeter kept the garden discreetly screened from the rest of the compound; a small pond with a fountain in the shape of a pagoda trickled away quietly behind him. He was positioned in such a way that the bright overhead sun reflecting off the surface of the water haloed his head in light, making his face hard to see. "Not at all, Horatio," he said serenely.

Horatio put on his sunglasses and stared directly at him. "Lieutenant Caine," he said.

"You seem agitated, Lieutenant. Is something the matter?"

"Very much so, Doctor. Maybe you can help me out with a little spiritual advice." Horatio stood on a flagstone path that wound its way around the garden; on either side, plots of white gravel were raked into patterns of smooth, gently curving symmetry. "You see, I know this person who's about to land in a lot of trouble. Unfortunately, he seems oblivious to just how bad things are about to get."

"In that case, he deserves to be warned, don't you think?" Sinhurma asked gently.

"Well, that's my problem. See, this person's grasp of reality isn't that strong . . . he labors under the illusion that he's beyond consequences, which makes any rational discussion pointless."

"Perhaps it is simply rationality that is pointless."

"In fact, when cornered he's given to making the kind of semiprofound statements first-year philosophy students spout while on their third beer . . . so apparently I'm going to have to introduce him to some of the harder sciences. I was just wondering which one I should start with."

Sinhurma's gaze was untroubled. "Perhaps your friend understands more than you think."

Horatio's smile was cold. "I never said he was a friend."

"Then his fate is hardly your concern—"

"Physics might be a good start. Every action has an equal and opposite reaction? For instance, the act of killing someone in Florida provokes the corresponding act of execution by the State."

"I think you're confusing the laws of Man with the laws of Nature—"

"The most appropriate method would be the electric chair, but lethal injection will still get the job done. . . ." A small gray pebble lay a few inches from Horatio's foot; he kicked it idly off the path and onto the white gravel. "Perfect symmetry is rarely possible, is it? No matter how carefully you plan."

Sinhurma's face still held a calm smile, but Horatio could hear the tension in his voice. "I don't think you really understand the nature of perfection."

"Or what about chemistry? Maybe I could make him see the light with some clever metaphor using acids and bases. . . ." Horatio shook his head and held up a hand in apology. "No, you're right, that's too esoteric. If I'm going to use chemistry, I should be more direct; I should just mention what we found in Ruth Carrell's blood."

Sinhurma paused. "Ruth was—"

"—troubled, right?" Horatio snapped. "That's the

word everyone uses when they want to imply that the person they're slandering was crazy or high on drugs."

"If Ruth was taking drugs, I had no knowledge of it."

"Uh-huh. Killing Ruth was a mistake, Doctor. We know every drug you were pumping into her without her knowledge or consent, and when we prove it you can kiss your medical license *and* your clinic good-bye. And we *will* prove it, because you're *still doing it.*"

Horatio took a step forward, leaning in just slightly toward the doctor. "You *have* to, now. You have to keep them on the drugs, or everything will fall apart. You're the one who's addicted . . . and I'm the one who's going to cut off your supply. I don't think you'll find a lot of acolytes in prison, Doctor."

Sinhurma laughed, lightly. "I think *you* are the one who's deluded, Lieutenant Caine. I am not going to prison. If I am going anywhere, it is to a better place, not worse. I am a successful, well-regarded man with many friends; my life is full, and will remain so. What happened to Ruth was a tragedy, but Miami is a violent place. Karma dictates our endings as well as our beginnings."

Horatio gave him the kind of smile that made most men flinch. "I'm not going to stand here and debate your New Age fortune-cookie credo with you, Doctor. I came here to put you on notice. Enjoy your little barricaded paradise while you can—because the next time we talk, I'll be reading you your rights."

Horatio turned and strode away.

Maxine Valera was, as usual, peering through a microscope when Calleigh walked in. She straightened up and said, "Let me guess. You want me to process feather DNA from an arrow."

Calleigh smiled ruefully. "Is there any chance you could?"

"Well, using regular PCR techniques it's highly doubtful. Researchers have recently developed a technique for pulling DNA from ancient hair samples, which suggests that surrounding keratin might protect enough cellular material for testing—but nobody's tried it on feathers yet."

"And you want to be the first, right?"

"Let me finish," Valera said with a smile. "Hair shafts are hollow—feathers aren't. Unless you have the base of the quill—"

"Which I don't—"

"—that method won't work. I also considered a Low Copy Number test."

"But the problem with LCN is contamination," Calleigh said with a sigh. "And these feathers—while not exactly Stone Age—are pretty old. Any result we get with LCN is going to be highly suspect and almost useless as evidence."

"Right. Sounds like you already figured all this out."

"I did. I didn't much like what I came up with, so I thought I'd try something else." She took the large brown envelope she had in her hand and dumped out a bunch of smaller envelopes on the worktable.

Valera picked one up and scrutinized the small amount of leafy green material within. "Bribing me with drugs won't change the facts," she said, deadpan.

"Really? Even with a selection like this?" Calleigh plucked a sheet of paper out of the envelope and held it out. "Samples from every major pot bust in Miami in the last six months. I'm trying to track down a lead with a drug connection in the Mulrooney case, and I'm hoping this'll help. The sample you're holding is from a suspect we busted with a brickyard worth of hash; I'm hoping you can match the DNA to another bust, which might just tell me where he was getting his dope from."

"Well, it's worth a shot," Valera said. "Unlike the arrow."

"Ouch," Calleigh said.

9

WOLFE HAD TRACKED DOWN the rocket. Now, he wanted the system that launched it—the launch pad and the igniter.

He already knew he was looking for a rail system with a broken or newly replaced ceramic blast deflector. He knew the fuel formulation the rocketeer had used. He didn't know what sort of launch system had been utilized, but they were always electric and usually physically wired to a controller. Remote systems existed, but they were rarer, more expensive, and there was always the possibility of interference; and even though the launch sequence itself could be triggered remotely, the electric charge that ignited the rocket still had to have wires to travel down.

That meant they had to lead from the launch pad on the roof to a control console nearby—probably inside the kitchen, where Wolfe stood now. The small window high up on the wall that Calleigh had spotted was the most likely route; two sets of wires had probably been fed through it, one up to the launch pad, and another from the launch pad to the hole behind the first-aid kit that led to the copper pipe.

The problem was that said wires would be in plain view—not to mention the controller itself. The kitchen wasn't that large, and the waitstaff would be continually moving in and out of it with food orders and dirty plates. Somebody standing there with a piece of electronic equipment and wires trailing out the window would definitely attract attention.

So, Wolfe thought, *assume they must have been hidden. How?*

He looked around. *Maybe something on wheels?*

There was a tall, multishelved aluminum cart in one corner, the kind usually used for bakery deliveries. Wolfe grabbed it, rolled it over to the window. The top shelf just obscured the sill—and it was wide enough to block any view of the first-aid kit as well.

The cart's shelves were open on two sides. *The controller could have been on one of the middle shelves, right at the back. Stick a few loaves of bread in front of it, you wouldn't be able to see it at all. Of course, there is the problem of when you'd set all this up—do it before the restaurant opens and you risk it being there all day, maybe being discovered. And then you'd have to get rid of it all afterward.*

He rolled the cart back out of the way, got a chair and put it against the wall. He climbed up on it and studied the sill of the window carefully.

"Huh," he said. "Interesting."

It wasn't what was there, though; it was what *wasn't.* . . .

"Scorch marks," Wolfe told Horatio. They were back in the computer lab, Horatio studying images of the end of the copper pipe on a large flatscreen.

"I didn't find any," Wolfe continued. "You said the lightning bolt vaporizes the wire connecting it to the rocket, right?"

"That's what my sources tell me."

"If the Kevlar-coated wire led directly to the pipe, we'd see charring along the pathway—it would have had to be in contact with the sill, the wall, probably the edge of the hole. So the fact that there wasn't any—"

"—means a heavier grade of wire was used to make the connection," Horatio finished. "Sure. I'd come to the same conclusion myself."

"You—had. Oh."

Horatio smiled patiently. "Good thinking. The question is, exactly what sort of wire are we looking for . . . and where is it?"

Wolfe looked over at the screen. "Studying the tool marks? Calleigh said she was having a hard time telling new ones from old."

"It is pretty marked up," Horatio admitted. A network of scratches crisscrossed the pipe, the heaviest concentration near the ends. "But I've got a theory. You see these gouges right here?" He tapped the screen.

Wolfe peered at it for a moment. "Looks like it was made by something with teeth—vise grips or pliers, maybe."

"Just what I thought. Could have been made when the pipe was installed, or even when it was cut. But Calleigh hasn't been able to match it to any tool, plumbing or otherwise."

"So what are you thinking?"

"I'm thinking that what we're looking for is a heavy-duty wire with a clamp at the end—at both ends, actually."

"Jumper cables?" Wolfe tried.

"Jumper cables. Not quite as common in Miami as the colder parts of the country, but even here vehicles sometimes need a boost."

"Could be in the bottom of a canal by now."

"True. But that doesn't mean we stop looking."

Wolfe hesitated, then said, "Sorry. Didn't mean to come across as negative."

"Negative or positive are equally wrong, Mister Wolfe. Objective, focused and patient are what we strive for."

"Right. What's next?"

"Well, we still need to find or at least identify the launch system. Any progress on that?"

"I think I know where in the restaurant it was placed, but that's about it. And unfortunately my contacts in the rocket community have sort of—blown up."

"All right. I have a contact of my own—I'll see if he can shed any more light on the subject. In the meantime, we're also looking for jumper cables; that means we check vehicles. I noticed a large white van parked at the clinic the last time I was there, and I'm betting that's how Sinhurma ferries his patients to the restaurant and back."

"Think we can get a search warrant?"

Horatio smiled. "We don't have to. The knives we found in the kitchen and the statement Ferra made about witnessing a drug transaction in the restaurant between Lucent and Humboldt tie The Earthly Garden to the hashish operation. That means, under the Florida Contraband Forfeiture Act, that we can impound anything connected to the business that might be the proceeds of drug-dealing, especially if those proceeds are seen to be highly mobile. That definitely applies to the van—and does not require a warrant."

"And once it's in in our possession, we're legally allowed to inventory its contents," Wolfe said. "But I don't think it's going to be that easy to tie Sinhurma himself to a drug-dealing operation."

"Maybe not," Horatio said. "But that's not our intention at the moment. If it also happens to make the doctor nervous, that's just a bonus. . . ."

Jason McKinley's office at Atmosphere Research Technologies was neat and sparse, the only clutter a row of action figures posed on top and around his monitor. There was a file cabinet along one wall, a corkboard covered in sheets of printout above it and a small desk that held his computer.

Jason himself was seated behind the desk, and stood up to shake Horatio's hand when he came in. There was no other chair, so Horatio remained standing when Jason sat down again.

"So, back to pick my brains?" Jason said. His voice sounded thick and phlegmy, and his eyes were red. "You keep this up, I won't have any left."

"You look a little—if you'll pardon the expression—under the weather," Horatio said.

Jason pulled out a wad of partially used tissue and blew his nose. "Excuse me," he said. "Allergies. Some people get 'em in the spring, I get 'em in the fall. If I take medication, I can't concentrate on anything more complex than making a cup of coffee—so, I suffer. Anyway, what did you need?"

"I was hoping you could tell me about launch systems."

"Sure. Pretty straightforward, really. There's two kinds, rod and rail—"

"This would be a rail."

"Ah. Okay, then, there are a number of options, most of which are electrical. You can use something called green fuse or Jetex wick to set off a rocket like an old-fashioned stick of dynamite—you know, light the fuse with a match and stick your fingers in your ears—but it's illegal and unreliable. Pretty unlikely, too, I'd say.

"There's an igniter kit sold under the name FireStar that's popular. Comes with a solution you have to mix up and then dip wires into—the voltage you need for ignition varies with the thickness of wire you use."

"How much voltage are we talking about?"

"Six to twelve volts. *Hachoo!* Excuse me. Now, if it was a single composite motor, they might have used a copperhead, which is made of two strips of copper separated by a thin layer of Mylar. That takes a lot of juice, though—twelve volts at least, and they're not that reliable."

"Twelve volts," Horatio mused. "Like a motorcycle battery?"

"Yeah, they get used a lot—smaller than a car battery, with enough of a charge to ignite black powder. Or you could go with a Magnelite, which doesn't take quite as much power and uses magnesium-tipped wires—they burn really hot, good for single high-power motors." He blew his nose again.

"What about lower-power systems?" Horatio asked.

"Well, there's an Electric Match—they only need two hundred milliamps. Or if you go really minimal, you'll use a flashbulb igniter. They fire at fifty milliamps, setting off a Thermalite fuse. You have to be careful with 'em, though—flashbulbs can be touchy. Easy to set off by accident if you don't know what you're doing."

"So if you were designing an idiot-proof, easily transportable launch system, you'd probably use a Magnelite igniter and a nine-to-twelve-volt power system—maybe a lantern battery?" Horatio asked.

"Maybe," Jason said. "You find the rocket yet?"

"As a matter of fact, we have," Horatio said. "It more or less fit the description you provided."

"I'm glad I could help," he said. "You know what? I think I'm gonna give in and take some antihistamines after all. Better to sit here with my brain fried than drown in my own mucus."

"Well, then, I better leave you to it," Horatio said, smiling. "I wouldn't want to have to arrest you for doing research while under the influence."

Jason tried to laugh, but it came out more like a wheeze. "Wouldn't be the first time. . . ."

After he left Jason, Horatio drove around for a while just thinking. A lot of CSI work was like that; you could only collect so much data before you had to sit down and actually figure out what it *meant*. Eric liked to mull things over while he was running,

Calleigh said she got some of her best ideas while on the shooting range, but Horatio did a lot of his processing behind the wheel. There was something Zen-like about all those activities, when the body was doing something it had done a million times before. It focused the will while leaving the mind more or less unoccupied, and therefore free to solve problems.

His drive took him past the Holocaust Memorial on Meridian Avenue, and as always, the forty-two-foot sculpture seemed to squeeze his heart as he looked at it. A gigantic hand of green-painted bronze reached up toward the sky in a desperate gesture that implied both hope and despair, grasping for . . . what? Help, certainly, but from whom? God, or Man?

A line of numbers—a concentration camp tattoo—ran down the arm and into the base of the sculpture, a writhing mass of naked humanity: men, women, children, some of them embracing, some of them trying to claw their way out, some of them trying to help others. A glimpse into hell. It never failed to move Horatio, and today it turned his thoughts toward questions he had no answers to.

They weren't questions of theology, though. Despite its trappings, this case wasn't about religion; as far as Horatio was concerned it was about a con man, plain and simple, one who'd lied and manipulated his way into his victims' lives and now threatened them. That was something he intended to prevent . . . because, in the end, it didn't matter who the victims were reaching out to.

What mattered was that someone take that hand, and pull them up.

* * *

"There are three kinds of DNA in plants," Valera said. She and Calleigh were looking over her data in the DNA lab. "Chloroplast, mitochondrial and nuclear. We use nuclear cells for IDing species, and PCR the chloroplast to generate a profile of a specific plant."

Calleigh nodded. Polymerase Chain Reaction, or PCR, was an umbrella term for DNA typing. It involved extracting DNA from a cell, then getting it to replicate itself millions of times over in a process sometimes referred to as molecular xeroxing.

"In a human subject," Valera said, "I'd use the Short Tandem Repeat method for further analysis." STR used an electrophoretic gel or capillary device to separate and identify a number of different DNA markers at the same time, in a process called multiplexing.

"Right," Calleigh said. She was familiar with the thirteen specific DNA sites, or core loci, that were used by law enforcement to ID a specific individual.

"But typing plants for forensic purposes isn't as advanced a science as human genetic fingerprinting," Valera cautioned. "The polymorphic loci aren't as firmly established, and they haven't been physically mapped to chromosomes yet—let alone done any multiplexing. I could have gone with RAPD testing, where we add random sequences of PCR primers, get the oligomers to bind with the template, then stain the gel with ethidium bromide to produce a band pattern—but there've been a few problems with that. Different labs have produced different results, probably because their thermal cycler ramp speeds vary."

"Your results are only as accurate as your equipment," Calleigh said.

"So I went with AFLP—Amplified Fragment Length Polymorphisms. It uses PCR to amplify restriction fragments with attached adapter oligomer sequences. We add fluorescent dye, which gets incorporated at the same time the PCR primers bind to the oligomers, which amplifies DNA fragments of varying sizes. A DNA sequencer with a laser makes the dye fluoresce and generates a banded pattern. This gets recorded by a CCD camera and we run the whole thing through an analysis program, which stores and interprets the pattern."

"Sounds fairly advanced to me," Calleigh said.

"Well, they're really just adaptations of the technology we use for human DNA testing—but it can produce a result you never see outside of science fiction movies." Valera gave her two pieces of paper, which Calleigh compared side by side.

"Identical genetic sequences," she said. "Clones."

"That's right. Dope growers have been refining and cross-breeding different strains for four decades; when they get a really high-quality product, they take a cutting and grow more of the same. And while they don't mind sharing seeds, they're more proprietary about cuttings."

"Like owning a prize bloodhound," Calleigh said. "You might put him out to stud, but there's a certain pride of ownership that comes with possession of the original."

"Well, none of your samples shared the same pedigree."

Calleigh frowned. "But these two are identical."

"Yes, but the one in your left hand didn't come from any of the samples you gave me. A lab in Wisconsin has been trying to put together a database of marijuana DNA; they've already got data from Connecticut, Florida, Iowa, Wyoming, West Virginia, Tennessee . . ." Valera paused, frowning, then added, ". . . Kentucky, Vermont, Georgia, Canada, *and* Taiwan. I went to school with one of the people working on it, and she was nice enough to give me access. One of the profiles in their database matched yours, so I tracked down the case file, too." Valera handed over a folder.

Caleigh opened it, scanned the first page. "Hmmm. Now that *is* intriguing. Looks like I should pay a visit to the pound . . ."

Horatio was about to tuck in to a Cuban sandwich at Auntie Bellum's when Salas strolled up.

"Mind if I join you?" she asked.

"Please," Horatio said.

She slid into the booth on the other side. "Eating alone, Horatio? No one wants the pleasure of your company?"

He smiled and picked up his sandwich. "You're here."

"Yes, but I'm a glutton for punishment. Other people apparently don't have my high Caine threshold."

"I sense I'm not going to like what you're about to tell me."

She reached over and stole one of his French fries, holding it delicately between a red-nailed forefinger and thumb. "That depends. If you enjoy being told you've pissed off the people that sign your paycheck, then you'll be ecstatic."

He took a bite of his sandwich, chewed thoughtfully and swallowed before answering. "And what, pray tell, would the brass be upset with me for?"

She stared at him skeptically. "Are you trying to tell me you don't know?"

Horatio drank some iced tea. "I didn't say that," he said, putting down the glass. "I just happen to like the way you deliver bad news."

"The mayor had a supermodel scream at him this morning."

"See? That's what I mean," Horatio said with a grin. "A screaming supermodel is vastly more entertaining than simply being told I screwed up."

"Horatio, you screwed up."

"Did I?"

She pointed the French fry at him accusingly. "You know, that habit you have of ending every other sentence with a question mark can be really annoying. And if you say 'Is that so?' I'm gonna clock you."

"All right then, I'll stick to making definitive statements. Statement number one: I know exactly what I'm doing. Statement number two: I'm sure the mayor has been yelled at by people a lot scarier than a professional mannequin. And statement number three: nervous people make mistakes."

"So impounding every vehicle at the Vitality Method clinic was just a scare tactic?"

"Not every vehicle. Just the ones owned by Sinhurma."

"Which, as it turns out, are basically all of them—his less well-to-do patients sign ownership over to him in lieu of payment, and his richer clients just give him cars."

"Yes, we took away three Mercedes," Horatio said. "Delko couldn't wait to start ripping them apart."

"Oh, wipe that smirk off your face. You really think you can get away with using the contraband act to pressure Sinhurma?"

"I needed to rattle him, Yelina. Locked away in that compound, surrounded by people who worship him, he thinks he's invulnerable. Nothing alters that point of view quicker than a few squad cars showing up and taking away your toys."

"And that's all you hope to accomplish? Shaking him up?"

Horatio shook his head. "No, I'm hoping to find more evidence. Specifically, evidence in the Mulrooney murder."

"None of which will be admissible if you can't make the forfeiture stand up in court."

"Sinhurma is drugging his patients without their knowledge or consent, and making a hefty profit out of it. It'll stand."

She sighed. "Okay. I'm just the messenger, anyway; personally, I hope you nail the bastard. But be careful; Sinhurma has a lot of powerful friends."

"Not for long . . ."

The man sitting across the scarred wooden table from Calleigh wore an orange jumpsuit, prison-issue sneakers and a sneer. His eyes were blue and his hair was no more than short blond fuzz covering his scalp like a peach; he was handsome, in a heavy-lipped, heavy-lidded kind of way. His name was Joseph Welfern Junior, and he was currently a resident of Dade Correctional Institute.

"Mister Welfern," Calleigh said. "I've got a few questions for you."

The man's sneer twitched into something closer to a grin. "Go ahead an' ask. I got nothin' better'n do than shoot the breeze."

Calleigh glanced down at the file she held. "I see you were arrested for transporting marijuana."

"Hell, that was just a little stash for personal use." His tone was friendly.

"Fourteen pounds?" Calleigh said. "What do you use it for, insulation?"

He laughed. "Okay, okay. But I was just the driver, all right? Didn't grow it, didn't sell it. Didn't even know what I was haulin', but that didn't stop the cops from takin' away my truck."

"Well, that's what you told the court, but apparently they found it somewhat hard to believe. So do I."

Welfern shrugged. "Believe what you wanna. Ain't gonna matter much to me."

"It might. A letter of recommendation from an officer can carry some weight at a parole hearing—and you've got one coming up in two weeks."

"So I do," he admitted. "And you wanna know what, exactly?"

"We've matched the strain of marijuana you were transporting to a hash-making operation in Miami.

We know where the dope was headed; we'd like to know where it was coming from."

He snorted. "Is that all? Y'all are wasting your time, blondie. Don'tcha think that was the first thing they asked me to give up? If I couldn't do it then, why could I do it now?"

She gazed at him levelly. "Maybe it's not that you couldn't; maybe you just wouldn't. Be strong, do the time. But you've been in here a while now, and what has it gotten you? I bet you spend a lot of time thinking about the guys that *didn't* get caught, that *didn't* go to jail. About all the things they're getting to do that you're not . . ."

She let that hang in the air for a moment, then smiled warmly. "I'll bet the closer that parole hearing gets the more you think about all those things. And how *terrible* it would be if they didn't let you out. Might make you wonder if you hadn't made a big mistake in the first place . . . but that's all water under the bridge now, isn't it? Any chance you had to make a deal is long gone. What a shame."

His grin had vanished. "You got no idea how it works," he said.

"Don't I? You roll over when you're arrested, it's obvious who talked. You do it now, nobody'll notice. Especially if the bust comes from a completely different direction—in this case, as part of a murder investigation."

He stared at her for a moment. "And if I keep my mouth shut, you screw me with the parole board, right?"

"No," Calleigh said. "I didn't come here to threaten

you, Mister Welfern—I came here to give you a chance to do some good. It's up to you to decide whether or not you're interested."

He leaned back in his chair, stared at her through half-closed eyes. "You'll come to my parole hearing?"

"I'll even wear a skirt," Calleigh said.

His grin came back. "Frostin' on the cake . . ."

"Nice ride," Wolfe said. He and Delko, both in overalls, were looking at the vehicles brought in from the Vitality Method compound. The one Wolfe was admiring was a Dodge Viper painted a lurid shade of purple.

"You should have seen the ones we *didn't* take," Delko said. "Some sitcom star was there for his daily injection, pulled up in his Maserati. I was tempted to wait until he came out again and arrest him for DUI."

"Why didn't you?"

"Hey, this is H's play. He's already getting a lot of flak for the compound bust—I wasn't about to turn us into the lead story for *Entertainment Tonight.*"

Wolfe crossed his arms. "So you just let him drive away?"

Delko grinned and shook his head. "No, I suggested to the man that if he were there for a medical procedure, it would be in his own best interests to have someone drive him home."

"How'd he take it?"

"With a very large, professional smile. I get the feeling it's not the first time a cop has given him advice instead of a ticket."

They got to work. Each of the vehicles had to be

gone through and all its contents listed; this consisted, for the most part, of writing down such mundane items as pens, tire pressure gauges, maps, combs and packages of tissues.

In the spare tire compartment of a large white van, they found what they'd hoped for: a set of jumper cables, coiled on top of the spare like a bright orange snake with twin heads at either end.

Wolfe picked up two of the alligator-tooth clamps, examined them carefully. "I think I've got something here, caught in the clamp," he said.

Delko picked up the other end and studied it. "I've got something, too—looks like copper. Let's get these to the lab and take a closer look. . . ."

Darcy Cheveau looked just as relaxed waiting in the police interview room as he had the first time Horatio had talked to him at The Earthly Garden. He looked up as Horatio and Salas came in and said, "Hey," as casually as if he were greeting someone he saw every day.

"Mister Cheveau," Horatio said, sitting down. Salas, as usual, remained standing. "I understand you're the one that usually drives the Vitality Method van."

"Not all the time," Cheveau said. "To and from the restaurant, usually."

"Uh-huh. How about maintenance? You ever have to tune it up, change the plugs, anything like that?"

Cheveau shook his head. "Naw, man. I'm a cook, not a mechanic. The Doc gets all that stuff done professionally."

"So it runs okay? Never broke down on you any-where?"

"Nah—oh, wait a minute. Does changing a tire count? I had to do that once."

"That would count, yes," Horatio said. "What about Albert Humboldt? He give you a hand?"

"No. I changed it myself—Albert wasn't even there. Why?"

"So can you think of any reason Albert's finger-prints would be on a set of jumper cables in the spare tire compartment instead of yours?"

Cheveau stared at him for a second, then chuckled. "I don't know, man. Albert's a neat freak. The Doc mighta had him clean out the van or somethin' when I wasn't around."

"We also found some epithelial cells on the handle of one of the jumper cables. I was wondering if we could take a DNA sample from you to eliminate you as a suspect."

Cheveau shrugged. "Sure. Whatever you gotta do." He stretched and yawned. "Just get it over with, huh? I gotta get back."

Looking at Cheveau, Horatio thought as he pulled out a swab, *you'd never figure him to belong to a cult.* He seemed like just another bad boy, the kind that always had a beautiful woman hanging off one arm and a six-pack under the other. From the way Salas was looking at him, she recognized his type too. Never thinking too far ahead, never worried about his health or his reputation or even the day after tomor-row. Guys like him seemed genetically predestined to wind up as an outlaw biker, a surfer, or a bass player in a rock band; usually, their idea of spiritual fulfillment was to live in a beer commercial.

It just showed, he thought as Cheveau opened his mouth and Horatio stuck the cotton swab inside, *that you never really knew what you were going to find when you went under the surface.*

"This is an OH-58 Kiowa," the Florida National Guardsman told Calleigh. "Specially outfitted for the Reconnaissance and Interdiction Detachment."

"RAID," Calleigh said. She squinted at the helicopter in the bright afternoon sun, shading her eyes with one hand. Matte black, with its oval body, pointed nose and tapered rear section, it reminded her more of something that swam than flew. "You military boys do love your acronyms."

The Guardsman, a lanky, beak-nosed man that had introduced himself as Chief Warrant Officer Stainsby, patted her canopy lovingly. "Yeah, and we love nicknames even more. They call us the 'Grim Reefers,' you know."

Calleigh smiled. "Well, considering how many marijuana crops you've been responsible for eliminating, that seems entirely appropriate. Shall we?"

"After you," Stainsby said, opening the door.

"I want to thank you again," Calleigh said as the rotors started up. "The directions I got were kind of vague. The person had only been there once, at night, and was being told how to get there by someone riding with him. If I tried to find it in a car I'd probably wind up hopelessly lost."

"Yeah, some of the roads out there aren't much

more than trails," Stainsby said, speaking loudly over
the sound of the engine. "But we won't be looking for
roads."

"What will we be looking for, exactly?" she asked
as they lifted off.

"Anything out of place. You got to keep a sharp eye
out, though; growers use all kinds of tricks. They hide
crops by mixing them in with other plants sometimes,
like corn or even tomato vines. The area we're headed
to, though, they're probably growing it in the middle
of a pine forest. Pot's a lighter green than pine, but it
takes a little experience to pick it out."

"Lucky I have you along, then," Calleigh said.

Law enforcement had been using Florida Natural
Guard choppers for aerial surveillance of suspected
drug crops for years. Calleigh and Stainsby were
headed for an area near the Georgia/Florida border;
Calleigh knew that growers near the state border liked
to live on one side of the line and plant their crops on
the other, hopefully confusing whose jurisdiction it
was under.

For a while they flew in silence, the racket of the
chopper's blades making it hard to talk. The landscape
below them was a series of low, sandy ridges, with
marshy swamps full of cypress, blackgum, bay and
maple between them. The trees on the ridges varied
from longleaf and slash pines to saw palmetto, and
the occasional expanse of wire grass.

"I hear some of these fields are booby-trapped," she
said at last.

"Oh, yeah. I've never encountered any myself—
we're strictly recon, just spot 'em from the air—but

I've heard stories. Fishhooks, sharpened stakes, bear traps—even shotguns wired to go off."

"Sounds pretty bad."

"They don't care so much about cops, it's thieves they're trying to stop. A seven-foot-tall plant can be worth a thousand dollars; that's a pretty good incentive to protect your investment. A lot of grow-ops are moving indoors—harder to find, easier to protect."

"But just as dangerous to officers," Calleigh said. "I read about a case where the growers electrified a steel door, rigged jars of nitric acid to dump on a trespasser's head and hooked a motion detector to a chemical spray. And then there was the lizard."

"Excuse me?"

"Crocodile monitor—relative of the Komodo dragon. The Komodo's the biggest lizard in the world—they can get up to three hundred fifty pounds—but the croc's the longest; they've found specimens over ten feet in length. They also have the longest fangs of any lizard, which apparently the owners of one particular grow-op thought would make a reasonably scary burglar deterrent . . . say, did you see that?"

They were up around five hundred feet, flying over acres and acres of gently rolling hills of pine forest. "I thought I saw a flash down there," Calleigh said, grabbing a pair of binoculars. "Can you circle around and get a little lower?"

"No problem."

She tried to focus the binoculars on the area the flash came from. She got a blur of green—and then, suddenly, two human figures. One was standing, one kneeling.

The flash had come from the shiny silver barrel of the large handgun the first held to the head of the second.

"Put us down!" Calleigh yelled. "*Now!*"

"Mister Humboldt," Horatio said. "Thank you for coming in."

Humboldt glanced around the interview room nervously. "Is this going to take long? I'm supposed to be helping prepare dinner at the clinic—"

"How long can it take to boil some rice?" Salas said. "But don't worry—this'll be over soon. We were just wondering if you could clear a few things up for us."

"What do you want to know?"

"Let's start with what I already know," Horatio said. "I know you have nothing to do with the driving or maintenance of the Vitality Method van. Correct?"

"It's—it's not really my area, no." Humboldt blinked several times rapidly. Salas smiled at him encouragingly.

"And I know the jumper cables from the van were used to hook the rocket on the roof to the pipe in the toilet," Horatio continued. "We found traces of Kevlar caught in one of the clamps, fragments of copper in another . . . and some skin. Guess you got a little careless when you were hooking it up, or maybe it was just awkward getting the clamp onto the pipe through that hole in the wall and your hand slipped."

"You—you can't prove that—"

"But I can. I already have your prints on the cable—and pretty soon I'll have your DNA."

Horatio slapped a piece of paper down on the table. "Which is the purpose of this warrant," he said. "I guess I owe you an apology, Albert; I don't seem to have any questions for you at all. But you"—he said, as he pulled out a swab—"definitely have something for me. . . ."

10

"Put down where?" Stainsby said. "There's no—"

"There's a clearing to your left!"

The men had noticed the copter, of course—it wasn't exactly quiet. The one with the gun, a large, bearded man in jeans, boots and a denim vest, was yelling something and waving the gun around. The one on his knees was dressed in camo fatigues and a black baseball cap—that was about all the details Calleigh had time to see before the chopper dipped down below the tree line.

"I can't set it down—the terrain's too uneven!" Stainsby shouted. They were about ten feet up.

Calleigh jumped.

She hit the ground hard and rolled with the impact. "Get some backup out here!" she yelled, and then she was sprinting, gun already out, in the direction of the two men.

"Miami-Dade police!" she shouted. "Put your weapon down—"

A shot rang out.

She darted behind a scrubby pine, which really didn't provide much cover. The Kiowa was already shockingly far away; in another few moments the sound of its motor had faded to a distant clatter, like that of a determined woodpecker. She knew Stainsby was getting out of range of the gun, which had looked large enough to bring down the chopper if the shooter hit something vital.

Smart move, she thought to herself. A lot smarter than her own; she was alone in the woods with an unknown armed maniac, who not only was probably more familiar with the area but apparently had a hostage.

And booby-traps. Can't forget about the booby-traps, she reminded herself. Somehow, she'd gone from being an observer, nice and safe in an aircraft, to starring in a Florida remake of *Rambo* in the space of about thirty seconds.

Dad always did say I was too impulsive, she thought. *Guess I'll have to tell him he was right.*

She crept forward, listening intently. Birdsong and insects, nothing else. She crested a small rise and saw a camo-suited body lying motionless at its base. Even from a distance she could see that he'd been shot in the head.

"Damn," she whispered. She was too late.

At least it meant she wasn't dealing with a hostage situation—any standoff was tense, but in a situation like this it might be an hour or more before any backup arrived. That was a long time to stare down someone with a gun.

Of course, now the shooter doesn't have to drag a captive along. He's free to be just as quick and sneaky as a fox . . . he's probably getting a hunting rifle from his four-by-four right now. One with a high-powered scope and a laser sight.

She shook her head, tried to stay focused. It was more likely he'd simply try to get away than get into a gun battle. All she had to do was keep her ears open; more than likely she'd hear a motor start up, and then she'd know where he was.

But the next sound she heard wasn't an engine. It was a deep, gravelly roar, echoing through the forest like the voice of some enraged ogre: "I AM GONNA KILL YOU!"

So much for him running away . . .

"Sir?" she called out. "I'm a Miami-Dade police officer! I'm going to have to ask you to discard your weapon—"

"I HEARD YOU THE FIRST TIME!" the man bellowed. "YOU AIN'T NO COP, AND YOUR PARTNERS AIN'T EITHER!"

"Oh, lovely," she muttered. What was she supposed to do now, stroll out and flash her badge? Recite the Police Officer's Oath of Office?

"You *did* notice the helicopter?" she called back.

"DIDN'T LOOK LIKE NO COP HELICOPTER TO ME! MORE LIKE ARMY SURPLUS!"

Good Lord, she thought. She was dealing with the most dangerous kind of felon: a complete idiot.

"BESIDES—WHAT KINDA COP WOULD SHOW UP OUT HERE ALL ALONE? EVEN YOUR BUDDY TOOK OFF! PROBABLY DIDN'T WANT HIS BARGAIN-BASEMENT WHIRLYBIRD GETTIN' ALL SHOT UP!"

She sighed. *I can't even argue with him—no cop with half a brain* would *get caught in a situation like this.*

"What's your name?" she tried.

"DON'T MATTER WHAT MY NAME IS! I'M JUST THE ONE GONNA PUT YOU IN THE COLD, HARD GROUND, THAT'S ALL YOU GOTTA KNOW!"

Wonderful. Even if he doesn't shoot me, I may die of testosterone poisoning before anybody gets here. "Well, I have to call you something!"

A pause.

"DOOLEY!"

"Excuse me?"

"MY NAME! IT'S DOOLEY!"

"Okay! Mine is—"

"BUT I'M STILL GONNA KILL YA!"

"All right! My name—"

"JUST SO'S WE GOT THAT STRAIGHT!"

"I got it, Dooley! I understand! Now do you *want* to know my name, or would you prefer to shoot a complete stranger?"

That, apparently, required enough thought to distract Dooley from bellowing for a moment.

"I AIN'T SURE!" he finally shouted. "MAYBE I'LL JUST CALL YOU *TOAST!*"

"It's Calleigh! CALLEIGH DUQUESNE!" she hollered back.

She was answered with a gunshot. "WHATEVER YOU SAY, TOAST!"

"Terrific," she muttered.

"I didn't fire the rocket," Humboldt said.

Horatio stared at him coolly. "You keep saying that, Albert. Almost like you expect me to believe it."

"It's true. That wasn't—it wasn't what I *did*." He pronounced every word very clearly, very carefully, as if he were walking a verbal tightrope and didn't want to fall off.

"Oh, I know what you did, Albert. You got caught—caught smoking hashish in Doctor Sinhurma's home. And he didn't like that, did he? He demoted you to washing pots and pans in the restaurant. You'd think that might stop you, but no—you kept on doing it. A little hot-knifing off a portable torch with your pal Samuel Lucent when no one else was around—what did you do, stay late to clean up and drive your own car back to the compound, or did he give you a ride?"

"You can't believe what he says. He's not—not—"

"Not what? One of you? No, he does his own thinking. . . . but you needed him, didn't you? Needed someone to sell you drugs. Needed someone to get high with. Is that when you got the idea to kill Phil Mulrooney? The whole rocket-and-lightning idea sounds like the kind of thing someone would cook up when they were stoned. . . ."

"It wasn't like that."

"Really? That's not what the evidence says. The evidence places those jumper cables in your hands—"

"I connected them, all right?" Humboldt gave him an aggrieved look. "I attached the clamps to the pipe and to a device on the roof. But that's hardly a crime."

"Considering it led to an event that stopped Phillip Mulrooney's heart, I think a jury would disagree with you . . . but for the sake of argument, let's say you're right. How would *you* explain your actions?"

"I was simply carrying out a task. I had no knowl-edge of any rocket or even what that pipe was connected to. And at the time I performed that task, Phillip wasn't even in the bathroom. That's not murder."

Horatio studied him intently for a moment. "And what, exactly, did you think was the purpose of your task?"

"I didn't know. I didn't *need* to know." Humboldt smiled. "It was part of a larger pattern; my heart told me I was doing the right thing."

"Right. You know what the military calls that, Albert? Plausible deniability. You claim you didn't really know the consequences of your actions, that you were 'out of the loop.' But *someone* told you to place those cables . . . and I'm going to find out who."

"Is that all you want?" Albert said, his smile widening. "Why don't you just ask me?"

Horatio smiled back.

"Dooley! Listen, I really *am* a police officer—"

"YEAH? COPS ALWAYS SNEAK AROUND WITH DUFFEL BAGS FULLA STOLEN DOPE?"

"I don't *have* any of your drugs, Dooley!"

"YOUR BUDDY SURE DID! RIPPED UP FIFTEEN OF MY BEST PLANTS BEFORE I CAUGHT HIM!"

"Look, I don't have anything to do with the man you shot!"

"NOT ANYMORE, YOU DON'T—'LESS YOU PLAN ON GOIN' TO HIS FUNERAL! WHICH YOU AIN'T GONNA HAVE THE CHANCE TO DO ANYHOW!"

A shot cracked out. She tried to keep as much of the tree between her and Dooley as she could, but it wasn't that thick; she had to find better cover.

Sounded like all he had was a handgun, which was good. She'd only gotten a brief look at it, from a distance, but she'd seen it was a large revolver; from the full-length underbarrel lug and stainless steel finish it was probably a Colt King Cobra.

Two point six pounds, empty. Six-round cylinder, double action, good to around a hundred and fifty feet. You can chamber it for a .38-caliber, but it's a cowboy gun—he'll be using the full 357 Magnums. He's got the six-inch barrel—too bad, the four-inch would have cut down on his accuracy. Not that he's hit anything farther away than point-blank, so far.

She looked around. There was a fallen tree to her left, which looked like good cover but wasn't—rotten wood wouldn't slow a 357 down enough to matter. It would hide her, but that was about it—and if he saw her duck behind it, she'd be out of luck.

Just past the fallen log, though, was a slight depression in the ground, with a boulder on the edge of it. Taken together, they should provide enough protection if she lay prone . . . but she'd have to cross his field of fire to get there.

Probably had his gun fully loaded. Might have fired a shot at the thief to get his attention, but probably not—Dooley seems more like a "Fire first, ask questions later" kind of guy. He's fired two shots at me, and one to kill the thief, which leaves him with three shots—unless he's reloading right now. Better not give him the chance.

She fired a quick two shots off in his direction. He responded, as she expected, with two shots of his own—and then she was sprinting toward the fallen log.

The last bullet sprayed her with decaying wood as she darted past the log, and then she was down in the pine needles, behind sheltering gray rock.

"WHERE YOU GOIN', TOAST? YOU WANNA BE CAREFUL OUT HERE—NEVER KNOW WHAT YOU MIGHT RUN INTA!"

Traps. He's talking about traps.

She looked around cautiously—then froze.

Less than a foot from where she sprawled, an almost invisible monofilament line was suspended six inches or so above the ground. It was so fine, at first she thought it was a spiderweb . . . but then she followed it to the hollow base of a stump. Something was inside—something hidden except for a single metal corner that stuck out. A metal corner painted a flat khaki green.

She had a pretty good idea what the object would look like when exposed: metal, smaller than a shoebox, with the words THIS SIDE TOWARD ENEMY stenciled on it in big white letters.

Antipersonnel mine. This guy's playing for keeps.

"IF YOU GO OUT IN THE WOODS TODAY, YER IN FOR A BIG SURPRISE. . . ."

And he's singing "The Teddy Bear's Picnic" at me. I almost wish I'd tripped the mine . . .

"IF YOU GO OUT IN THE WOODS TODAY, YOU'LL GET IT BETWEEN THE EYES!"

All right, then—no more running around. She'd stay where she was, and wait him out. Sooner or later Stainsby would be back with reinforcements—all she had to do was hang on until then. Maybe she could even learn a few things in the meantime.

"Hey, Dooley! You planning on serenading me to death?"

A bullet *spanged* off the rock in response. Well, he knew where she was—and he obviously had more bullets.

"YOU GONNA BE SORRY YOU EVER CAME UP HERE, TOAST!"

The only thing I'm sorry about is that I didn't bring a little more firepower with me. . . . "You might want to ask yourself *how* I found this place, Dooley!"

Silence.

Then, "WHAT THE HELL'S THAT SUPPOSE T'MEAN?"

"Think about it!" she called back. *If that's possible.*

It was a calculated gamble. Dooley might assume she'd got the information from Joseph Welfern—but that would be a correct assumption, and so far Dooley hadn't made too many of those. If, on the other hand, he made the same kind of wrongheaded guess he'd been making so far—

"THAT GODDAMN LITTLE PEAR-SHAPED BAS-TARD! I'M GONNA KILL HIM DEADER'N I KILL YOU! *NOBODY* SELLS ME OUT!"

Calleigh smiled.

"And why should I believe you?" Horatio asked. "Forgive my skepticism, but it seems to me that one of Doctor Sinhurma's tenets is loyalty . . . so what would make you suddenly betray one of your own?"

Humboldt gave him a superior look. "He was never one of us, not really. The best strategy is to turn an enemy's strength against him—that's the only reason he was allowed to join."

"The only reason you recruited him, you mean. . . ." Horatio frowned. "That was Ruth Carrell's job, wasn't it? She brought him in, made him feel welcome—on Sinhurma's orders."

"Doctor Sinhurma had nothing to do with this."

"Forget it, Albert. That dog won't hunt. You might think you can pin this whole thing on a martyr, but that's not going to happen."

"I don't know what you're talking about," Humboldt said primly. "The person who told me to connect those cables obviously hates our organization and is trying to destroy it."

"I thought you were following your heart, Albert. Which is it? Were you doing the right thing on the orders of your leader, or doing the wrong thing because you were ignorant of the facts?"

"I—I was doing as I was told."

"By whom?"

Humboldt locked eyes with Horatio. "His name is McKinley. Jason McKinley, the rocket expert."

Calleigh thought she had a pretty good idea where Dooley was located now. From the sound of his voice and the angle of the shots, she thought he was holed up in a deer blind, about twenty feet above the ground, around a hundred yards away. She was lucky; the terrain sloped up toward her, negating most of his height advantage—otherwise, he could have taken his time and picked her off. As it was, they were almost at the same level.

Except he was sitting up in a tree.

She thought she could make out the shape of the blind, a slightly darker, squarish blob in the trees, no doubt covered with camouflage netting. She wondered why he was still using the Magnum; a sentry post like that one should have a rifle with a scope in it at the very least.

Maybe it does. Maybe he's trying to draw me in closer, get a better shot.

Maybe he's not as dumb as he sounds.

"I'M COMIN' TA GET YA, TOAST! AIN'T NO PLACE TA HIDE!"

The voice didn't sound any nearer. He was obviously trying to get her to rabbit, maybe stumble into one of his traps—which gave her an idea.

"You just stay where you are!" she yelled. She tried to put just a little fear in her voice. "I've got friends coming!"

"SURE YA DO! CAN'T WAIT TA MEET 'EM!"

She scooted to the side, careful to avoid the trip wire, and examined the mine. There were hundreds of varieties of antipersonnal mines, and she wasn't familiar with all of them—but lucky for her, this was one she recognized. It was an M18 Claymore with a simple trigger: pull on the wire, activate the mine. She took a deep breath, reached out and grabbed the metal box, lifting it up slowly.

Nothing happened. She let her breath out and put the box down, facing away from her, with the trip wire no longer taut. Then, keeping low, she crawled back to where the other end of the line was attached.

She clipped it off with a multitool from her pocket, and hung on to the end.

"You stay away!" she yelled, crawling as far from the mine as she could without exposing herself. She plugged both her ears with her fingers—and yanked on the line.

THWOOM!

A Claymore was loaded with seven hundred steel balls that could turn a target into hamburger from 150 feet away. Fortunately, they were directional, spraying their shrapnel into an arc in front of them—the only thing Calleigh had destroyed was some foliage.

"HA! YOU RUN INTO A LITTLE SURPRISE, TOAST?"

She kept quiet.

"TOAST?"

Okay, Mister Dooley—it's your move. Come on down and take a look for yourself.

And then you'll get a little surprise of your own. . . .

"What was that name, H?" Wolfe asked.

"Jason McKinley," Horatio said.

Wolfe scanned the membership list he'd gotten from the rocketeer club. "McKinley, McKinley . . . yeah, here it is. Jason McKinley. Who is he?"

"At the moment, our prime suspect," Horatio said. "I talked to him about rocket-triggered lightning, but at the time he had no connection to the case—he was just a resource." *And the last time we talked, you weren't having an allergy attack, were you? You'd been crying—in mourning for Ruth. Somehow, you kept it together during our conversation, then got rid of me as quickly as you could.*

Horatio was on the move, striding down the corridor and toward the stairs. Wolfe hurried to keep up.

"Looks like you weren't the only one to draw on his expertise," Wolfe said. "If Kim is really as clueless about rockets as he seemed, then McKinley must be the one who built the rocket."

"Which is why he was recruited into the organization in the first place," Horatio said, taking the stairs two at a time. "Somebody aimed Ruth Carrell at him like a missile—and from what she told me, it was Sinhurma himself."

Wolfe and Horatio exited the building together. "What do you want me to do?" Wolfe asked.

Horatio headed straight for his Hummer. "Get a search warrant for Jason's home address," he said as he yanked open the door and climbed in. "I'll meet you there. I'm going to check out the place he works first."

The big silver vehicle roared off. Wolfe sprinted back inside.

"Dammit," Horatio said under his breath. *Should have checked that membership list personally.* He knew that it wasn't always possible to have each and every scrap of information in an investigation undergo his personal scrutiny—and there hadn't been any obvious reason to flag McKinley as a suspect—but he hated it when something important slipped past him.

Or someone.

The question now was the extent of Jason's involvement. He hadn't seemed like the rest of the Vitality Method patients, obsessed with appearance and popularity—but that was probably what made him an easy target. Having someone like Ruth pay attention to him was probably all the encouragement necessary; no drugs or fasting needed.

Despite its science-fiction trappings, the lightning-rocket stunt wasn't that hard to pull off. It was entirely possible that Jason had been used only as a source of information, and that someone else built and launched the rocket. Except . . .

Except someone else wouldn't have used a custom blend of fuel. That was the mark of a tinkerer, of someone who knew what he was doing and was always trying to do it a little better.

He didn't want to believe Jason was guilty. It was somehow easier to think of him as a victim than a killer—someone who'd been used for his knowledge and then discarded.

Maybe Jason was an innocent dupe. Or maybe Sinhurma's influence had corrupted him much further than Horatio wanted to admit . . . and that was the crux of what was really bothering him. That a decent, rational man—a man of *science*—could have his intelligence subverted by Sinhurma's brand of shallow, egocentric nonsense just stuck in Horatio's craw.

But loneliness could get to anyone. Reason and logic couldn't keep you warm at night . . . and all the precision and symmetry of the laws of physics could vanish in the depths of a pair of green eyes.

He didn't know how deep Jason had gotten.

But he was going to find out.

Kyle "Dooley" Dolittle was no fool.

No, sir. He'd heard the Claymore detonate, and he

was pretty sure it had blown that thieving little tramp's legs off, but that didn't mean he was going to take anything for granted. No, he was going to go down and check on the body personally, make sure she was dead. Then . . . well, he wasn't exactly certain what he was going to do. Maybe grab as many plants as he could and hightail it out of here—maybe stick around and shoot anyone else that showed up.

The deer blind worked just fine for that. It would've worked even better if he hadn't gotten bored sitting up there and used up all the rifle ammo shooting at birds and squirrels, but hell—he didn't figure anyone would actually show up and try to rip him off. And he still had the Cobra, didn't he? Big-ass handgun wasn't too good at long range, but it worked just fine close up. It was all he'd needed to kill the first poacher, and it would take care of anybody else that got in his way, too.

He climbed down with the gun stuck in the waistband of his jeans, jumping the last few feet and landing with a thump. He drew the gun immediately and started making his way forward, darting from tree to tree. If she was still alive, she might try to shoot him as her last act—and while he could respect that, it didn't really fit into his plans.

The light seemed unnaturally bright to him; adrenaline plus the speed he'd been popping for the last two days had his heart racing like a Harley on a mountain road. His skin was all atingle and he swore he could feel the hair on his head growing.

He wondered who the hell the guy in the helicopter had been. Whoever he was, Dooley was going to

track him down and put a bullet between his eyes—
nobody but *nobody* ripped him off. Not even somebody with a helicopter.

And how the hell did they figure they were going
to land, anyway? There wasn't even a dirt track leading to this place, let alone a patch big and flat enough
to land a chopper. He and Jimbo had to pack the
whole damn crop out by hand, and when they were
this close to harvest they took turns guarding it
twenty-four/seven.

He stopped for a second and considered whether or
not Jimbo had sold him out. He'd known the guy for
twenty years and done time with him too, but anything was possible. Maybe he'd have to have a little
talk with his partner after he was done burying the
bodies.

He approached cautiously. The trees around where
the mine had blown looked like someone with a shot-
gun had been using them for target practice.

Funny, though—he thought he'd placed this Claymore facing more toward the east—

"Drop the gun, Dooley," a soft Southern voice said
from behind him. "Don't make me shoot you in the
head."

He let the Magnum fall to the ground, cursing as he
did so.

"Now turn around." He did, slowly.

There was no one there.

"And look up."

A blond woman was perched in the branches of a
tree, pointing a gun down at him steadily. "High
ground is always a good idea—but you don't always

need a platform. I was quite the tree climber when I was younger." She sighed. "But I'm not happy, Dooley. I think I've *ruined* these pants."

"Guess you're gonna shoot me now, huh?"

She tossed down something that landed at his feet with a metallic clink. "Depends. If you cuff yourself to the nearest tree and promise to behave yourself until my backup arrives, probably not." Her voice got a little colder. "On the other hand, if you call me 'Toast' one more time, all bets are *off*."

11

"I'M SORRY," Doctor Wendall told Horatio, "But I haven't seen Jason in two days. He's just vanished."

Horatio was in Wendall's office at the Atmosphere Research Technologies. The scientist rubbed the top of his smooth skull and added, "I really don't know where he would be. Is he involved in the case you were telling me about?"

"I can't say yet," Horatio said. "Tell me, has Jason been acting different lately?"

Wendall hesitated, then said, "Well, yes. We all thought it was a girl—he was acting like he was in love. You know, sort of giddy, always in a good mood, dressing better—not at work, here he was still pretty casual, but afterward. I actually saw him in a suit once."

"Uh-huh. What about his eating habits? Were they different?"

"I believe he's recently become vegetarian, come to think of it."

Horatio nodded. "Did he ever talk about adopting a new set of beliefs?"

Wendall frowned. "I don't understand. You mean going into a different field of study?"

"No. I mean religious or metaphysical beliefs."

"No. No, he never mentioned anything like that."

That was a good sign. If Jason hadn't gotten around to mentioning his new outlook to his coworkers, maybe he still had doubts. Maybe he hadn't completely given in to Sinhurma. . . .

"He seemed a lot happier," Wendall said, his thick eyebrows coming together as he frowned. "I thought we only had to watch out for disgruntled people in the workplace—is sudden joy a warning sign now too?"

"This kind of joy comes with a very high price tag," Horatio said. "One I don't think Jason wants to pay. . . ."

"*How* much?" the man in the pink T-shirt and white suit jacket asked again, disbelief in his voice.

"Cover's twenty bucks," the bouncer repeated. "*If* you want to stand in line, *and* you don't look like an idiot. Or you could pay the fifty-dollar surcharge."

"And what would that be for?" the man asked. He was in his late thirties, trying to look like he was in his mid-twenties, and from his unshaven chin and Ray-Bans obviously still thought *Miami Vice* was the height of cool.

"That would be to get you to the head of the line, *and* to suppress my natural idiot-detecting abilities," the bouncer said. His name was James Collinson, he stood six foot two, his hair was brown and wavy and he had arms like tanned tree trunks. "Which, I gotta say, are being severely strained at the moment. Find that jacket at a yard sale? Or you been saving it since your high school prom?"

The man glared at Collinson, glanced down at the oak-size arms folded across his chest, and slunk away to try his luck farther down Ocean Drive.

The bouncer didn't give him another thought. Collinson dealt with people like him every night, people who thought charm, arrogance or—laughably—politeness would get them through the portal he guarded. None of the above impressed him. He kept an eye out for sexy women in a minimum of clothing, celebrities, and cash, in that order—and even the cash didn't impress him that much. He enjoyed his job for the perks, not the profit, and the two main ones were sex and power.

He yawned and stretched, showing off his massively muscled biceps at the same time. The night was hot and humid, threatening rain, but the line to get in was just as long as ever. Garth's was the newest, hottest spot on the beach, and if you wanted in you had to convince the giant at the front door you were worthy. Life was good.

He checked the counter in his hand—which showed how many people were inside and kept him from violating the fire code—and then looked up and down the street, his gaze passing over the people lined up behind the velvet rope like they weren't even there. South Beach was always entertaining; on the street, the traffic that crawled slowly past was a mix of black and white limos, tourists in rental vehicles, and tiny Italian sports cars that looked small enough to dart between the wheels of the hulking, tinted-window SUVs. The art-deco facades of the buildings were lit up in spotlights of pink, green, orange, blue;

across the street, out in the bay, the lights of a thousand pleasure craft twinkled and bobbed like drunken stars.

Tonight, though, it all seemed kind of boring. He fished the paperback out of his back pocket, flipped it open to where he'd left off and started reading.

"Is that *The Vitality Method?*" a voice asked. Only the fact that the voice sounded young and female prompted Collinson to look up.

"That's what the cover says," he said. The speaker was a woman, but she wasn't that pretty, that young, or showing that much skin; he dismissed her almost immediately as a middle-aged tourist wanting to experience a hot Miami nightclub with no actual idea of how unlikely that was. There was something familiar about her, though. . . .

"I just finished reading that!" the woman said. "Are you vegetarian?"

He was almost about to snap, *No, but* you *might want to skip your next few cheeseburgers*—she wasn't fat, but he hated being interrupted—when he suddenly realized where he knew her from. A grin spread across his face.

Collinson considered himself to be a lucky person. In the few years he'd been in Miami, he'd landed in one fortunate situation after the other; he'd made tons of cash, spent most of his off-time partying, and had slept with some truly outstanding women, including an underwear model. But the moment he was about to enjoy made all those previous blissful experiences seem like a short beer in a bad bar.

Careful, he thought. *Take it slow. Savor this holy sacrament, for lo, it shall not pass this way again.*

He gave her his best, most disarming smile and said, "Hey. Don't I know you?"

She smiled back and said, with just a trace of a Southern accent, "I don't think so."

"You sure? My name's James—that ring any bells?"

"Sorry, I'm afraid not."

"Well, then—what do you do for a living? Maybe that's it."

"I'm a public servant."

He spread his arms expansively. "Just like me."

She laughed. "I don't think so. My job's a lot more boring."

"Oh, I doubt that," he said. "I'll bet you have lots of fun . . . I know *I* do. Been waiting long?"

"Seems like forever."

Good, good, he thought. *The more time she's got invested the longer she'll stick around.* "Yeah, I know what you mean," he said. "Me, I'm outta here in a few more minutes—soon as my replacement shows up."

"Lucky you. Um—looks like somebody else just left," she pointed out, a trace of hope in her voice.

"You know the great thing about the jobs we have?" he asked in a friendly voice. "The control we have over other people's lives. I mean, it's not like we're in charge of anyone's destiny, but we do have a big influence in the short term. It's like there's a big switch over people's head, with two settings: 'good day' and 'crappy day.' And we're the ones that get to flip the switch. I tell 'em to go on in, they have a good day; I tell 'em to get lost, they have a crappy one. You know?"

Suspicion had kindled in her eyes. When she replied, her voice had that cold, irritated tone to it he remembered. "Not really, no."

"Sure you do. You get to flip that switch every day, just like me. The difference between us is that you like switching it to 'crappy' a lot more than I do."

There it was. The flat look in her eyes that had made him want to throttle her, the last time they'd met. *But this is gonna be even better. . . .*

"It's all about the *power,* isn't it?" he said. "I mean, yeah, it's nice to make people happy, yadda yadda, but it's nothing like the charge you get when you really, truly *screw* someone. Doesn't matter if they deserve it or not, doesn't matter what they've done or who they are—'cause it's not about *them,* is it? It's about *you.*"

"I don't—"

"See, you and I are privileged," he said, on a real roll now. "Other people who deal with the public every day get driven crazy, because they have to treat their customers with respect. No matter how many times they get asked the same stupid question, they have to grit their teeth and smile. But *we* don't, do we?" He leaned in abruptly, getting right in her face. "Nah, *we* can tell 'em how we really feel. If we're hungover or mad at our neighbor or just pissed off because the world ain't fair, we can dump that anger all over the next person in line. I do it right here . . . and you do it down at the Federal Building."

She wanted to leave, he could tell, but she was

torn; she'd waited a long time to get in, and maybe his replacement would be nicer. *Besides,* he thought, *what she really wants to do is let me have it with both barrels. That's what she's* used *to. Well, come on, girl—show me what you got.*

"Look, I just do my job," she said coldly. "It's not my fault if you don't—"

"If I don't *what*?" he snapped. "If I don't like being treated like some kinda *bug*? Like I'm some kinda *annoyance* that's keeping you from doing something more *important*? C'mon, be honest—your job gives you a license to treat people like crap, and you use it more often than you shave your damn *armpits*."

Her eyes went wide, and he knew he'd finally pushed her into losing her temper. *About time, too.*

"Who the hell do you think you are, talking to me like that?" she demanded. He knew she was about to unleash a verbal tirade, but he had no intention of enduring it; there was something he could do at his job that she couldn't do at hers.

He stepped to one side and yelled to the line of people stretching out behind her—many of whom had been following the exchange with interest— "Hey! How many people here been screwed around by the government?"

He got a few immediate cries of "Yeah!"

"Income tax? Trying to get a permit or something?" he called out. The whole line erupted with shouts of affirmation, drowning out whatever the woman was trying to say.

"Yeah, I know!" he hollered. "Well, this woman right here works for the *DMV*!"

This time, there were insults and boos mixed in with all the noise. The woman looked like her eyes were about to spit flames.

"Think I should let her in?" he hollered, and was met with a loud chorus of *no's* and profanity. You could always count on a crowd to act like a bunch of third-graders.

"You think she *deserves* the right to party with us?"

"NO!"

"What? You don't think she's *nice* enough?"

The responses were getting uglier. He looked down at her, saw her wince, just a little.

"You don't think she's *hot* enough?" he continued.

More denial. Comments about her weight, her clothes, her parents. Was that a tear he saw in her eye?

Struck by a sudden inspiration, he waved the book he still held at her with one hand. "You say you just read this book? Well, I'm not done with it yet, but so far it seems to be saying, 'Ugly on the inside, ugly on the outside.' Which makes *you* the ugliest bitch I've ever met . . . see, I have a *responsibility*. I am here to keep a certain kind of people out of this club—and honey, you are *it*. Nobody here *likes* you, nobody here *wants* you, and nobody here wants to hear a single goddamn word you have to *say*."

That did it. She bolted, reduced to tears. He watched her run with a grin on his face, savoring the victory. *Make me wait six months for a goddamn motorcycle license, huh? Let's see how* you *like getting jerked around for no reason.* "Come on back anytime," he called after her. "I'm here all night. . . ."

He waved the next three people inside, showing

how magnanimous he was, nodding and smiling as they congratulated him and confirmed that "she had it coming." Life wasn't just good, it was *grand*.

And then the guy in the bad suit walked up. Mid-forties, almost bald, built like an ex-linebacker with a face to match. "That was quite the performance," the man said. "You feel that way about all public servants?"

"Just the jerkoffs," Collinson said.

"Yeah, well, I'll be sure to pass that along to the desk sergeant down at County," the man said, pulling a badge out of his pocket. "Lieutenant Frank Tripp. Y'know, I would have done this sooner, but when you started waving that book around I thought you might actually tell me something useful. Wishful thinkin', I guess."

"What, this? A friend gave it to me."

"Yeah, and I bet I know which one," the cop replied. He pulled out a pair of handcuffs, grabbed the bouncer's wrist and spun him around. "James Collinson, you are under arrest."

"For what?" he demanded. "Getting a little pay-back?"

"Marijuana cultivation and trafficking," the cop said. "Let's go, Jimbo."

Damn, the bouncer thought as he was led away. *Guess the switch just got set to crappy. . . .*

Horatio gave Doctor Wendall his card and told him to get in touch if he heard from Jason, then got back in the Hummer and called Wolfe. He'd had better luck—Jason wasn't at home, either, but the CSI had managed to get a warrant to search his residence.

Horatio met him in front of the place, an art-deco apartment building painted a vivid shade of green. The super, a rotund woman wearing heavily tinted glasses and a floral-print sundress, let them in.

Jason's apartment wasn't quite what Horatio expected. The carpet was spotlessly white, the furniture a combination of Danish modern and designer originals that incorporated a lot of curving chrome and blond wood. Track lighting on the ceiling, tasteful art posters in silver frames on the walls. Bookcases that incorporated Lucite panels and aluminum strutwork.

"Pretty stylish for a geek," Wolfe said, looking around.

Horatio walked over to the bookcase. "Only on the surface, Mister Wolfe." He pulled out a book with one gloved hand and read the title out loud: "*Advanced Dungeons and Dragons Players Handbook.*"

"Doesn't quite go with the room," Wolfe said.

"The room doesn't really go with the tenant," Horatio said. "Let's see if the rest of the place is the same."

The bedroom, at the end of a short hall, told a very different story. The bed was unmade, the walls covered with tattered posters: *Apollo 13, Buffy the Vampire Slayer,* scantily clad heroines from Japanese *manga.* Dirty clothes were piled in heaps on the floor, food-encrusted dishes balanced on top of stacks of magazines or books. A computer with a flatscreen monitor was set up on a desk under a window, a towel thumbtacked to the window frame as a makeshift curtain.

"Seems a little more like the guy you described," Wolfe said.

"Yes, it does," Horatio said. "The living room looks

formal and artificial—it's the image he's trying to project to the outside world. This room is what he's really like."

"You think he's been playing us, H?"

"No. I think somebody's been playing him . . . somebody who preaches the importance of appearances."

Wolfe glanced around the room. "Doesn't look like the sermon was entirely effective."

I hope not, Horatio thought. "Let's see what the evidence says. . . ."

Wolfe searched the living room; Horatio took the bedroom.

By the time he was done, Horatio was fairly sure that if Jason had slept with Ruth Carrell, he hadn't done it in his own bed. The sheets hadn't been changed in a while, and there was no evidence of sexual activity. That made sense; if Ruth had seduced Jason, it would probably have taken place at the compound.

"Hey, H? Take a look at this."

Wolfe was in the small kitchen off the living room. A deep fryer sat on the Formica counter, next to a sink piled high with dirty dishes. "He may have developed a sense of style, but his sense of hygiene hasn't quite caught up," Wolfe said. "One of the rocketeers told me he makes fuel in a deep fryer. Check this one out."

Horatio peered into the appliance. A yellowish, waxy substance was encrusted around the edge; he scraped a little off with his finger and sniffed at it.

"Sugar," he said. "And I'm betting when we test it,

we'll find ten percent ammonium perchlorate as well. This is where he cooked up the fuel for the rocket."

"Think the launch system's here too?"

"We won't know until we look, will we?"

They went through the entire apartment, room by room. They found books on rocketeering, old rocket parts, and a small tool kit under the sink. From the scraps of wire and plastic scattered on it, Jason used his kitchen table as a workbench.

More disturbing was what they didn't find. "No toothbrush, no shaving supplies," Horatio noted. "Hard to tell with that mess in the bedroom, but I'm guessing clothes and a suitcase are missing too. He's taken off—but I'm guessing he hasn't gone far."

"The Vitality Method compound? You think Sinhurma would try to hide him?"

"I do. But not," Horatio said grimly, "the way Jason is hoping for."

Calleigh walked into Charette and Sons with a big smile on her face. Oscar Charlessly was talking to a woman in a green sweater over by a large industrial fridge, grinning and patting the appliance like it was a big, friendly dog. The woman was nodding and laughing, obviously very much at ease.

He is *one hell of a salesman,* Calleigh thought.

She strode right up to them and said, "Hello again."

He turned, beamed when he saw her and said, "Good to see you! Hold on a sec, darlin', I'm just finishing up here—"

"I'm sorry, Oscar," she said sweetly, "but I'm in

kind of a hurry. If I wait for you to run down, I could be here all day."

He laughed. "I do go on a bit, don't I? Well, then, what can I do for you, Miss Duquesne?"

"You can tell me how much dried marijuana you can pack into one of these," she said brightly, looking over at the fridge. "Sort of a custom-made packing crate, isn't it? I'd guess you could use all sorts of large-scale appliances for the same thing—stoves, washing machines, dryers. . . ."

His laugh got heartier. "My, my, my! I suppose I'm smuggling cocaine in my shorts, too, right? Plenty of room in those!"

The woman in the green sweater laughed too, but she sounded a little uncertain.

"No, I think you just stuck to the green and leafy stuff," she said. "Old appliances aren't hard to find—for your purposes, they didn't even have to work, did they? They just gave you a convenient excuse to drive a big truck back and forth from the Georgia border to Miami. So much dope comes into Miami from the Caribbean, you thought you could slip under the radar by bringing it in from the other direction. Undercutting the competition by using a local supplier? Lower-grade product than Jamaican *ganja*, but you got around that by using high-grade clones—kind of a designer knockoff. And lastly, you maximized your profit by turning some of the dope into hash, like a winemaker turning bad grapes into brandy. You even had a Rastafarian front man—picked for promotional reasons, right? Really, Oscar, you're quite the merchandiser."

The woman in the green sweater gaped at them. Calleigh turned to her, smiled and said, "You can go." She did.

Charlessly was shaking his head, but he still looked cheerful. "I don't know what to say, Miss Duqesne— that's quite the story. I suppose my lawyer will have to sort everything out—"

"Oh, I'm sure you'll be giving him all sorts of business. But first, you and I have a little business of our own." She pulled a folded piece of paper out of her back pocket and handed it to him. "This is a warrant to search your property, your vehicles and your computer records. The thing about old appliances is they tend to have all sorts of corners and edges and flanges inside—you know, the kind that accumulate grease and dust and various types of debris? You think maybe a speck or two of plant material might have gotten stuck in one of them?"

"Even if that were so," he said, "all these items are second-hand. I don't think a jury will hold me responsible for the history of an old fridge—"

"You can't sweet-talk DNA, Oscar. Because you used clones, any trace I find I can link to three previous arrests: the one in North Florida, the hash lab—and the grow-op Kyle Dolittle was supervising. And Dooley himself has been telling us quite a bit. . . ."

The smile on his face was beginning to look a little frozen. Calleigh motioned through the glass door to the two officers outside, and they came forward.

"One of the marks of a good businessman is keeping good records," Calleigh said. "I'm thinking that when we get into those files of yours—you know, the ones you couldn't remember the password to?—we'll find all sorts of things."

Charlessly didn't have a reply to that.

Silencing a salesman, Calleigh thought. It *almost* made up for ruining her pants.

The big wrought-iron gates of the Vitality Method compound were locked. Calls to the inside went unanswered. Horatio was forced to use more direct methods.

"Break it down," he said. The officer behind the wheel of the cruiser nodded, put the vehicle in gear and rolled forward. The iron battering ram jutting from the front bumper hit the gates with a resounding *CLANG*, throwing them open in a second.

Horatio, gun drawn and torso sheathed in a bullet-proof vest, followed the cruiser in. He was flanked by four cops in SWAT gear.

No one was in sight. The officers spread out around the perimeter, checking the archery range, the pool, the auditorium. All empty.

Horatio checked the front door: open. He led the way inside, gun leveled in front of him. There was no one behind the receptionist's island.

"Not good," he muttered. He was afraid of what he'd discover in the dorms . . . but all he found were small, plain rooms with neatly made beds.

Sinhurma's office and living areas were deserted as well. In the Japanese garden where Horatio had last talked to the doctor, he found a single slip of folded paper, weighed down with a small gray stone. On the paper, a few precise brushstrokes formed four Japanese ideograms in black ink. Horatio didn't know what it represented . . . but he knew it was meant for him.

"The ideograms mean *sayonara*," Delko said. "Goodbye."

He, Wolfe and Horatio were working the scene at the clinic; Calleigh was still busy at Charette and Sons.

"You know Japanese, Eric?" Horatio asked.

"Just a little. Dated an exchange student from Tokyo for a while—she used to leave me little notes. If I could figure out what they said, there was a reward."

"Well, our reward here is to prevent a massacre," Horatio said. "Eric, you start on the dorms. Wolfe, take the clinic. Both of you keep on eye out for a security center—all those cameras have to feed somewhere. I'm going to tackle Sinhurma's private space. We're looking for anything that might tell us where they've gone or what their intentions are. Anything that might indicate a timetable is important, too. Let's go."

Delko headed off at a trot. Wolfe hesitated, then said, "You really think we're looking at some sort of mass suicide?"

"Hard to say," Horatio said. "Sinhurma's a master manipulator—this might just be a feint. I've been trying to rattle him, get him to make a mistake; he's smart enough to try the same strategy on me. If we overreact, he can very easily use public opinion to make us look like a bunch of 'paranoid storm troopers.' Not my words—the judge's. We're lucky we got a warrant at all."

"But you think Sinhurma *could* be serious?"

"I think we better track him down and ask him," Horatio said. *"Fast."*

Sinhurma's private quarters were as sumptious as the dorm rooms had been monastic. A huge central living space looked out over the Japanese garden through one glass wall; the blinds had been closed when Horatio was here last, preventing him from seeing what he was now.

The floor was polished hardwood, overlaid with thick Persian carpets big enough to smother elephants. Recessed alcoves along one wall displayed a variety of items: a jeweled dagger, a sculpture of a bird being engulfed by flame, a golden mask that looked vaguely Egyptian. Huge, brocaded pillows were scattered around the room, the only furniture in it a raised platform of transparent Lucite set against the window, with a thin foam pad on top. Sinhurma's throne.

You sat right there, haloed by Miami sunshine—time it right and you could put the setting sun right behind your head. With that Lucite platform you could almost look like you were levitating, couldn't you?

Only your inner circle would be allowed in here, and they'd all be seated on the floor looking up. After a long day of strenuous exercise and little food, those big soft cushions probably felt like heaven . . . and that's when you would reveal the secrets of the universe. After, of course, you'd pumped all your followers full of drugs . . .

He went over the room carefully, but there was nothing in it to suggest where Sinhurma had taken his disciples.

Sinhurma's bedroom was next. It was so undistinguished that at first Horatio thought it was for guests, but after looking at the other rooms he realized the truth.

The bed was king-size—of course—with a purple velvet duvet draped over it. Antique dressing table and bureau made of some dark, polished wood. A closet full of expensive suits and shoes and a rack loaded with silk ties. Other than the clothes, the room was as sterile as an empty hotel suite.

Horatio had searched many bedrooms, had looked into the private nooks and crannies of every kind of life. This was the first time he'd been confronted with this kind of *blankness*; it was as if someone had gone through the room with some sort of cosmic vacuum cleaner and sucked it dry of any trace of personality. It was like a display in a furniture store, dressed to give the impression of being real.

This isn't you. This is just another convenient fiction, left for me to find. You've erased yourself from this room as completely as you erase people's defenses. As completely as you erase lives.

But Horatio wasn't as easy to fool.

No trace of personal items except the suits and shoes. He could have taken them, too—why leave them behind?

As a message.

Another "good-bye"—but this one aimed at what the clothing represents. The conventions of mainstream society, the conservative uniform of those who fit in. Wherever you've gone, you don't plan on ever wearing a suit again.

The bathroom off the bedroom was just as devoid of life. No medications, no toiletries, not even towels. If Sinhurma's vanishing act was a setup, he'd gotten all the details right.

He hoped Wolfe and Delko were having better luck.

Sinhurma's office wasn't the wood-paneled, bookshelf-lined room Wolfe was expecting. Instead, it was filled with plants from floor to glass ceiling, with a small fountain in one corner and an actual stream running through it. The desk was made of rattan, with a chair of the same material behind it and a wireless keyboard resting on top. The monitor and CPU were hidden inside a wall unit disguised as a bamboo wardrobe; double doors swung open to reveal a hermetically sealed, climate-controlled glass cabinet that kept the humidity at bay. Another bamboo-fronted bureau beside it did the same for shelves of books and drawers full of documents—or would have, if any papers were left. The books—medical texts, mainly—had been abandoned, but all the files appeared to be gone.

He tried booting up the computer, but nothing happened. A quick check of the equipment—once he figured out how to open up the glass case—revealed that the internal drives had been removed. From the cables leading into it, he deduced that this was where the security cameras had fed to, as well. There were no tapes or disks.

Wolfe sighed. Unless the potted palms started talking, the room didn't look like it was going to give up any secrets.

And then he noticed the picture.

It hung on the wall to the right of the desk. *The thing about pictures on walls*, Wolfe thought, *is that you see them every day. And after a while, you* stop *seeing them—they're just part of the landscape.*

He went over and took a closer look. It showed a group of beaming patients standing in front of the clinic, clustered around a grinning Sinhurma like chicks around a mother hen. He did a quick count of the faces and came up with twenty-six.

Ruth Carrell and Phillip Mulrooney were standing next to each other. Both of them looked proud and happy.

"And they say pictures don't lie," Wolfe murmured.

Delko found the same thing in each of the dorm rooms: a single cot, a chest of drawers, an empty closet. At least, that's what each room appeared to hold at first glance.

Under an Alternate Light Source, it was a different story. He didn't find blood, but other bodily fluids—seminal, vaginal—showed up readily. Different colors of hair on several pillows, and a used condom under a bed that had been missed by whoever did the cleaning. Despite the narrowness of the beds, it seemed that the residents of the dorms had made room in them for company.

The communal bathroom yielded a wastepaper

basket that hadn't been emptied. Used tissues, and lots of them.

"Either someone had a cold," he murmured, "or people were doing a lot of crying. . . ."

They met in the kitchen to compare notes.

"The office was cleaned out," Wolfe said. "Computers are all missing their drives, no hard copies of anything but textbooks on the premises, including recordings from the security cams."

"What about the clinic itself?" Horatio asked.

"I found medical supplies and equipment, but everything was sterilized and scrubbed down. No drugs, no used syringes, no swabs or medical waste. I did, however, find this." He showed Horatio the picture.

"The dorm rooms?" Horatio asked.

"Empty—but not quite as clean," Delko said. "I found used tissues, a condom and fresh sexual traces. In almost every bed."

"So either they were having a lights-out party," Horatio said, "or they thought this might be the last chance they had."

"What about this room?" Wolfe asked.

"I already went through it," Horatio said. "No fresh fruit or vegetables, no canned or dry goods. A few plates and cooking utensils that apparently they didn't want."

"That's a good sign," Delko said. "People planning on a mass suicide don't usually make dinner plans."

"Unless their plans and Sinhurma's don't coincide,"

Horatio said. "The problem is, we just don't have enough information on what those plans are. We need to get inside Sinhurma's head. . . .

"Wolfe, get back to the lab. See if the Vitality Method Web site is still up, check for recent postings and go through everything on it. If he's really planning something drastic, he won't be able to resist some sort of announcement.

"Delko, hit the outbuildings and grounds. I'm heading over to The Earthly Garden, see if there's anything there."

The arresting officer in the case of both James "Jimbo" Collinson and Oscar Benjamin Charlessly was Lieutenant Frank Tripp, a gruff, balding man whose bulldog determination and level headedness Calleigh was well familiar with. He was with her now as she talked to Charlessly in the interview room, glowering at the suspect from across the table. Calleigh liked Frank; though she didn't approve of smoking, anytime she thought of the cop she imagined him with a cigar clenched between his teeth.

"Well, Oscar," she said brightly, "it seems that some awful person had crammed your used appliances full of high-grade dope."

The salesman still hadn't lost his poise; though he'd insisted on his lawyer being present, he'd agreed to answer a few questions.

"It's a terrible thing," he said with a grin. "But I really don't see how I can help you in that particular area."

"Well, that's not the area I need help in," she answered. "What I need to know is whether or not you had any partners other than Samuel Lucent, Kyle Dolittle and his friend, James Collinson."

"I wish I had," Charlessly said. "Got Jimbo too, huh?"

His lawyer, a pale man with curly black hair and watery eyes, said, "My client has no knowledge of any of the persons so named—"

"Oh, relax, George," Charlessly said. "We're just having an informal chat—right, Miss Duquesne?"

"Sure, Oscar. So no one else was involved?"

" 'Fraid not," he said affably. "I mean, if I could spread the blame around a bit, I would—but y'all seem to have caught all the fish in one go, haven't you? Mind you, I'm definitely the small fry in all this; how was I supposed to know my trucks were bein' used to haul illicit material around? I didn't do any of the driving or loading—that was all Jimbo. Samuel was just this guy I sold a few hand-mixers and blenders to. If you ask me," he said, leaning forward and dropping his voice to a whisper, "the real brains of the operation was *Dooley*." He winked.

Calleigh smiled despite herself. "Nice try, Oscar. The files we pulled from your computer showed the kind of profit you were making from this operation, and everyone else agrees it was your idea to begin with."

He shrugged and sat back. "Guess it'll all come down to finger-pointing in court, then. Believe you me, if there was some criminal mastermind I could finger instead of two brain-dead bikers and a Rastafarian plumber, I would."

"I'm surprised, Oscar," Calleigh said. "I would have

thought that a slick operator like yourself would have been better prepared."

He chuckled. "Have a patsy all set up, y'mean? Well, Miss Duquesne, I guess I'm just not that hard-hearted. I may or may not be guilty of dealin' a little herb, but that don't make me some kinda monster."

"Maybe not," Calleigh said, "but nice guys don't set Claymore mines to guard their investments."

Horatio found The Earthly Garden closed and locked. It had been released as a crime scene the day before, but apparently hadn't reopened since. He peered inside through the glass of the front window, but didn't think the place had anything new to tell him. In any case, the restaurant hadn't been covered by the warrant, and there was no one around to ask for permission to enter.

The clouds overhead were heavy and dark, lightning flashing as it had the night of Phillip Mulrooney's murder. Horatio drove back to the crime lab, expecting a downpour to start at any second; the thunderheads grumbled and roared but refused to give up anything but sound and fury.

Had he pushed Sinhurma too far?

The dorms had room for two dozen people. Twenty-five souls, including Sinhurma himself. Were they already dead? Had they drunk Kool-Aid laced with cyanide, like the Jonestown cult, or were they planning on doing something worse? The Aum Supreme Truth doomsday cult in Japan had released sarin gas in a subway, killing twelve people and injuring thousands—were they going to do something similar? Sinhurma's medical degree gave him access to all sorts of drugs; the amount of havoc he could wreak with twenty-four dedicated followers to disperse them was horrifying to consider.

Had he pushed Sinhurma too far?

The sky offered its own cacophonous opinion; Horatio didn't know what it meant, but it didn't sound approving. . . .

12

THE PHONE RANG TEN TIMES before someone picked it up. "Ms. Murayaki, please," Horatio said. "Tell her it's Lieutenant Caine."

"Hello, Horatio," Sun-Li's cool voice replied. "My assistant's not in and I'm in the field—my calls are being forwarded. I'd love to help you out, but I'm a little busy at the moment—"

"Too busy to help prevent another Heaven's Gate?"

There was the briefest of pauses. "Okay, you've got my attention. What's the situation?"

"I have a cult group that's vanished. Two dozen people gone. Their leader is under suspicion for murder and I have to find him before he decides to do something drastic."

A burst of static cut off her reply. "—ammit. Horatio? You there?"

"I am, but I didn't quite catch that."

"Look, we should talk in person. Can you meet me?"

"Certainly. Where are you?"

"A little off the beaten track, at the moment. I'll give you directions."

He pulled out a pen and notebook and jotted them

down. "I'll see you in about half an hour," he said, and hung up.

The place she'd told him to go was past Florida City, on a citrus farm; he could smell the warm tang of grapefruit half a mile before he got to the place. Night had just fallen, and the crickets were loud enough to sound like they were seriously considering a march on the city.

He pulled up in the Hummer outside a small farmhouse. Murayaki was waiting for him on the screened-in porch, sitting on an old-fashioned porch glider and drinking from a bottle of water. She was dressed much more casually from the last time he'd seen her, in loose-fitting jeans and a white hooded sweatshirt with UNIVERSITY OF CHICAGO printed on it. Her long black hair was pulled back in a ponytail.

He got out of his vehicle, walked up the front steps and opened the creaking screen door. "Ms. Murayaki," he said. "Thank you for seeing me. Am I interrupting something?"

"You mean, do I have some raving cult member inside, strapped to a chair while we attempt to unbrainwash him?" she asked. "Thereby putting you in an extremely untenable situation vis-à-vis legal responsibility?"

He smiled and put his hands on his hips. "Well, now that you bring it up . . ."

She smiled back. "Don't worry—we rarely do that anymore, except in cases of court-ordered intercessions or legal guardians interceding with minors. The big cults can afford more lawyers than we can, and they've been grinding away at us for years."

"So why the remote location?"

"This is where his parents live," she said. "Not everyone can afford a condo in Miami Beach." She motioned for Horatio to sit and he did so, easing himself down on the glider and feeling it move beneath him like an animal adjusting to his weight.

"I would have come in to the city to see you, but I'm at a sensitive stage in the process," she said. "It's important to establish a bond of trust, and that means staying close during the intervention."

"For how long?"

"The average is about four days, depending. The longer the subject's been in, the harder it can be—after a certain point they're not just leaving the cult, they're leaving friends, lovers, sometimes even children."

"So what do you do? Or would that be giving away trade secrets?"

She leaned back, the motion making the glider move ever so slightly. "There's nothing mysterious about it, really. The one thing all cults try to take away from the individual is the capacity for critical thought; I just give it back to them."

"As easy as that? After all, you can lead a horse to water—"

"—but you can't make him think? Well, fortunately most of my subjects are more intelligent than your average horse—they just need to be reminded. That's really what I do; I teach people how to think for themselves again."

"In four days."

She shrugged. "So I like a challenge."

Horatio leaned forward, clasped his hands together

in front of him, elbows on his knees. "I notice you're not being that forthcoming with details."

She glanced at him sharply, then sighed. "Look, all I do is present the subject with information. That's it. There are interventionists who club the subject over the head with evangelism, but most of us rely on objectivity and honesty as opposed to dogma. Besides, any argument based on religious grounds always boils down to one belief system against another anyway, with no real proof involved. I like to have reason on my side; nothing makes a better weapon in a debate than a good hard *fact*."

"It sounds," Horatio said mildly, "as if the police aren't the only ones you have an adversarial relationship with."

"People don't hire me to hold their child's hand," she said. She put her bottle down on the arm of the glider. "You know what I really am? I'm an *assassin*. The cult imposes a new persona on top of an old one—even gives it a new name—and that persona is no more than a big, bloodsucking *leech*. It's a parasite that exists to suck money out of the community, work without questioning or complaining, and attract more victims. The longer it's in place, the weaker the original personality becomes. It's my job to *kill* that leech, and yeah, I get a lot of satisfaction out of that."

Her voice sounded steady, but Horatio could feel her body trembling through the glider, both hands locked tight around the edge of the bench, down by her legs. "It's always the same at the beginning," she said, her voice low and intense. "They're like *cows*, dumb and stubborn and slow, and for every question you ask you get a rote answer. You have to find a crack, an opening, something you can get your fingers into and *pry*."

"Ever push someone too far?"

"That's not a relevant question. By definition, I push every single one of them too far."

"So you've never had a subject do something extreme in response?"

"Like what—attack me physically?"

"I was thinking more in terms of trying to harm themselves," Horatio said.

She frowned. "Only once. Tough case, I should have taken better precautions. But it was early in my career, and I didn't fully understand what I was getting into yet."

"What do you mean? I thought you used to be a cult recruiter yourself."

She sighed and leaned back. "Yeah, and when I reversed direction I went as far as I could go the other way. Nobody hates smoking more than an ex-smoker, you know? So my attitude in those days was *rabidly* anticult."

"As opposed to how kindly disposed you are these days?"

"Oh, I used to be *much* worse. So much so that it clouded my judgment." She grabbed her water bottle, took a long sip of water. "What I couldn't see—what I *refused* to see—was that for some people, the cult was better for them than what they'd left behind."

Horatio's eyebrows went up. "That seems hard to believe."

"I'm not saying that joining a cult is a good choice,"

she added quickly. "It never is. But when you take a person out of a carefully controlled environment, they have to have someplace else to *go*. Otherwise, all you have is a puppet with the strings cut."

Horatio thought about that. The people at the Vitality Method—did they have someplace better to go?

Of course they do. They have friends, families; Sinhurma didn't recruit from the streets, he targeted people with money.

It wasn't that they had no place better to go—it was that Sinhurma's patients thought they'd already arrived. The compound was the doctor's little enclosed utopia, a place of manufactured beauty, youth and joy. *So if the Vitality Method is the Promised Land, where have they gone from there?*

"See," Murayaki continued, "most cultists, contrary to popular belief, aren't running from shattered homes or child abuse. They're usually well-off and well-educated. But every so often there's an exception. . . ."

"Which you ran into."

She was silent for a moment, lost in thought. Then, "Don't get me wrong. It wasn't like the cult rescued him; they don't care about anything but the survival of the group. But this guy . . . he was mentally challenged. No family, no friends, barely getting by on a disability pension. The cult adopted him the way you'd adopt a puppy, except they found a way to capitalize on it. He was great for fund-raising, great for showing people how caring and trustworthy they were."

"And when there was nobody to perform for?"

She gave a bitter little laugh. "Oh, you mean when they beat him and kept him locked in a cage and fed him nothing but scraps? I wish it was that simple. No, he was probably treated better than anyone else in the cult—they didn't have to starve or brainwash him to get obedience. All they had to give him was some attention, and he'd do anything they said. Yeah, he was being used, but he was happier than he'd ever been in his life."

"And you took all that away."

"Yeah," she said quietly. "I did. I tried to show him where all the money was going, but that was too complicated. So I had ex–cult members talk to him, showed him tapes of breaking sessions. What finally got to him was when he understood they were portraying him as an idiot in order to turn a profit. It was a hard idea to get across, but I did it. I hammered at him with the truth until I finally broke through that thick goddamn skull."

She sounded even angrier than she had before. Horatio waited.

"He cried for a day. A full day. Then he broke a glass and tried to cut his wrists."

"But he didn't succeed."

"No. I got him patched up and into counseling. I didn't even have a paying client—like I said, he had no family or friends—so I paid for that out of my own pocket. And then he went back to his tiny little apartment and his tiny little life."

"If no one paid you to deprogram him," Horatio asked, "then why did you take him on in the first place?"

She gave him a bleak look. "I thought he'd be a challenge. And I was right—I just didn't understand what kind."

Horatio studied her. "And how's he doing now?"

"What makes you think I know?" she asked neutrally.

"Let's just say I have a hunch."

Her expression softened. "He's doing all right, I guess. He likes to play checkers."

"How often do you visit him?"

She hesitated, then said, "Every Thursday."

"Then he still has at least one friend, right?"

"For what it's worth." Her eyes narrowed. "But you didn't come all the way down here to talk about my bad choices." Suddenly she was all business, with almost no transition. "You said you might have a cult gearing up for a mass suicide?"

"I might." He told her about Sinhurma, about how he had confronted him and the deserted clinic. He didn't go into detail about the homicide investigation, but told her Sinhurma and his people were prime suspects.

"I see," she said thoughtfully. "And you have no idea where they went?"

"I have people working on that. What I'd like from you is some idea of what to expect when I find them."

"Hard to say. Paranoia is more or less a given when it comes to cult leaders, but that doesn't mean he's planning on suiciding. Pushing him like you did was almost guaranteed to get a response, but I don't think this was the one you wanted."

"Not exactly."

She shrugged. "On the other hand, sometimes the only way to get through to someone is to get in their face. Before you can start a dialogue, you have to get their attention, and it sounds like you did that."

"Hard to have a dialogue when the other person disappears, though," Horatio said.

"You know what that tells me? He's worried. You're not wrong about the size of this guy's ego, and if he's got the connections you say, he should have gone on the offensive. Called in some favors, cried religious persecution, that sort of thing. The fact that he didn't stand his ground means one of three things."

"Which are?"

She held up a finger. "First, that he's messing with you. Possible—screwing with people's heads is what he does, after all—but unlikely. It takes time and preparation to make a group disappear, and reactionary tactics are usually more spontaneous."

She uncurled a second finger. "Two, that you really got to him and he's just on the run. Again, having a group with him slows him down and makes it hard to vanish—if he really wanted to be gone, he'd probably just hop on a plane by himself, take an extended vacation in a country without extradition."

She added a third finger. "And three, that he's gone to ground someplace isolated. Cults often own property in remote locations—they're easy to fortify, which lets them control people's entering and leaving."

"So he's just relocated?"

She shook her head. "Not that simple. The vanishing act suggests he had an exit strategy already in place, maybe even something they rehearsed over and over. That indicates a dangerous frame of mind."

"Dangerous how?"

"Jim Jones had his people run mock-suicide drills several times before the real thing. At first, all they drank was Kool-Aid. . . ."

"And then," Horatio said, "something a little more final."

"It may come to that, yes."

"There's something else," Horatio said. "I have reason to believe that one of the members is a recent convert—in fact, that he was recruited specifically for his role in a crime. Is there any advice you can give me on how to reach out to him? Is there any particular approach I should make or avoid?"

"Well, some people feel that trying to intervene with a new cult member is actually more dangerous— they call it the honeymoon phase, when the recruit is still feeling the initial euphoria. I don't agree, though—the longer someone's in a cult, the more likely they are to form long-lasting cult relationships, to become dependent on the cult, to distance themselves from their previous existence. If you have the chance to communicate with this person, honesty is your best weapon. Don't try to mislead him or hold anything back—just give him the truth. No matter how much he refuses to accept it at first, some part of him will recognize it."

"No matter how painful it is?"

She took another sip of water. "Yeah. People *need* the truth. Sometimes, I think that's the only reason any of them wind up listening to me at all—that after all the sweet lies their leaders feed them, they have this craving for a grain of salt."

She glanced at her watch. "Look, I have to get back inside. But—well, just hang on a second. I'll be right back."

Horatio stood up with her. She ducked inside the house, then returned a moment later with a DVD case in her hand. She handed it to him and said, "I'm sure you can understand why I can't let you watch an actual session, but I've recorded some in the past—clients often want to see just what they're getting into when they hire me to counsel their son or daughter. This'll give you some ideas of the techniques I use—maybe they'll come in handy."

"Thank you," Horatio said. "And good luck."

"Same to you . . ."

Despite being the CSI team's scuba diver, Eric Delko's preferred method of exercise was running. He tried to get in at least an hour a day, usually early in the morning; though Miami tended to be better known for its sunsets, its sunrises could be pretty too. It made him a member of a particular tribe, the predawn joggers: there were a whole group of people he never saw in anything but shorts, T-shirts and sneakers. It wasn't always that social a tribe—breath was often too valuable to be wasted on conversation, and most people liked to run listening to music through headphones or earplugs—so most communication between tribe members took the form of waves, smiles and nods.

The residents of the Vitality Method compound had taken the idea of exercise as a bonding ritual a lot

more seriously. Delko knew that Japanese corpora-
tions often started their day with communal calis-
thenics, but he found the whole idea disturbing; one
of the reasons he ran was the feeling of freedom, and
one of the reasons he ran early in the morning was
the isolation. A nod from an iPod-wearing stranger as
they passed each other was all the interaction he
wanted at 5 A.M.

Still, a group that did everything together multiplied the chances of one of them leaving some sort of
trace of where they'd been. Delko was hoping the
grounds of the compound would prove more inform-
ative than the main building had.

The swimming pool and the changing rooms next
to it yielded nothing of interest. The same went for
the archery range and the auditorium.

Then he found the gardening shed.

He almost didn't recognize it as such, because it
was completely empty—only a bit of spilled fertilizer
and the empty hooks on the walls betrayed its purpose. He stepped inside and realized it had stored
more than just gardening implements—from the
hooks on the walls, it had held hammers and saws
and various other tools. None were there now.

He took pictures of every surface, trying to figure
out what was missing. He found several tire tracks in
the spilled fertilizer and in the dirt by the front door;
he deduced that the wheels had rolled through the
fertilizer first, then deposited bits of it along the tires'
path as they rolled out the door. From the way the
tracks crisscrossed each other, it looked like several
one-wheeled objects.

Wheelbarrows, he thought.

Behind the shed was another interesting find—several depressions in the earth, the grass in those areas crushed and yellow. Something heavy had rested there recently, and from the shape of the depressions Delko thought it was probably several wooden pallets.

They had confiscated the clinic's vehicles, but obviously Sinhurma had access to more; Delko found fresh tire tracks next to the depressions in the earth as well. From the size, tread and wheelbase it was a large vehicle, probably an SUV or truck.

So something had been loaded up and taken away. Something they needed tools for?

The ground around the depressions told the story—a scattering of sawdust and a few small splinters meant the cargo had to be lumber. *They're building something—but what?*

He thought about it as he headed back toward the lab, then decided to take a brief detour to grab a bite to eat.

Horatio watched the disk in the computer lab. The screen showed him a logo of the company, the Mental Freedom Foundation, then cut to a shot of Sun-Li Murayaki herself. She wore a business jacket over a fuzzy white top, and perched casually on the corner of her desk—trying to project professionalism and warmth at the same time, Horatio thought.

"Hello," she said. "What you're about to see is typical of the interventions I conduct. The subject is free to leave at any time; the reason he doesn't is because he has something to prove. Luckily for him, I have more proof than he does."

The camera cut to a static shot of a living room. Fireplace in the background, brown leather sofa and matching overstuffed chairs, big pink ceramic vase stuffed with flowers on a small table of dark, highly polished wood. Lots of natural light.

Sun-Li sat on the sofa, dressed in black track pants and a gray sweatshirt. Across from her, on one of the chairs, sat a young man with a shaved head, wearing a shapeless white garment somewhere between a toga and a smock.

"So, Brad—I understand that your leader, Reverend Joshua, is an honest man," Sun-Li said. She sounded casual, relaxed.

"Of course he is," Brad said. He sounded calm, almost sleepy. "He believes in The Truth. And my name is Abraham now."

Sun-Li picked up a thick folder from beside her on the couch, flipped it open and pulled out a newspaper clipping. "Then how do you explain this?" she said, holding it out to him.

The recording wasn't nearly as dramatic as Horatio had expected. There were no large bodyguards preventing Brad from leaving, no shouting, no tears. Brad was given a lot of information to process, in the form of news reports, government documents, videotapes and even police reports. For every question he had, Sun-Li had an answer. She refused to be drawn into metaphysical arguments, always returning the discussion to the provable facts. Brad's parents made several appearances, usually to bring him food—food rich in protein, Horatio noted. When Brad complained about feeling overwhelmed, they suggested he take a nap. The recording stopped, then resumed again sometime later.

It had no dramatic finale, either; Brad didn't suddenly see the error of his ways, or break down in tears and embrace his parents. Instead, the tone of his questions changed—they became less about challenging Sun-Li and more about genuine requests for information. By the end of the recording, Brad was obviously deeply unsettled; Horatio could almost see the neurons starting to fire again.

The last shot was of Sun-Li, in her office again. "This process took place over five days, slightly longer than average. Brad continued to talk to his parents, agreed to attend group sessions, and eventually left the cult. It's been estimated that recovery times for such an experience range from six to eighteen months, but it can take much longer. It's a slow process . . . but once they begin to think for themselves again, they don't want to stop."

The camera moved in, ever so slightly, on her face. "Just make sure," she said, "that they don't have a reason to."

"Amen," Horatio said.

Yelina walked in on Horatio in the layout room, staring at the objects on the light table: a bloodstained blue T-shirt, a pair of shorts, socks and underwear, a pair of sneakers. Ruth Carrell's clothing.

"We'll find them, Horatio," she said.

"Of that," he said, "I have no doubt. The question is—before or after?"

"There may not even be an 'after,' " she pointed out.

"I wish I could believe that. . . ."

"Any luck with the drug connection?"

"Afraid not. Calleigh's questioned all the principals and none of them implicated the clinic or Sinhurma."

"You think they're covering for him?"

Horatio selected a slide and put it under the microscope. "If they are, there's no reason I can see. They're not cult members—and despite Sinhurma's delusions of grandeur, he doesn't have the kind of rep that would keep them quiet out of fear. No, I think we just kicked over enough rocks that something else crawled out."

Yelina yawned. "Excuse me—it's been a long day. So, any other developments?"

Horatio peered into the eyepiece, adjusted the focus. "There just might be. . . ."

"What are you looking at?"

"Grains of sand I found in Ruth Carrell's shoe. If I can identify them, they might tell us where Sinhurma's gone."

"Good luck. I'll let you know if anything turns up on the street."

Normally, the TV hanging from one corner of Auntie Bellum's ceiling didn't get a lot of Delko's attention unless it was flashing sports scores; today, though, as he was about to dig into a bowl of jambalaya, he heard the phrase "Miami-Dade crime lab" and glanced up.

The face he saw on the fuzzy color screen was vaguely familiar, in the way that veteran character actors on television always were. *It's that guy,* Delko thought. *The one that played that jerk on* Seinfeld, *and the weirdo on* Friends. *Or was it* Everbody Loves Raymond? He couldn't remember the man's name, but it didn't matter—he always played the same role anyway, the instantly unlikeable guy who sneered, glared and whined his way from one commercial break to the next as a succession of dishonest car salesmen, grouchy principals and bad blind dates.

Not a good choice for a spokesman, Delko thought, though the man didn't seem nearly as reprehensible at the moment. Whatever his career choices, the actor was plainly upset about something, and Delko wasn't surprised to learn that something was the closure of the Vitality Method clinic. When he asked the waitress to turn up the sound, she had to stand on a chair to do so; either they'd lost the remote or the set was so old it never had one.

"—really don't understand what the problem is," the actor said. "I've been attending Doctor Sinhurma's sessions for six weeks now, and I think they're fantastic. I've never felt better in my life."

I'll bet you haven't, Delko thought.

"I got an e-mail from the clinic canceling my appointment without any explanation, and when I tried to drive up here the police wouldn't let me in. I don't know what's going on."

The reporter's voice cut in as the camera panned

over the front gates of the clinic and the two squad cars parked in front of them. "Phone calls to the clinic went unanswered, and a police representative who declined to be interviewed on camera simply stated that the Vitality Method was part of an ongoing investigation."

"Well, that didn't take long," Delko sighed. He tossed some money on the counter and left without touching his food—he had to get back to work, and he didn't have time to get it to go.

You can't bring food into the lab anyway, he thought as he crossed the street. *Somebody should tell that actor to forget about the Vitality Method and try the CSI diet instead. . . .*

Delko found Horatio in the lab, going over the evidence they'd collected from The Earthly Garden. "Hey, H," he said. He gave him a quick summary of what he'd found at the compound and then told him about the news story.

"Now the media will be all over it," Horatio said. "And it's only going to get worse. Well, we have other things to worry about."

He studied the plug of the burned-out blender Delko had found in a Dumpster. "Ruth told me they were planning on expanding, but she didn't mention another site. I found sand in her shoe, and Trace is trying to identify plant matter from the sole; hopefully that'll give us a location as well."

"That why you're checking the restaurant stuff again? Think it'll point us in the direction they've gone?"

"I already know that," Horatio said. "They're headed straight for crazy . . . no, I thought I'd take another crack at matching the pattern you found burned into this plug."

"I thought for sure it was one of the knives," Delko said. "But the pattern's too squared off and thin."

"Yes, it is," Horatio said. "On the exposed end, anyway." He picked up one of the charred knives by the blade, then took hold of the wooden handle with his other hand. He tried to pull them apart, with no success.

The second knife, though, pulled apart easily. The base of the blade was thin and squared off.

"Is that what I think it is?" Delko said, pointing to the exposed metal.

Horatio examined it critically. "Only one way to find out," he said.

"The Garden of Eden," Wolfe said out loud.

"Excuse me?" Calleigh said.

Wolfe glanced over from the screen he'd been studying intently. "Sorry, didn't notice you there," he said.

"Would it help if I was wearing a snake and offered you an apple?"

"Huh? Oh, right. No, I mean Sinhurma has this Garden of Eden fixation. It didn't really register when I scanned the site before—there's so much pontificating and so few facts I sort of classified it as noise, not signal. But I've been studying his Web site, and he refers to it in one way or another over and over."

"Well, it's a story that features religion *and* food,"

Calleigh said. "That would seem to be right in the doctor's comfort zone."

"More like his obsession zone. If I'm interpreting this right, he thinks the apple doesn't just symbolize original sin, or even self-awareness; he thinks it's a literal representation of how evil enters the body."

"Through fruit?"

"Through eating. Certain foods are more evil than others, and preparing foods in certain ways can increase or reduce how evil they are . . . it gets pretty twisted. But that's not the important part."

He tapped a few keys. Calleigh came over and studied the screen from behind his shoulder.

"This passage, right here," Wolfe said.

" 'For the Garden is still within our reach,' " she read. " 'It still exists, not just in our hearts but on this Earth, as well. It has been waiting for us to reclaim it, to return to the bosom of its embrace as a child returns to its mother.' Sounds like he has someplace specific in mind."

"That's what I was thinking. Later on, he refers to a 'lush and verdant paradise, where the promise of Eternal Youth becomes a legend fulfilled.' "

"Wait a second," Calleigh said. "That sounds familiar."

"Sure it does," Wolfe said. "Substitute the word 'fountain' for 'promise' . . ."

"—and it's a reference to Ponce de León," Calleigh finished. "The 'legend fulfilled' becomes the Fountain of Youth. Which is supposedly located—"

"—somewhere in the Everglades," Wolfe said. "He thinks the 'glades are the Garden of Eden. That's where he's gone."

"Well, that only give us four thousand square miles to search," Calleigh sighed. "He's somewhere in the River of Grass—but *where*?"

"Cape Sable," Horatio said.

He'd called a meeting in the lab's conference room, all of them clustered at one end of a big wooden table. "The plant material found in the tread of Ruth Carrell's shoe was *Chamaesyce garberi*," Horatio said. He rubbed his eyes wearily. "Also known as Garber's spurge. It's on the federal list of endangered species—only five sites in Florida where it grows. One's Big Pine Key, the other four are in the 'glades."

"How do you know which one it is?" Calleigh asked.

"Garber's spurge grows in pine rocklands, coastal flats, coastal grasslands, and on beach ridges, either on exposed limestone or in Pamlico sand. I found Pamlico sand in her shoes—and Cape Sable has plenty of that." Pamlico sand was composed of sand, limestone and tiny, carbonaceous fossils called eolianites from the late Pleistocene; it underlay much of Florida and surfaced at certain points.

"Cape Sable's also on Ponce de León Bay," Calleigh pointed out.

"What are they doing out there?" said Wolfe.

"Carpentry, apparently," Delko answered. "I found traces of a large amount of lumber that had been stored at the compound, and all their tools were gone."

"Maybe they're building an ark?" Calleigh said.

All heads at the table swiveled to look at her. She

shrugged and smiled. "Religious cult, woodworking, lots of coastline? Makes as much sense as anything else."

"Maybe we should put out a security alert for the Miami Zoo," Delko said with a grin.

"I don't think so," Wolfe said. "Sinhurma's obsession is with the Garden of Eden, not Noah. If there's a religious script he's following, it's Genesis, not . . . whatever the story of Noah's ark was in."

"That would be . . . still Genesis," Calleigh said.

"As long as it's not Revelations," Horatio said. "If he wants to run around naked in the swamp and pretend he's Adam, fine. But he's not alone out there . . . and I'm not going to let him sacrifice anybody else."

13

CAPE SABLE WAS AT THE SOUTHERN tip of Florida, on the west coast of the Everglades. It had several beaches along its length that were open to camping, but most of the Cape was a mangrove swamp inhabited only by wildlife.

Horatio considered several approaches. He could go in by sea, but that would give the members of the cult plenty of time to see them coming. He decided instead to travel overland as far as possible, then go the rest of the way by airboat.

He told Delko, Wolfe and Calleigh to get ready. He wanted his whole team with him, for two reasons: first, because they had all worked on the case—and second, because there might be as many as two dozen bodies to process.

"You mind if I stay behind, Horatio?" Calleigh asked.

"What's up?" Horatio asked. "You have enough of the Great Outdoors after your tree-climbing adventure?"

"It's not that," she said. "But I have an idea I'd like to follow up on in the lab."

"Sure. We'll be fine."

They took three airboats on trailers and a SWAT team. Horatio, Delko and Wolfe traveled in the Hummer, while two other police vehicles followed them.

"What do you think we're going to find, H?" Delko asked. He was in the front seat, Wolfe in the back.

"If we're lucky," Horatio said, putting the Hummer in gear, "two dozen extremely fit people, covered in mosquito bites."

"And if not?" Wolfe asked.

"Same number of people," Horatio replied, "but more bugs . . ."

Calleigh Duquesne was not the sort of woman to give up easily.

Not being able to link the arrow that killed Ruth Carrell to the arrows recovered from Julio Ferra's garage still bothered her. Despite nailing Charlessly and shutting down his drug operation, she couldn't ignore the fact that it had still been a lead that turned into a dead end.

Sometimes, though, following a trail that didn't go where you wanted still took you somewhere interesting. Perched in a tree, waiting for a homicidal maniac to climb down from his deer blind and come looking for her, she'd found herself thinking about Julio Ferra. According to Horatio, he'd learned to shoot a bow from his father; they'd gone on hunting trips together. She'd wondered who had hand-fletched the arrows, the father or the son—it was the kind of thing you'd show your child how to do, the kind of thing you'd keep later.

The arrows she'd examined from Ferra's garage

hadn't been new. They were worn, dusty, their paint starting to peel. The heads had been glued on, not screwed on like more modern arrows. The evidence told her they were probably made in the late eighties or early nineties, and she was willing to bet the feathers were a product of one of those father/son hunting trips. If they'd stuck close to home, it also meant the feathers were almost certainly from a Floridian bird.

That had given her an idea, but right about then Dooley had shown up with an extremely large gun in one hand, and she'd been a little busy for the next while.

Now, though—now she had time to see if she was right.

She clipped a tiny sample from the quills of the killer arrow, then did the same with one of the Ferra arrows.

"All right, guys," she murmured. "Incredible Hulk time . . ."

Airboats were noisy. Flat-bottomed skiffs with large, caged props at the back, they were essentially surfboards with an oversized fan bolted on. They were perfect for skimming along the shallow, marshy water of the Everglades, where something with a deeper keel or standard outboard motor would get stuck, but they made a racket reminiscent of a mosquito the size of a Cessna.

This was why Horatio had them shut off the engines while still a mile away, and pole the remaining distance. He sat in the front with a GPS locator in his hand, making sure they were still on course while Wolfe and Delko provided the muscle power. The SWAT team in the other two boats glided along behind them, half a dozen muscular men in short-sleeved shirts and bulletproof vests, dark blue ball caps shading the sun from their eyes. Not that there was much sun to be protected from; the black thunderheads rolling overhead promised a downpour, and soon. The air held the heavy, thick stillness that preceded a major storm, and the combination of physical activity and humidity had everyone drenched in sweat.

"Think they heard us coming?" Wolfe asked under his breath. "Sound carries a long way on the water—"

"And there's nothing unusual about hearing an airboat out here," Delko said back in a low voice. "As long as they don't hear one up close, they shouldn't think anything of it."

The Sea of Grass slid by, saw grass rippling in the wind like yellow waves. A flock of storks flew overhead, long white wings almost seeming to beat in slow motion. The Everglades themselves were a slow-motion phenomenon, overflow from Lake Okeechobee making its gradual way to Florida Bay over a vast, level expanse of wetland; the water they were moving through was no more than a foot deep in places. A flood creeping along at the pace of a snail, supporting a thick gumbo of life along its unhurried way. In many ways, Horatio thought, it was the opposite of a hurricane, nurturing life instead of taking it, creating instead of destroying, calm instead of violent.

Is that why Sinhurma came here? Does he see this as a birthplace of life, not death?

He wondered about what they'd find at the end of their journey. He couldn't believe the cult had come all the way out here simply to kill themselves; Sinhurma's ego was too big to suicide anywhere but in the spotlight. Of course, by coming after him they were providing that spotlight. . . .

But that's what we do. We shine a bright light on the dark places, no matter what we might find. We can't back off because something might lunge out of that darkness; we can't let sleeping demons lie.

The saw grass gave way to mangrove islands, tangled masses of tree trunks crested with birds and bromeliads. An alligator drifted past, eyeing them coldly before submerging without a sound.

The Garden of Eden. And who does Sinhurma see as the serpent? Me? Have I been written into whatever twisted scripture he's writing for himself?

He didn't know. He also didn't know how Sinhurma could have convinced Jason to join them after Ruth Carrell was killed—she was obviously murdered to keep her quiet.

But maybe not so obvious to someone being drugged. And someone grieving over the loss of a loved one fits the profile Murayaki gave me of potential cult recruits.

So Sinhurma steps into the void created by Ruth's death. He offers peace-filled answers in a world suddenly filled with violent questions . . . and somehow convinces Jason that the cult couldn't possibly be responsible.

But someone is. It wasn't a bolt from the blue that killed

Ruth, it was an arrow. Jason must know she was mur-
dered—so who does he think killed her?

Whoever Sinhurma points his finger at.

Whoever gets branded the serpent . . .

Every now and then, Calleigh would have a moment
when she would step back, mentally shake her head
and say, "Wow. I feel like I'm living in a science fiction
novel." Despite all the high-tech equipment she
worked with on a regular basis, occasionally a particular process or piece of technology would just strike
her as being a little surreal.

Like bombarding a piece of evidence with radia-
tion.

The process was called neutron activation analysis.
Its purpose was to detect and measure the gamma ray
level of any given substance, thus identifying the elements it was composed of.

First, she put each sample in a dark bottle with a 25
percent solution of nonionic detergent and shook the
contents up thoroughly. When she was done, she
carefully removed each sample from its bottle with a
pair of plastic forceps, and rinsed it five times in
deionized water. Then they went into a desiccator,
under a vacuum, to dry.

When they were ready, she sealed them in reactor-
grade polyethylene containers for bombardment in a
pneumatic irradiation reactor. There, a process called
the neutron capture reaction would cause thermal
neutrons to collide with the target, forming a compound nucleus. The new nucleus would be in an ex-

cited state, causing it to emit one or more gamma rays; by using a gamma ray detector and a computer program to compare it with the known half-lives of radioactive materials, she could tell exactly what element was now radiating.

The GPS unit in Horatio's hand told him they were approaching the right area. The ocean was close enough that though they couldn't see them, they could hear waves crashing against the beach; the wind had picked up and the barometric pressure had dropped. They angled to one side, paralleling the coastline.

"Stay alert and stay quiet," Horatio said. "We may hear them before we see them—and we don't want them to hear us first."

A sharp *crack* sounded in the distance. Horatio narrowed his eyes, listening intently. Several more followed in quick succession.

"Gunshots?" Wolfe said.

"I don't think so," Horatio said. "More like a hammer on rock . . ."

They followed the sound. When Horatio thought they were close enough, they beached the boats on a muddy spit of land and proceeded on foot, guns drawn.

They were very close to the shore. The Everglades existed on a broad, flat plain, a lip of limestone encircling it and providing a natural dike. That lip rose up before them now, crested by dunes that provided cover while they surveilled the activity on the other side.

What they saw were three house trailers on a large, raised wooden platform, arranged in a U-shaped formation facing down the beach. A wooden boardwalk on stilts ran in a straight line from the platform into the ocean itself, extending at least fifty yards from the shore.

Cult members were hard at work. Most of them were on the beach itself, using picks, shovels and sledgehammers to excavate or break up limestone boulders; others would load chunks of rock into a wheelbarrow, which would then be trundled up a ramp and down the boardwalk to the very end, where it would be dumped into the sea. They reminded Horatio of a line of busy ants.

"What do they think they're *doing*?" Wolfe whispered.

"Building paradise," Horatio said. "Unless I miss my guess, Sinhurma's trying to construct an island."

"That's insane," Delko said softly.

"For a control freak like Sinhurma, it almost makes sense," Horatio said. "Like having your own little country . . ."

"Except it's still inside the boundaries of a national park," Delko said. "Which is all kinds of illegal right there."

"We'll add it to the list," Horatio said. "I count seventeen bodies down there, but I don't see Jason McKinley, Caesar Kim or the doctor. They must be inside one of the trailers."

"How'd they get all this stuff out here anyway?" Wolfe asked.

"Must have used a barge," Delko guessed. "Build

the support structure first, then come in at high tide when the water's deepest and use a crane to unload the trailers directly onto the platform."

The leader of the SWAT team, a burly man named Hernandez with a thick, black mustache, moved over beside Horatio. "How do you want to play this?" he asked.

"Divide and conquer," Horatio said. "We'll take them in three teams—half of your men isolate the ones on the beach, the other half pin down the people on the boardwalk. We'll concentrate on the trailers."

"Targets on the pier'll be easy," Hernandez said. "No place for 'em to go except the surf. The ones on the beach might have weapons, though—a lot of tall grass down there. And there could be anything in those trailers."

"Then let's hope the doctor is a lousy shot," Horatio said.

The thunder was almost constant now, which Horatio was grateful for; it helped disguise the sound of their movements. With the element of surprise on their side, it was possible they could take the whole group into custody without bloodshed.

The first of Hernandez's teams moved into position, creeping into place as close as they could get to the group on the beach but still in sight of Horatio. He would lead a charge on the main structure, with the second group of SWAT officers continuing onward, trapping the cultists on the boardwalk.

"Go," Horatio snapped.

*   *   *

"Is Horatio around?" Alexx said, sticking her head in the door.

Calleigh put down her cup of tea; she'd been taking a break while waiting for the test results. "No, he's somewhere out in the Everglades at the moment, chasing bad guys. From the look of the weather out there, I hope he brought rain gear."

Alexx walked into the break room and pulled up a chair. "Well, I'll tell you, then. I took another look at Ruth Carrell's tox screen, trying to figure out exactly what Sinhurma was trying to accomplish. Some of the drugs that came up didn't make much sense at first—I thought maybe they were there to suppress the side effects of some of the others. One of them, though, I just couldn't figure out—mefloquine."

"What's it do?"

"It's highly toxic, for starters. It can produce headaches, nausea, dizziness, difficulty sleeping, anxiety, vivid dreams and visual disturbances. On a hunch, I took a look at Sinhurma's Web site—it says he travels extensively. He just got back from a trip to Mozambique, in fact."

"So?"

"So, mefloquine is used as an antimalarial."

"And countries like Mozambique have a high incidence of malaria." Calleigh frowned. "So if Sinhurma was taking this drug, why would it show up in Ruth Carrell's blood? She wasn't traveling with him, was she?"

"Not that I could tell—she didn't even have a passport. I do have a theory, but it's not good news. See, mefloquine has all sorts of neurological effects: in some cases it can cause depression, seizures, even psychosis. Somebody with an already overdeveloped messiah complex might get worse . . . and some religions have a tradition of using chemical means to commune with the Divine. If Sinhurma interpreted his own reaction to the drug as a metaphysical one, he might decide to share that experience with his followers—and it takes the body a long time to get rid of it. Months, sometimes. I checked Phillip Mulrooney's tox screen, and sure enough, he had traces of it too."

"So the drug makes Sinhurma crazy, and he gives it to his patients," Calleigh said. "That might explain why he thought murdering someone with a rocket was a rational decision."

"That's what's worrying me," Alexx said. "If Sinhurma was giving his patients the same drugs he's on, he may be taking the same mix of drugs he's giving them. And if that's true, then Sinhurma's just as irrational as the people following him. . . ."

Everything happened very fast.

Hernandez's first team crested the dune, two officers scrambling down it while a sniper with a rifle covered them from the top. Horatio and everyone else charged straight for the trailers, guns out.

"Everyone freeze!" Hernandez yelled.

Horatio's attention was on the trailers. They had windows, but he could see no movement through any of them. He went for the trailer on the right, Delko and Wolfe right behind him. Horatio flattened himself against the wall to the side of the door and yelled, "Doctor Sinhurma! Come out of the trailer *now*!"

He spared a glance at the action on the beach and the boardwalk. Hernandez's teams had both groups covered; nobody had their hands in the air, but nobody seemed to be going for weapons, either.

"Stop! Don't come in!" Caesar Kim's voice, sounding terrified. *"He'll kill us all!"*

Horatio called back, "Take it easy, Doctor! Your people out here are fine! Nobody has to die—"

And then all hell broke loose.

One of the cultists on the beach shouted, "BASTARDS!", raised the pickax in his hands, and charged Hernandez. At the same moment, a woman dove for a clump of tall beach grass.

Hernandez shot the man with the pickax three times in the chest. The woman came up with a semiautomatic rifle—screaming incoherently, she began to spray the area with bullets.

The cultists on the boardwalk took this as a sign. When the officers covering them turned toward the gunfire, they jumped off the makeshift pier and into the surf. They splashed through the shallow water as fast as they could, heading for the beach.

The sniper on the crest of the dune took down the woman firing the semiauto with a single shot. The remaining cultists on the beach bolted—not away from the fracas, but around it, toward the nearest trailer.

"Stop them!" Horatio yelled. "Don't let them get inside!"

Officers on the beach took it as a warning they were going for more weapons. They opened fire on the fleeing cultists, hitting two in the back. Four more made it to the trailer, the farthest one from Horatio.

The cultists in the water were on the beach now, racing for the same building.

"No! Hold your fire!" Horatio shouted. He holstered his gun and sprinted for the group surging toward him. "Delko! Wolfe!"

They followed his lead, holstering their guns and charging forward. Neither Horatio nor Wolfe were large men, but neither hesitated, either; they slammed into the cultists like a defensive line trying to stop an offensive rush. There were seven cultists and only three of them, but Horatio and Wolfe tackled one each while Delko managed to clothesline two of them. The others didn't stop to help their fallen comrades; they continued their mad dash away from the water like hydrophobic lemmings.

Horatio managed to get his opponent's arm behind him, cuffed one wrist, then snagged an ankle and cuffed that. *"Stay,"* he barked, then helped Wolfe, who was wrestling with an energetic woman with long blond hair and a crazed look in her eye. One of Delko's targets lay on the beach, unconscious; he had the other in a headlock and was shouting, "Stop it! Just *stop*, dammit!"

The others managed to get inside. The door banged shut.

An instant later the trailer exploded.

The detonation was so loud Horatio couldn't hear it at all. The shock wave knocked him flat with an invisible punch—he lay there for a moment, face against the damp sand, semiconscious. When his ears began to ring, he wondered for a second if it was his alarm clock. He'd been having this odd dream about playing football on a beach. . . .

He picked himself up groggily. "Eric! Ryan!" He could barely hear his own voice.

"Right . . . here, H," Delko gasped. He was already on his feet.

"What?" Wolfe managed, sitting up. "That was—oh, *man.*"

The remains of the trailer were burning, black smoke billowing skyward. Lightning flashed through dark storm clouds overhead. People were screaming, shouting, weeping.

Horatio yanked the walkie-talkie from his belt. "Lieutenant Caine to Coast Guard Cutter *Alhambra,*" he said. "We need the support team here, *now.* We have a hostage situation and survivors of a bomb attack needing immediate medical attention. . . ."

Then it was time to round up the prisoners, see who else was hurt and wait for backup to arrive.

And pray the other two trailers didn't follow the first one.

Calleigh knew a lot about the compound bow in front of her. She knew what its draw weight was, what it was made of, and how many inches it measured from tip to tip, strung and unstrung. What she didn't know was who had fired it last—besides her, that is.

With a firearm, she could have done a GSR—a Gunshot Residue Test. She'd tried dusting the bow for prints, but it had already been wiped clean. But there had to be *something.*

She slipped on a pair of gloves, picked up the bow and hefted it. She pretended to nock an arrow, drew back on the string until it was level with her cheekbone. . . .

She glanced to the side. Her eyes widened and she whispered, "Of *course*."

She let the bowstring out slowly, then put the bow back on the table. She had one more test to run. . . .

"So much for the element of surprise," Delko said. He winced as a medic taped a gauze pad over a cut in his forehead.

"It could have been worse," Horatio said. They were in a makeshift command post, a tent set up on the other side of the dunes by Coast Guard personnel. They'd come ashore in a rigid-frame zodiac, bringing reinforcements and equipment and taking away the badly injured. "We didn't lose any cops; we have four prisoners that would have been corpses. And there are six cult members unaccounted for and presumably still alive."

"Where do you want this?" a reservist in fatigues asked, hefting a blocky aluminum case. Horatio took it from him, snapped open the latches and lifted out a square electronics unit.

"Yeah, but for how long?" Wolfe asked. He was staring at the the closest sand dune like he could see through it. "For all we know, they're taking cyanide right now—"

"No," Horatio said firmly. "Kim's still alive—we heard his voice. What he said—'He'll kill us all'—indicates Sinhurma's alive as well. And he won't go out by shooting himself or taking poison."

"Why not?" Wolfe asked.

"Because he can't stand to be upstaged," Horatio said. "Whatever he used to blow up the first trailer, you can be sure he's got ten times that much planted in his own."

"So why hasn't he set it off?" Delko asked.

"I don't know—"

Horatio's cell phone vibrated in his pocket. He frowned, pulled it out, and checked who was calling. "Well, here's our chance to learn," Horatio said, flipping the phone open.

"Hello, Doctor," he said.

"Hello, Horatio," Doctor Sinhurma said. "I thought we should have a little talk."

"I'm surprised you can get reception way out here," Horatio said. "You must have a good plan . . . what would you like to talk about?"

"My imminent departure from this plane of reality," Sinhurma said matter-of-factly.

"You don't have to do this, Doctor. All these people don't have to die—"

"Die? Nobody's going to *die*, Horatio." He sounded mildly puzzled. "At least, none of my disciples will. We are all going to *return*."

"I don't understand."

"Of course not. You are standing on holy ground, Horatio. This spot—this *very spot*—was where the race of Man originated. I have been all over the world, searching for the cradle of humankind, and I have finally found it. It was not in the Tigris-Euphrates river basin; it was not in Ethiopia, nor in Brazil. It is *here*."

"I see," Horatio said evenly.

"No—you do *not*," Sinhurma said, and now the fervor in his voice flared into anger. "You see *nothing*. You see swampland and alligators and flamingos. You see the leaves of the cypress, but you do not see the *roots*. The rich ecosystem all around us, Horatio, is nothing more than life nurtured by death. It is meant as a beacon, an immense, living message for those with the vision to truly *see*. From death comes life. To die here—to die *knowing the truth*—is to be reborn into this place as it once was. Our souls will be drawn back through time, to the Garden known as Eden, the womb of life itself. . . ."

"There must be something you want, Doctor. Otherwise, you would have already made your exit."

"I will leave when the correct time arrives—and that time is fast approaching, Horatio. The next sunrise I see will be in Paradise. And as for what I want . . . I want you to join me, Horatio."

Horatio nodded, slowly. "And if I do?"

"Then you will be redeemed."

Of course. In his script, he not only gets to return to Eden, he rehabilitates the serpent, too. "That's a very interesting offer, Doctor. I know you think of me as your enemy, but really, we're not so far apart. We both have the well-being of your disciples uppermost in our minds . . . and there's something you may not have considered."

"Such as?'

"You say that those who truly believe will go to the Garden if they die here. But what about those who are having doubts? Their deaths will be meaningless."

"All of those with me are filled with faith."

"Really? Have you *asked* them lately how they feel about leaving this 'plane of existence'? Or are you afraid of not getting the answer you want?"

Horatio held his breath. This was a delicate game, and the sanity of one of the players was uncertain. He couldn't afford to push Sinhurma too far . . . but if he *didn't* push, he wouldn't get any results.

Other than six more bodies to process.

The voice on the other end of the line chuckled. "You play your role well," Sinhurma said. "But I don't see what you hope to accomplish. Surely you see I cannot allow doubt to infect my followers now?"

"You don't want them to talk to me. I understand that. But that's not what I'm asking. What I'm asking for . . . is a second chance. A second chance for *them*."

"What?"

"If any of your followers have doubts—maybe doubts that they've been afraid to express to you— then they will be dying for *nothing*. And I know that's not what you want." He paused, hoping he was right.

"Go on," Sinhurma said neutrally.

"Any doubts your followers have are *your* fault. *You* lead them; *you* taught them. You can't condemn them to a meaningless death for your failings, can you?"

"What are you proposing?"

"Let them decide. Let the ones who have doubts leave."

"I will *not* abandon my flock—"

"You're *not* abandoning them, Doctor," Horatio said. "You're giving them an opportunity for redemption. Because they can always come *back*, can't they?

The Everglades—the Garden—will still be here. It's eternal, remember?"

"Yes. Yes, the Garden is forever—"

"Maybe some of them aren't ready yet. Maybe they need more time to think, to contemplate what you've taught them—"

"Oh? More time to debate my 'New Age, fortune-cookie credo?' " Sinhurma's voice was cold.

"Don't make this about you and me, Doctor—"

"But it is about you and I, Horatio. I knew that from the very first time I talked to you. Did you think I would not *recognize* you? Not *know* you? Or perhaps the dance of karma is such that you have no more choice than I. . . ."

"Doctor, *listen* to me. I'm not the snake in this morality play you've constructed—"

The burst of laughter in his ear sounded very close to hysterics. "Snake? Don't attempt to distract me with irrelevancies, Horatio. I know exactly who you are . . . Mister *Caine*."

The line went dead.

"Well," Horatio said ruefully, "I guess I should have seen that one coming. . . ."

"So he's even crazier than we thought," Wolfe said.

"If what Calleigh told Horatio is accurate, yeah," Delko said. "A friend of mine had to take antimalarials when he went to Africa—he told me they gave him nightmares every night for months afterward."

"Big difference between nightmares and religious mania," Wolfe said. "And if Horatio's Cain, then who's Abel?"

Delko sighed. "Don't ask me. Sinhurma's got his own version playing in his head; for all I know, Adam and Eve are porn stars and the apple is a—I don't know, a banana."

Wolfe and Delko were sitting on folding chairs in a corner of the tent, drinking coffee from a thermos while Coast Guard reservists set up equipment. Horatio was a few feet away, on the phone.

"But no matter how warped his logic is, there's still a pattern," Wolfe said. "Hostage negotiation is all about getting inside the hostage-taker's head. If we can figure out what he's thinking, maybe we can find a way to give him what he wants without anybody else dying."

Delko blew on his coffee. "Yeah, well, that only works when the person in charge wants something that you can actually give him—or you can convince that person that it's within your power. With a head-case like Sinhurma, it's not so easy. So far, the only thing he's asked for is Horatio."

"You think he'll go for it?"

"He'll draw it out as long as he can, buying us time. But if we're out of options . . . yeah. Yeah, I know he will."

"But that's crazy. The minute Horatio steps inside that trailer Sinhurma will blow it to Kingdom Come."

Delko shook his head. "Horatio knows that too. And if he thinks it'll buy the hostages even a minute more time . . . he'll do it."

Horatio, still talking on the phone, walked over to them.

"—all right, Doctor. Yes, I understand. I'll live up to

my end of the bargain if you live up to yours." He closed the phone with a snap. "All right, gentlemen," Horatio said, "time to go to work."

"What do you want us to do, H?" Delko asked.

"We have a crime scene to process, Eric. Just over that dune."

"You mean the trailer that just blew up?" Wolfe asked. "How do we know he won't set off another blast while we're out there?"

"We don't," Horatio said coolly. "But he's agreed to let us do our jobs, as long as we don't approach the other two trailers. That means we can get the bodies under cover, and examine the site itself. Hopefully, we'll learn something useful in the process."

"Why would he do that?" Wolfe asked. "I mean, I don't see the logic behind it."

"Logic and the doctor are not really on speaking terms at the moment," Horatio said. "But he seems to feel that he and I have some sort of link, and I was able to appeal to that."

"All right," Delko said, getting to his feet. "I'll get my kit."

"Uh, H?" Wolfe said, looking uncomfortable.

"Yes, Mister Wolfe?"

"It's not my place to say, but—I really don't think you should go out there with us."

Horatio smiled humorlessly. "And why would that be?"

"Well, if Sinhurma thinks he can take you with him, he might set off the explosives anyway."

"Thank you for your concern, Mister Wolfe. I had

come to much the same conclusion myself . . . so I'll watch this one from the sidelines."

"Oh. Okay, then."

What Horatio didn't mention was that he'd be holding his breath every second they were out there. . . .

14

HORATIO HAD SEVERAL PROBLEMS.

First, he needed to know who was alive, and who was dead. More importantly, he needed to know who was in which trailer.

Kim was in trailer one—that much he knew. That, and the fact that Sinhurma's second-in-command didn't seem happy with the direction things were going. Sinhurma was probably in the trailer with him, but that wasn't a certainty; Kim could be restrained in some way, preventing him from leaving, and the doctor could be in the other trailer with a detonator in his hand.

That was his second problem: the explosives. The distinctive smell in the air—somewhere between shoe polish and almonds—told him the blast had probably been TNT. . . . But how much was left? Exactly where was it, and how would it be set off?

His best hope was that the entire group wasn't in one trailer. If they'd followed Sinhurma this far, they'd probably be willing to follow him all the way—but Sinhurma's actual presence would make all the difference. If one of the groups were separated from their leader, he might be able to work on them, get them to see reason. The longer the process took, the more chance for the drugs in their systems to wear off.

And was Jason McKinley still alive?

He hadn't been on the beach or the pier, that Horatio was sure of. But he might have been in trailer three . . . might even have been the one who blew it up. Horatio wouldn't know until Delko and Wolfe had IDed all the bodies, and at a bombing site that could take a while.

He just didn't have enough information . . . and he was running out of time. Sinhurma wouldn't wait forever.

The question was, what exactly was he waiting *for*?

Delko and Wolfe walked to the top of the ridge, where a SWAT sniper lay prone, and peered over. A few flames still guttered in the wreckage, but that and the waves were the only sign of movement. Even the lightning seemed to have stopped for a moment.

Processing a blast site was never easy. It was messy, of course. Debris was scattered everywhere, including body parts. The odor of charred flesh mixed with the smell of burning wood and hot metal. In this instance, the rich miasma of the Everglades itself added to the mix, with the humid air coming off the Atlantic giving it the salty tang of blood.

They started by estimating the radius of the blast, looking for the farthest piece of debris then adding another 50 percent to be safe. They planted numbered flags, marking off a numbered grid for the entire area.

Wolfe snapped pictures while Delko did a preliminary examination of the scene.

"Okay," Delko said. He was hunkered down in the midst of the wreckage, studying the ground. "We know the seat of the explosion was somewhere in the trailer. We figure out exactly where, it might tell us how the other two are wired."

Wolfe glanced over at the other trailers; the center one was no more than thirty feet away. The outside of it was charred on the side facing the explosion and the windows were all broken, but someone had used blankets and towels to block any view inside.

"Take a look at this," Delko said. He pointed to a blackened piece of wood jutting up from the foundation. "See the way the nails are all bent facing the same way?"

"Uh, yeah. Same thing over here, but facing the other way." Wolfe took a photo, then glanced back at the other trailers.

"So the bomb must have been planted somewhere between the two. Floor's pretty much gone, but see here?" Delko motioned toward a pipe that was sticking up at an odd angle. "Pipe would have been below the floorboards. If the bomb was in the trailer itself, it would have been blown down and into the ground. This one's bent backward and up, meaning the blast came from beneath it."

Wolfe was still staring at the center trailer. "Right. Bomb was under the trailer."

Delko smiled and shook his head. "Staring at it won't help, Wolfe. It's going to blow up or it isn't—ei-

ther way, obsessing about it won't change anything.
Focus on the job at hand."

"Yeah, okay. Sorry."

Normally, the scene would have been checked
thoroughly for further explosives before the CSI team
went in, but that wasn't possible here. Even as they
examined the site carefully, using tweezers and mag-
nifiers to sort through the debris and documenting
everything with photos, both Wolfe and Delko
couldn't help but wonder how long Sinhurma would
let them work.

And what he'd do to stop them.

By the time Wolfe and Delko got to the bodies, Horatio already knew a lot.

He knew how many people had been in the trailer:
thirteen. He knew because some of the bodies—or
parts of them—had made it over the crest of the dune.
Others had been counted by scanning the area from
the top of the ridge with binoculars. Between torsos,
heads and various limbs, he'd worked out a total that
meant one person had already been in the trailer in
addition to the twelve who had bolted for it.

*So. Two shot, four in custody, a baker's dozen blown to
hell. That leaves six: Sinhurma, Kim, and four unknowns.*

Who are they?

*Try to think like Sinhurma. You're the star of the show,
the main attraction—which trailer do you pick?*

The center one. Of course.

*Mister Kim, your faithful right-hand man, is not beside
you at your hour of greatest need. Why?*

Because his faith, it turns out, is not as strong as you had thought. He's been exiled, isolated, banished. Your love is being withheld to punish him.

So who do you keep close? Those you trust?

No. Those you need.

"Jason's still alive," Horatio murmured.

Still alive, because he's Sinhurma's go-to guy for blowing things up. And he's got to be in the center trailer, along with Sinhurma himself. The other building either holds a trussed-up Kim and a guard—or maybe just Kim himself. After all, you don't want his doubts spreading to anyone else. . . .

Kim's alone. If there was a guard, Kim would have been gagged.

And that gave Horatio an idea.

The SWAT officer approached the end trailer from the far side, out of view of the other building. He carried a TacView 1400, a high-tech periscope that let him look in windows and around corners without exposing himself to enemy fire. It had a tiny infrared/color camera mounted on a telescoping aluminum pole, linked to a five-inch TFT screen at the base. He was in contact with Horatio via his headset.

"I'm beside the building," the officer, Eskandani, said softly. "No sign of booby-traps. There's a broken window on this wall—I'm going to take a look inside."

"Take it slow," Horatio told him.

Eskandani raised the pole carefully. What the camera showed him was a long room with bunk beds down either side—a barracks. The room was empty, but there was a door ajar at the far end. Through it,

Eskandani could make out what looked like a figure tied to a chair; he described what he saw to Horatio.

"Okay," Horatio said. "Is there any sort of device or wire attached to him?"

"Hard to say—I don't have a full visual."

"What about the barracks? Does it look like it's rigged in any way?"

"Checking . . ."

Seconds ticked by.

"No," Eskandani said. "No trip wires or anything obvious, anyway. Could be pressure switches in the floor, though."

"My guys tell me the first bomb was probably placed underneath the trailer. Try to get a look under the platform with the camera, but do *not* enter the space."

A latticework of wooden slats in a crisscrossing pattern ran from the edge of the raised platform to the ground. Eskandani poked the camera between two of the slats.

"All right, I'm looking around . . . got it. There's some kind of plastic tub attached to the bottom of the platform. No wires I can see . . . uh-oh."

"What?"

"I have a camera in one corner. We're being watched—"

Horatio's cell phone rang.

"Get out of there, *now!*"

Horatio flipped open his phone. "Doctor, don't do anything rash—"

"I'm disappointed in you, Horatio. I thought we

had an agreement. But I suppose it's simply your nature to be untrustworthy."

"Don't do this, Doctor. If you kill Kim, you'll be making a huge mistake."

"Mister Kim is no longer one of our brethren. His fate is of no concern to me."

"It would if you knew what I know."

Horatio held his breath. He prayed that Eskandani was clear.

"What could you possibly know about Mister Kim that would interest me?"

"He's your business partner, Doctor. His heirs will have a say in the disposition of your assets once you're gone. Have you given any thought to that? I understand his brother owns a chain of fast-food restaurants—six months from now, The Earthly Garden will be selling cheeseburgers and milk shakes. That the legacy you want to leave?"

Horatio had no idea if Kim even had a brother—it was a flat-out gamble, a desperation move to give him some breathing room. If Sinhurma sensed he was being played, though, it could backfire in a moment.

"That is regrettable," Sinhurma said, "but I see no solution to the problem."

"It's not that difficult to solve, Doctor. Simply have Kim sign his portion of the business over to you, right now. I promise you, we'll get the documentation to the proper place."

"And I'm supposed to trust you? After you broke your word?"

"I haven't interfered with your plans, Doctor. You can't blame me for wanting verification, can you?

Better if I know you can do what you claim—that way, there's no chance of a misunderstanding."

"I see. You were only seeking the truth."

"That's what I do, Doctor. Believe it or not."

"And why would you care about my legacy?"

Horatio thought carefully before he replied. "Maybe I'm just hedging my bets, Doctor. You've already proved to be a quite a handful in this life—I really don't want to make an enemy of you in the next as well."

Sinhurma laughed sharply. "Ah! Lieutenant Caine, you are a formidable opponent yourself. I regret that you and I will never have the chance to play chess together—but then, I suppose that is exactly what we are doing. Very well. I will allow you to withdraw your knight . . . and I will consider the business arrangement you suggested. But I would hurry if I were you, Horatio; my time here is almost up."

The phone went dead.

Horatio took a deep, deep breath, and let it out slowly.

Delko and Wolfe stood on either side of a table set up in the tent. Along its length lay a grisly display of body parts: arms, hands, and fingers. There were more, in plastic bags underneath the table, but for now they were concentrating on the items that could give them a positive ID.

Both of them had handheld wireless IBIS units, which resembled oversized cell phones with a short handle jutting from the bottom. They used these to scan fingerprints into a laptop, which would then connect to the central AFIS system and look for a match. They also kept track of hands that were identifiably male or female, and made note of skin color and any tattoos or distinctive scars.

Horatio walked up to them just as they were finishing. "All right—what can you tell me?"

"We've found parts of all thirteen bodies—just a finger in one case," Delko said. "Must have been right at the seat of the blast. We've IDed six as female, four as male, three unknown. We've got positive IDs on eight of the bodies through AFIS." He handed Horatio a printout.

Horatio scanned it, nodded. "Leaving five corpses and four cult members inside whom we can't identify."

"We can narrow it down a bit further," Wolfe said. "According to the photo we found at Sinhurma's, three cult members were African-American, two were Asian. Cross-reference that with what he have and we know that one of the deceased unknowns was an Asian woman and one was a black man."

"Leaving seven unknowns," Horatio said. "Four inside, three outside. And you know what? I think I know who the ones on the inside are. . . ."

He handed the list back to Delko. "Tell me who you *don't* see on that list."

Delko studied it. "Any of our initial suspects," he said. "Shanique Cooperville, Darcy Cheveau, Albert Humboldt, or Julio Ferra."

"Looks like they're back in the doctor's good graces," Horatio said. "Or maybe he just doesn't want them telling stories after he's gone."

The next table held various pieces of debris,

arranged carefully on top of a white sheet. A silver and black device around the size of a boom box stood to one side, a small folding screen set into the top showing a graph in red and a table of numbers.

"The ETD detected trinitrotoluene and ammonium nitrate," Delko said. The device was a portable High-Speed Gas Chromatograph, with a micro-differential Ion Mobility Spectrometer that could isolate and identify explosive or narcotic traces down to a trillionth of a gram."

"Amatol?" Horatio said. "The smoke was awfully white for that—must be close to a fifty/fifty mix."

Wolfe looked visibly impressed. "Forty-eight/fifty-two," he said.

"Jason, Jason," Horatio muttered. "Anybody else would have just gone with half-and-half—but you had to tweak it, didn't you?"

"These are all the components we could find and identify," Wolfe said. It used to be thought that all parts of a bomb were completely destroyed by an explosion, but forensics experts had known that wasn't true for decades—up to ninety-five percent of a device could survive. Trained investigators could detect those pieces by spotting distinctive traits like soot patterns and jagged breakage.

Horatio examined them critically. "No timer, which is no surprise. . . . Ah." He picked up a small piece of wire. "This looks familiar."

"Looks the same as the fragment we found on the rocket," Wolfe said. "Copper with a Kevlar coat."

"Which makes sense," Horatio said. "Model rockets are usually triggered by wire, not remote. I'm guessing that the other explosives are actually hard-wired as opposed to using a radio detonator."

"Which means our bomb-jammer isn't much use," Delko said. One of the pieces of equipment Horatio had offloaded from the Coast Guard vessel was an electronics countermeasure device, which jammed radio frequencies that might be used to set off a bomb.

"It's not much use now," Horatio said. "We turn on the jammer, we also disrupt cell phone transmission. Right now, communication with the doctor is paramount . . . and his ego won't let him take a subservient position. Trying to negotiate by bullhorn will just reinforce a siege mentality—it may even push him over the edge."

"What if he's just talking to you to keep us from jamming him?" Wolfe said. "They could even have the bomb rigged to a phone."

"I don't think so. Sinhurma's paranoid and Jason is smart—between the two, they'll know we can jam radio frequencies. And if they've figured that out, they won't use a method we can easily block. No, I think we're looking at a wire-controlled system."

"Which means we have a chance to find and cut the wires," Delko said.

Wolfe shook his head. "Sinhurma will never let us get that close. If there's a camera watching the bomb, there's probably a camera watching the area between the trailers."

"True," Horatio admitted. "But knowing there's a link that can be cut is a good first step."

"What's our second?" Delko asked. Wolfe frowned— the question seemed a little insolent, as if Delko were insinuating Horatio didn't know what the next step could possibly be.

In fact, it was exactly the opposite—Delko was so sure Horatio had a plan that it never ocurred to him his remark could be taken as other than a request for information.

"Our second, gentlemen," Horatio said, "is establishing a link of our own. . . ."

"All right, Doctor, I've downloaded and printed out the forms you'll need," Horatio said. "I'm going to send an officer into the trailer with Kim to deliver them. I assume you have a camera trained on him as well?"

"Your assumption is correct."

"Then you know the officer will be on his best behavior. He won't approach Kim in any way—he'll simply leave the forms in plain sight."

"And then?"

"I understand if you don't want to leave the trailer yourself. I know you're not alone in there—you can assign one of your disciples to travel between the buildings. She can get Kim to sign the documents and take them back to you. You can sign them and get them to me."

Horatio mentally crossed his fingers. What he needed was for Sinhurma to send Jason over—but he couldn't specifically request that, or the doctor would suspect he was up to something. He was hoping his use of the word "she" would push the doctor in the other direction, increasing the chances that he would choose Jason. Of the other three men, Ferra was unlikely—too unstable, too nervous—but both Cheveau or Humboldt were possibles. Cheveau seemed unshakable, while Humboldt was a born follower.

"And how do I know you will not attempt something foolish? How can I guarantee my envoy will be safe?"

The doctor's voice was calm, but Horatio sensed something else. As long as the doctor held the detonator, he had all the cards; he could blow the trailer sky-high with Kim and the officer in it, and still have the upper hand. His envoy had nothing to fear, but Sinhurma was still worried.

Getting a little nervous up on the high-wire, Doctor? Horatio thought. *I think it's time to point out just how far away the ground really is.*

"No guarantee at all," Horatio said. "But if I wanted you—or any of your people—dead, I'd just lob a tear gas grenade through a window and see if you fish or cut bait. Frankly, I'm tempted to do just that."

A pause. "Yet, you have not. Why?"

"I'm not sure, Doctor. I know you'd like to believe it's because we have some mystical connection, but the more I think about that, the less certain I am. See, I'm a man of science. The people I work with, they're scientists, too. Those are the people I feel a connection with, those are the people I care about. I can relate to you as a member of the medical profession, as someone who took an oath to do no harm; as a messiah. . . ." Horatio paused. "Let's just say you're a few miracles short of sainthood."

"I see. Being impoverished of faith, you require some sort of sign. Spiritual collateral, if you will."

"I don't require anything, Doctor; I'm fully aware of what you can do. Harming somebody else won't prove—"

"It's too late for that, Horatio. But I understand, I do. We all need to be shown, sooner or later. My own sign will be arriving any minute . . . and so will yours." Sinhurma hung up.

Horatio took out a handkercheif and mopped sweat off his forehead. Would it work? Had he planted enough hints, without tipping his hand?

And even if Sinhurma did choose Jason, Horatio had no idea what frame of mind the scientist would be in. As a recent convert, he might be having doubts right about now, might be willing to listen to reason— but if Sinhurma had convinced him that Horatio was somehow to blame for Ruth Carrell's death, he could be consumed with hatred.

Horatio had to fight to suppress a smile. Ironically, what it came down to was his belief in someone else's rationality—belief being what you were left with when evidence wasn't available.

Horatio's instincts against Sinhurma's. Science versus superstition.

In the end, no matter how you looked at it, it all came down to faith.

15

HAVING AT LEAST GOTTEN a glimpse of the layout, they sent Eskandani in again. Sheathed in body armor, carrying two sheets of paper in one hand and a ballpoint pen in the other, he felt like a postapocalyptic accountant. *All I need is a semiautomatic briefcase and a calculator chain saw,* he thought.

Officer Eskandani didn't have either of those—he wasn't even carrying a sidearm. He did, however, have something else concealed inside his bulletproof vest.

Lieutenant Caine watched him from the ridge of the dune through a small pair of binoculars as he approached the trailer. Caine didn't think Sinhurma would destroy the trailer just to make a point, but acknowledged it was within the realm of possibility.

Which was the sort of statement, Eskandani reflected as he trudged up to the building, that didn't exactly fill him with optimism. Still, he knew Caine would have gladly gone in his place if he could—his loyalty to his team was legendary. There were also a few ugly rumors floating around, mainly because Caine's brother had turned out to be dirty, but Eskandani didn't much care about that. Eskandani had started his career in New Orleans, and after a few years in the Big Easy you acquired a different attitude toward bribery. As far as he was concerned, making a little money off the books had nothing to do with how good a cop you were. That came down to dedication, loyalty and compassion; taking a bribe was one thing, letting innocent people get hurt was another.

He glanced over toward the center trailer, but he couldn't see any movement through the towel-shrouded windows. He reached out, took a deep breath, and grabbed the doorknob.

It wasn't locked.

He swung the door open, peered inside. Short hallway, no windows. He took a step inside.

"Mister Kim?" he called out. "I'm a police officer. Don't be alarmed."

The voice that replied came from the left, and was filled with terror. "Get out of here! There's a bomb! He'll kill us both!"

"It's all right, sir! He's given us permission to enter!" He stepped down the short hall to the end, where it branched to either side. Kim was in a windowless room on the left, three walls lined with lockers and one with a floor-to-ceiling mirror. The shock wave of the explosion had shattered the mirror; a few shards still clung to the frame, but most of it was scattered around the room in silvery fragments.

Kim was tied to a chair in the center of the room. He had a few minor cuts on his face from broken glass, but seemed otherwise unharmed. "Get me *out* of here," he hissed.

Eskandani glanced around, looking for the camera. He couldn't see one, but that meant nothing; it was probably stashed in one of the lockers, spying on Kim with a pinhole lens.

"I'm sorry, sir, I can't do that," he said. "If I attempt to free you, Doctor Sinhurma has made the consequences clear." He looked around, then settled for placing the pen and paper on the floor.

"Then what are you doing here? What are you putting there? At least untie me!"

"Just calm down, sir," Eskandani said. "We're doing our best to get you out of here, but for now you'll just have to be patient. These papers are documents that Doctor Sinhurma wants signed; I'd advise you to do so."

"What? Documents? This is—this is crazy. *He's* crazy. . . . And how am I supposed to sign anything with my hands tied?"

"Someone will be along in a moment to take care of that. Are you aware that the doctor is monitoring this room?"

"I—yes." Kim glanced nervously at the bank of lockers on the right. "But I don't think he can hear us—it's video only."

"Good. For now, just play along. We're doing our best."

Eskandani turned and left the room. Once he was out of sight of the camera he reached into his vest, pulled out a BlackBerry Personal Digital Assistant and placed it on the floor of the hallway. He exited the building quickly, shutting the door behind him.

*   *   *

Horatio waited.

Eventually, the door to Sinhurma's trailer opened and his envoy stepped out. A few seconds later he was inside the other building. Horatio gave him a few more, then used Delko's cell phone to place a call to the PDA Eskandani had left behind.

It rang. Once, twice, three times. Horatio waited.

On the eleventh ring, someone answered.

"Hello, Jason," Horatio said.

Silence.

"I don't know what the doctor's been telling you," Horatio said, "but I can't believe someone as intelligent as you are would make up his mind before getting all the facts."

Still no reply. This time, Horatio let it stretch out.

Finally, Jason said, "I shouldn't be talking to you." His voice sounded angry, suspicious, defiant. The voice of a teenager who knows he's in the wrong but refuses to admit it.

"Why? Because I'm evil incarnate? Because all I'll do is lie to you, try to confuse you?"

"Something like that."

"That sounds like the doctor talking, Jason. I didn't realize you let other people do your thinking for you."

"Thinking is vastly overrated, Horatio," Jason said, and suddenly his voice didn't sound angry at all; it sounded bone-weary. "I've been thinking my whole life. You know what happens when you think all the time? You don't *do* anything. You spend so much time scrutinizing data that the situation it pertains to becomes meaningless. Life passes you by. Knowledge without action has no value."

"What about life, Jason? Does that still have value? Because you're about to throw yours away."

He laughed bitterly. "Not all life is created equal, Horatio. My life wasn't worth much of anything before I met Ruth—did you know sometimes I'd go to a stylist to get a shampoo and haircut just so I could feel a woman's hands on my skin? And then everything changed, it was good, *too* good, it was like a dream and then suddenly it was a nightmare, she was dead and everything *hurt* so much. I just wanted it all to go *away*. And the doctor helped, they all did, they were *there* for me."

"I know, Jason. I understand that—"

"Do you? *Do* you? Doctor Sinhurma says *you're* responsible. He says Ruth was killed as a warning to all of us, that we threaten the status quo. That we're outsiders, and outsiders are *always* the ones to get blamed."

"And what about Phil Mulrooney, Jason? Am I responsible for that, too?"

Another long pause. When Jason spoke, his voice was barely more than a whisper. "No. That was . . . that was my fault."

Horatio's heart sank. He didn't want to ask the next question, but he knew he had to. "Jason—are you saying you killed Phillip Mulrooney?"

"I might as well have," Jason said miserably. "I built the rocket. I showed him how it worked. I—I didn't know anyone would *die*."

"*Who* did you show, Jason?"

"Doctor Sinhurma. He wanted to use it to set off fireworks, he said—it was supposed to be part of a big celebration. And then Phil got killed in that—that accident."

"Listen to me, Jason—Mulrooney's death was *not* an accident. He was set up—"

"He was a *traitor*!" Jason snapped. "*You* sent him to us! He was *spying* on us and God struck him down!"

"You're not making any sense, Jason. Was Phil's death an accident or holy retribution? Which is it?"

"There *are* no accidents. Phil was messing around where he shouldn't and God sent a thunderbolt to *punish* him. It *looked* like an accident but Doctor Sinhurma could see the *truth*. He told me what you're doing—trying to make it look like we're guilty of something so you can destroy us. But you can't frame God—that's ridiculous! So you assassinated Ruth instead. . . ."

It almost made sense. If you were paranoid enough, drugged to the gills and overwhelmed by grief, that is.

"I'm not trying to frame anyone—least of all, you," Horatio said. "I know you don't trust me right now, but I don't think you're willing to discard a lifetime's worth of trust in science, either. Evidence doesn't lie, Jason, and I know you still believe that."

"I don't know what to believe. . . ."

"Then take a look at the facts yourself. *Decide* for yourself. I promise you, I won't try to influence your judgment."

"What . . . what facts?" Tiredly.

"Let's start with why you're feeling so light-headed, why it's so hard to think. The vitamin shots you've been getting are laced with hypnotics, stimulants, antidepressives and other potent drugs. I can prove that, Jason; Ruth's blood was full of the same thing."

"He—he said that was just a temporary side effect of the vitamins—"

"Phillip Mulrooney didn't set off that rocket by accident. He died holding on to a steel toilet seat that was connected via jumper cables from a pipe in the wall to the Kevlar wire of the rocket. He was on the phone to Sinhurma at the time."

"The doctor said—he said Phil was trying to *sabotage* the rocket—"

"The doctor's the one who's been lying to you, Jason. He killed Mulrooney because Mulrooney had stopped taking his shots and Sinhurma was afraid he'd reveal the scam. Ruth came to me with a few suspicions of her own, and Sinhurma had her killed too."

"No—no he wouldn't, he *loved* Ruth, he loves all of us—"

"He doesn't love you, Jason. Everything I've been telling you, everything I've been saying, I can *prove*. I have lab reports, I have photos, I have DNA."

"That—that can be faked—"

"Is that the approach you want to take? That it's all one big conspiracy, that my team and I spend our time creating elaborate deceptions instead of uncovering the truth? Because this is the fork in the road, right here; you're going to have to pick a direction, and you don't seem to understand which way you're headed The road you're on means you're going to have to renounce everything you've ever learned, the entire foundation of knowledge your world is built on.

You're going to have to reject Newton, Galileo, Copernicus, Einstein. If you buy what Sinhurma's selling, the whole world becomes unreliable; everything is suspect because no one can be trusted. Is *that* what you want?"

"He said I could trust *him*," Jason said plaintively. "That Ruth and I would be together again in the Garden of Eden. . . ."

"The man you want to trust has you sitting on top of a *bomb*, Jason. Thirteen of the people he professes to love just *died* as a result. I'm out here trying to match severed limbs to charred torsos, wondering how I'm going to tell their families, and I do *not* want to have to do that for yours."

Horatio stopped. He could hear Jason on the other end of the line; it sounded like he was crying.

"It's so *hard*," he sobbed.

"It's okay, Jason. It's okay. The hard part is over. There's only one more thing you have to do."

"What. What do I have to do?"

"You have to tell me about the detonator. You have to tell me how it's wired and how Sinhurma's going to set it off."

"I need to *see*, Horatio," Jason said, sniffling. "I don't know who to trust, who to believe. I need to *see*."

"Then look through the menu of the BlackBerry you're holding. I've loaded it up with all the data we've collected so far: the toxicology report on Ruth Carrell's bloodstream, the DNA sample we took from the jumper cable that matches Albert Humboldt, photos of the tool marks on the pipe that match the jumper cables—"

Horatio's phone went off.

"It's all there, Jason," Horatio said. "But you better make up your mind fast. I've got a call coming in from Doctor Sinhurma right now, and I guarantee he won't wait forever for either of us."

Horatio switched phones and answered.

"You promised you would not interfere with my envoy," Sinhurma said tersely.

"I haven't gone anywhere near that trailer, Doctor. It's not my fault if your lapdog won't come when he's called."

"Lapdog? You sound betrayed, Horatio. Could it be that seeing where Mister McKinley's loyalties truly lie is bothering you?"

"He's not a prize for us to compete over, Doctor. He's a human being, just like the rest of your followers. Don't lose sight of that."

"I have lost sight of nothing, Mister *Caine*. I know what you're trying to do. The wolf separates the weakest sheep from the flock before he *springs*."

Horatio ran a hand through his hair; it came away damp. "Just take it easy, Doctor. I think Mister Kim may be a bit recalcitrant when it comes to signing those documents. Mister McKinley is obviously trying to convince him, and that may take a little time—"

"You don't have as much time as you think, Horatio." The line went dead again.

Horatio immediately switched to the other phone. "Jason? Jason, I hate to rush you, but you need to make a decision before the doctor makes it for you."

No response. Then: "Horatio?"

"Yes?"

"You've—you've got a lot of data here."

"I know it's a lot to take in, but—"

"No, no, it's fine . . .reminds me of cramming for finals with a head full of No-Doz and three pots of coffee sloshing around in my gut." He sounded almost wistful. "I'm . . . impressed. You must have some pretty cool stuff in that lab of yours."

Horatio smiled. "Not quite a batcave full, but we try. If you'd like to take a look sometime, I'd be happy to show you around."

"Yeah? I—yeah. Okay. I'm—I'm sorry, Horatio. I'm really, really sorry." His voice trembled.

"It's all right, Jason. All you did was provide information; you're not responsible for what was done with it—"

KA-*THOOM!*

The explosion that cracked the air wasn't the trailer going up, but a thunderbolt ripping across the sky. Static ate the cell phone signal with a deafening crackle, and the clouds overhead stopped spitting and released a torrent of water. Between the rain drumming against the tent overhead and the interference on the phone, Horatio could barely make out what Jason was trying to say.

"—don't let him—QZZZSSKKK—bomb—ZZZX—buried—CRKK—waiting for signal—"

"Jason! *Jason!* What signal? *What's Sinhurma waiting for?*"

"KRZZZXX—*shazam*—"

"Shazam," Horatio whispered.

He bolted out into the rain, heading for the sniper still on the crest of the dune—he couldn't count on the walkie-talkie. By the time he got there, he was drenched from head to foot.

"Sinhurma's going to launch a rocket!" he barked. "If he does, shoot it down!" The sniper nodded, as if being told to shoot down rockets in the Everglades was pretty much an everyday occurrence for him.

Forty-four feet per second, Horatio thought. *Not exactly easy to hit . . .* He hoped the sniper included skeet-shooting in his daily regimen; either that, or trying to pick off hummingbirds.

He sprinted back to the tent, trying to raise Jason on the way. He finally got a clear signal.

"—Horatio?"

"I'm here. If the rocket doesn't work, can Sinhurma set off the charges manually?"

"Only the one under this building. Wires are buried between the trailers at the northeast corners. He has a camera there."

"I figured as much. . . . Can you defuse the explosives under your trailer from the inside? Without Sinhurma seeing you?"

"I—I think so."

"Do it. Do it *now.*"

Light flared above Sinhurma's trailer, a shooting star ascending to the heavens. *The rocket.* It was followed by the sharp *crack! crack crack!* of rifle fire . . . but to Horatio's dismay, the star continued to rise. *He missed. It's up to the storm now. . . .*

He waited for the brilliant line of electricity to race down the wire and spark chaos. Waited. Waited . . .

Nothing happened.

He keyed the walkie-talkie and shouted, "Take the middle trailer! *Go, go, go!*"

And then things did happen, fast.

SWAT officers swarmed through the front door—Sinhurma hadn't even bothered to lock it behind Jason. Gunshots echoed through the rain. Horatio waited for the trailer to go up and take everyone with it.

But it didn't.

16

"HE'S DEAD," Horatio said.

Jason sat in a folding chair, shivering and wet, a blanket draped around his shoulders. His hands were cuffed, but Horatio had insisted they be in front of him. Jason looked like he hadn't slept in days, his eyes dark and haunted.

"We found Sinhurma inside," Horatio said. "When the rocket failed to trigger a lightning strike, he injected himself—we're not sure with what. He was in convulsions by the time we got in."

"And the others?"

"In custody. Shanique Cooperville tried to slash her wrists, but we got to her before she seriously hurt herself. The others surrendered—apparently you weren't the only one having doubts."

"What's going to happen to me?"

"Not as much as you might think. Between your cooperation and the fact that you were drugged without your knowledge, I think we can work something out."

"I didn't fire the rocket, Horatio—the one that killed Phil? I swear I didn't."

"I know," Horatio said. "I had someone look into it—you were working with Doctor Wendall that day, weren't anywhere near The Earthly Garden. No, the rocket was launched by someone at the restaurant."

"Who?"

"The same person who killed Ruth . . ."

"I don't get it," Delko said.

He and Wolfe were processing the trailer. Sinhurma's body lay sprawled on the floor, his carefully crafted poise and dignity stolen by death. The hypodermic they'd found jutting from his arm had already been photographed and bagged; a thin line of foam drooled from the doctor's open mouth to the floor.

"What's to get?" Wolfe said. He was taking pictures of the interior. "He was crazy, he killed himself."

"Not that," Delko said. "Shazam. What the hell is *shazam*?"

"It's the magic word Billy Batson says to change into Captain Marvel," Wolfe said. He focused carefully on the body and clicked off several photos. "Calls down a mystical bolt of lightning that gives him his superpowers."

"Oh," Delko said. "Well, I guess that makes sense, then, in a deranged messiah-complex kind of way."

The explosives, bolted to the bottom of the trailers in waterproof tubs, had been found and disconnected by Horatio with Jason's help. The launch console, though, still sat on a table beside Sinhurma's body. It had several gauges for reading local electrical fields, and three toggles: one for firing the rocket and two others for detonating the trailer charges.

Wolfe lifted it up, examined it. There was an access plate at the back that he pried off, revealing a twelve-volt battery inside. "Look at this. If anyone had taken the time to rig a simple bypass, Sinhurma could have blown himself up with the flick of a switch."

"Yeah, well, be thankful they didn't. Sinhurma was so sure God was on his side that he let the storm make the call."

"But Sinhurma didn't build this," Wolfe said. "Jason did. And he knew there was a fifty percent chance the rocket wouldn't trigger a lightning strike."

"So?"

"So Sinhurma didn't leave it in the hands of God," Wolfe said. "Jason did."

"Guy thinks like a CSI," Delko said. "Trust . . . but *verify*."

Calleigh and Horatio gazed across the interview table at the prisoner in the orange jumpsuit. He'd been held in county lockup since the standoff in the Everglades had ended; the fact that he'd narrowly escaped being blown into bloody fragments seemed to have altered his attitude since the last time Horatio had talked to him. His cocksureness was gone, replaced by a hollow-eyed, twitchy nervousness.

Of course, Horatio thought, *he could just be missing his daily vitamin shot.*

"Darcy Cheveau," Horatio said. "You're lucky to be alive."

"Yeah. Yeah," Cheveau said. "I didn't know how crazy he was, man. It just—it all made sense at the time, you know?'

"I suppose," Horatio said. "I wouldn't suggest using that as a defense at your murder trial, though."

"What? Hey, *I* was the one that almost got killed—"

"You may be yet," Horatio said, and now there was an undertone of steel to his calm voice. "But it'll be the State of Florida putting a needle in your arm as opposed to a religious fanatic with a homemade bomb."

"No. No way. If anybody killed anyone, it was the Doc—"

"That's not true," Horatio said, "and we both know it. Sinhurma wouldn't dirty his hands with something like murder. That's the sort of thing you get your loyal followers to carry out."

"I don't know what you're talking about," Cheveau said. He looked away, putting a hand up in a dismissive wave.

"I'm talking about Ruth Carrell," Horatio said. "Roll up your sleeve, please. The left one."

"Why?"

"You can do it," Calleigh said, "Or we can get an officer to do it for you."

Cheveau shrugged. "Whatever." He rolled his sleeve up to the elbow.

"Nasty welt you've got there," Calleigh said. There was a swollen, reddish mark on the inside of Cheveau's forearm.

"Just a scrape."

"Yes it is," Calleigh said. "And I can tell you exactly what scraped it. You're not really that familiar with archery equipment, are you, Mister Cheveau?"

"Not really. That was more Julio's thing—he was always practicing at the clinic's range."

"Which is why Sinhurma didn't use him," Horatio said. "Too obvious. Julio supplied the equipment, but someone else shot the arrow. Novice archers often have welts like yours—if you don't hold the bow just right, the string strikes the inside of the forearm on release."

"Sure," Cheveau said. "Like I couldn't have gotten a mark like this a million other ways."

"A million other ways wouldn't leave your epithelia embedded in the bowstring," Calleigh said. "Which we matched to the DNA sample you gave. I can prove you used that bow."

"All right, so Julio lent it to me and I fired a few shots at the target range. Doesn't mean I killed anyone."

"No, it doesn't," Calleigh said. "And you know, that really bothered me. I figured a way to link the bow to the arrows found with it, and I figured a way to link you to the bow, but I couldn't tie the arrow that killed Ruth Carrell to you or them. But I don't give up easily . . . and finally, the clouds parted. And you know what I saw?"

Cheveau forced a laugh. "I have no idea."

"Pollution."

"What?"

"Did you know that Florida's weather systems turn it into the nation's storm drain?" Calleigh asked. She opened the file folder in front of her on the table. "And I mean that literally. A large proportion of the pollution spewed into the air by Eastern industry gets blown toward the coast, where it runs into moisture from the Atlantic. Big old thunderstorms form, and the rain scrubs the chemicals right out of the sky. Unfortunately, it just transfers them from one medium to another—from the air to the ecosystem. The ground, the water, and everything that lives in it.

"During the 1980s, this was a major problem. Incinerators for medical and industrial waste were extremely popular, and were commonly used to dispose of things like batteries. Environmentalists finally got legislation passed in the early nineties, but it took about seven years before anyone started seeing concrete results."

Cheveau stared at her and tried to look bored. Horatio favored him with a smile that made it impossible.

"And one of the ways those results manifested was in Floridian birds," Calleigh continued. "See, the bird population of the Everglades went down almost ninety percent between 1950 and 1980, largely because of all the toxic materials that were winding up there—especially mercury. They know this because mercury is covalent with keratin, the substance feathers are made out of. It's stable over a long period of time—once it's there, it more or less stays there."

"And why should I care about any of this?"

"Because, Mister Cheveau, the way that they tracked these environmental changes was to measure the amount of mercury present in feathers from Florida birds. The arrows from Julio Ferra's garage *and* the arrow that killed Ruth Carrell were hand-fletched, meaning the feathers were probably local. I couldn't DNA-type them . . . so I tested them for mercury contamination instead."

She took a sheet of paper out of the folder and

pushed it across the table toward him. "The results show an identical level of mercury in both sets of feathers, right down to parts-per-million. All those feathers came from the same bird . . . and together with the hand-fletching, it links the arrows together."

"It probably doesn't make much sense to you right now," Horatio said. "You're still suffering from the effects of Doctor Sinhurma's 'treatment.' But don't worry—the prosecutor will spell it all out in court."

"Whatever. Are we done?" Cheveau tried to sound casual, but he couldn't hide the nervousness in his eyes; they twitched from Horatio to Calleigh and back again.

"Not quite," Horatio said. "There's still the matter of Phillip Mulrooney's death."

"What, am I supposed to be guilty of that, too?"

"Yes, Mister Cheveau," Calleigh replied. "You are."

"You were Sinhurma's button man," Horatio said. "The one he turned to when he needed something unpleasant done. But he was smart enough to borrow a technique used by street gangs—use one person to obtain the weapon, another to fire it, a third to dispose of it afterward. Tribal loyalty keeps everyone's mouth shut, and blame is supposedly too widely dispersed to nail any one suspect. But the chain of evidence, no matter how long it gets, is still there . . . and my team always uncovers it. Link by link.

"Jason built the rocket, but someone else fired it. Humboldt supplied the jumper cables, but someone else hooked them up. Ferra donated a bow and arrow . . . but someone else used them to kill Ruth Carrell. And that someone else, Darcy . . . is you."

"You can't prove that," Cheveau said. His voice had taken on the same kind of blankness Horatio had heard before; under extreme stress, he was reverting to the rote behavior Sinhurma had programmed into him. "Phillip was killed by an act of God."

"Actually, it was the act of a blender," Horatio said. "Or at least one was used as an accomplice. A burned-out appliance we found in The Earthly Garden's Dumpster had a distinctive pattern melted into the head of the plug. We couldn't match that pattern to anything we found in the restaurant—not at first. . . ."

Horatio looked up from the comparison microscope. "The tool marks near the blade match the clamp of one of the jumper cables," he said. "There's even a trace of melted plastic on the end. This is what was jammed between the plug and the outlet."

"But who put it there?" Delko asked.

"Somebody who knew where they were hidden when not in use," Horatio said.

"Albert Humboldt?"

Horatio studied the knife, his eyes narrowed. "I don't think so," he said. "As a matter of fact, I think both ends of this knife have left their mark. . . ."

"Samuel Lucent told me he thought Albert was getting high with someone else at work," Horatio said. "I know it was you."

"I don't know what you're talking about."

"Oh, I think you do," Horatio replied. "Archery isn't the only thing you're a little clumsy at. . . . The technique used for hot-knifing hash is to compress the drug between the heated blades of two knives underneath a bottle with the bottom broken out—but the bottle isn't actually necessary, is it? If you're experienced, you can simply hold the knives close to your mouth and catch the smoke with one well-timed inhalation. Experienced or lazy, I suppose . . . Which one was it, Darcy? Were you trying to show off, or did one of you break the bottle and were too stoned to manufacture another one?"

Cheveau stared at him, but didn't reply.

"Whichever it was, the results are plain to see. As plain as the burn on your face." Horatio pointed to the whitish, crescent-shaped scar on Cheveau's upper lip. "A very distinctive mark—one that matches the end of the knife jammed into that plug.

"Jason told you that there was only a fifty percent chance that the rocket would attract a lightning strike, and that just wasn't good enough, was it? Sinhurma was confident that Fate was on his side and against Mulrooney's . . . but you weren't. You didn't want to risk failing your beloved leader, so you cheated. You connected one jumper cable to the rocket and the pipe, and the other just to the pipe. You dumped a bucket of water under the door to provide a path from Mulrooney's knees to the metal drain, removed the knife's wooden handle and clamped the remaining end of the cable to the exposed base, then jammed it between the plug and the outlet on the nongrounded side. You zapped Phil at the same time you fired the rocket—reasoning that even if lightning didn't strike, Mulrooney would still be electrocuted. Afterward, Humboldt was supposed to dispose of the rocket equipment, which he did—except he was stupid enough to keep the jumper cables. You couldn't get Humboldt to get rid of the knife or the blender—you didn't want anyone else to know you had doubts about Sinhurma's plan—so you threw the blender in the trash, replaced the handle of the knife and hid it. You figured that even if it was found, it would be dismissed as drug paraphernalia."

Cheveau's eyes dimmed as realization set in. "I couldn't chance it," he said dully. "I was already on kitchen duty. I had to have a little insurance."

Horatio studied Cheveau coolly. " Oh, ye of little faith . . ."

Calleigh and Horatio watched two officers take Cheveau away. Outside, the rain was finally starting to let up; it would smell fresh and new and clean tomorrow.

"Kind of funny," Calleigh said. "The effects of a thunderstorm are what started this case—and what helped solve it."

Horatio looked out the window; lightning still flashed occasionally, but it seemed to be diminishing. "I suppose so," he said, "but I prefer to consider our success the result of hard work as opposed to divine intervention."

"Well, there was plenty of that, too," she said. "Not to mention paperwork. What kind of charges are the other cult members looking at?"

"Kim, Ferra and Humboldt are all facing conspiracy to murder. With Sinhurma gone, I'm guessing there'll be a scramble to see who can make a deal first; my money's on Kim, but Humboldt's testimony will help the most in locking down the case against Cheveau."

"What about Jason McKinley?"

"That's still being decided. The DA's talking accessory to murder, but I'm pretty sure I can convince him to drop that. Criminal negligence at the most, I think; I doubt he'll do time."

"Well, that's something. Poor guy."

"Yes. He lost his heart, his mind, and very nearly—"

"His soul?" she asked him, half-seriously.

"I was going to say his life," Horatio said. "If that's the price of popularity, I think I prefer to stay unacknowledged."

"No chance of that, Horatio," Calleigh said with a smile. "You'll always be popular with us. And for the record? For a guy with blue eyes and red hair, I think you've got *plenty* of soul."

"Thank you. And for the record, as far as my belief in souls goes . . ." He paused.

"Yes?" she prompted.

"Let's just say," he said with a smile, "that all the evidence isn't in yet. . . ."